ADAM - BEGIN]

ADAM Beginning and Re
A "Spirit" Mate Love Story &
Paranormal Romance &

© EJ Brock 2013

DEDICATIONS

This book is dedicated to my many readers who have encouraged and supported me. Your enthusiasm, for the next book, has been the driving force that keeps this series going.

THANKS

To Kim Davis and Emma Brock, for spending your time working with me to get this book completed.

A special thanks to **Charles Bell**, owner of H.I.T.M. (History In The Making) Studios in the Bronx, for allowing me to use his photo on the cover.

WARNING

Satan

Comes

to

steal,

kill

and

destroy...

John 10:10

ADAM - BEGINNINGS and REVELATIONS

PROLOGUE

§

Deep below the earth's crust...

Far beneath city streets and the ocean's deep...

Way down under every cave, cavern and grotto…

Just beyond the earth's mantle…

There is a, well-known, place that is hotter than the noonday sun.

It is a pit of darkness; where the only light is the amber flickers of a continuous flame.

Its ambiance is fire and brimstone. Its fragrance is smoke and sulfur.

It is where wicked spirits, have an open ended reservation.

The only music to be heard is the gnashing of teeth, echoing in tandem.

The only singing is the continuous chorus of remorseful screams.

And agonizing shouts of 'I'm sorry' fall on *deaf* ears.

Tears of regret, sorrow and pain aren't seen by anyone that matters.

Hope for another chance doesn't exist.

Or does it…?

Akibeel would beg to differ.

ADAM - BEGINNINGS and REVELATIONS

§

They say the temperature there is around 9,800° F. Scientists calls this place the center of the earth; aka the *'core'*.

But for the spiritually enlightened, its true name is **HELL!**

§

However, even in Hell, there is a hierarchy. In Hell, *Lucifer* ruled!

§

He turned one of the dungeons into his 'thrown' room. His imps have fashioned a faux royal chair, made of stone, for him to sit upon. The arms are large with sharp pointy fingers, at the end. On each side of the chair, stone sconces hang with fire blazing.

This room was fashioned for the Great Day of Judgment, when the remainder of his followers will join him.

It was already filled with hundreds of imps who serve as his army. They stand in formation along the walls, from front to back. Two are stationed at the entrance. In his mind, they are better than, or equal to, the Archangels. After all, they stood by their convictions, didn't they?

§

Some of the most powerful Archangels followed his lead, and refused to bow down to those puny humans.

They refused to be in servitude to creatures who should have kissed *their* feet.

They would get their *reward* before it was all said and done. They may be trapped down here physically; but they sent their spirits forth continuously. More often than not the 'so loved' answered *his* beckoning call. So who was more powerful?

§

Doubt is his General. Liar is his Chief Counsel. Hatred, Revenge, Malice, Murder and Chaos are his foot soldiers. Fear is his right hand man. Apathy is his overseer. Lust, Gluttony, Greed, Sloth, Wrath, Envy and Pride, are his seven most *deadly* followers.

All of them are powerful, in their own rights; but they yielded to his command.

A ritual bowing is performed three times a day. After all, he is equal to God, isn't he? He deserves the homage.

§

From where his throne sat, he could look beyond the mantle to the crust of the earth. He was always aware of what was happening on earth.

Today was not a good day. Not good, at all. Something big was about to jump off at Samjaza's boy's estate.

This turn of events was not good for his army's ego. And they were *not* happy. Several had requested a conference to discuss the situation. He'd already put them off as long as he could.

No pun intended, but all Hell was fixin' to break loose.

§

Chapter 1

Brock paced back and forth, outside of his suite. He resembled an expectant father anxious to hear...*it's a boy!* He did have another baby on the way; but that wasn't the reason for his pacing.

For the second time in their marriage, Jodi had locked him out of their suite. She'd locked herself in there with their son, Adam; two days ago.

Today was Adam's first birthday. But, at the exact second of his birth, he will not be *one year old*. In less than five hours, he'd be a *grown* man.

She thought she was okay with it, but she wasn't. She wanted her baby to stay a baby. She didn't want to release him to a life of fighting *demons*. Not her baby.

§

She was furious with Brock, because Adam wasn't going to be on his team. Brock had assigned him to Yomiel's team of Watchers. They'd been arguing about it for the last week. She did not want him on Doc's team. She was afraid that he, and Akibeel, didn't love Adam enough to protect him. But, she wasn't being rational. His brothers were crazy about all of his children.

Brock tried to reason with her. He told her that even though Adam wasn't on his team, he'd keep a watchful eye on him. He told her just like he snooped for everyone else's safety; he'd do the same for his son. But, she wasn't buying it.

He let her get away with shutting him out for the last two days; but enough was enough. That woman was just going to have to get over it. What the hell did she think? That he was going to be deprived of holding his son, one last time? He'd be *damned* if he wasn't going to be in the room when Adam made his transition.

He could hear her crying and talking to their son. But he had no sympathy for her. Not this time. Not about this.

"Open this door, Jodi Mae!"

§

"I'm not ready," Jodi sobbed. "Why can't you stay a baby, for mommy?"

For the first time, Adam spoke to her. He reached his tiny hand up and wiped her tears. *"I will always be your son, mom."*

She held him up over her heart, and rocked him back and forth. In just a few hours she'd never be able to do this again. She cried harder. "I'm going to miss holding you, Adam."

"You won't be able to hold me in your lap, but you can still hold me, Ma. I ain't going anywhere. Besides, you got another baby on the way."

"But he won't be you," she sobbed.

"No, he won't. But, he will grow up normally, just like Lizzie and Hans."

[2]

Jodi paused. "He will?"

"He will be Nephilim, but not Watcher."

"Why couldn't you be just Nephilim?"

"I don't know. But I'm glad I'm like my dad. I have three sisters and a brother on the way to help keep safe. Not to mention my beautiful mom."

Jodi smiled. "I'm supposed to keep *you* safe, baby."

"For twelve months you've done that. You are a good mother. I know you love me, but it's time to cut the apron string. I'm going to be a man, Mom. A thirty year old man."

Jodi sobbed again, "I'm not even old enough to have a thirty year old son."

"Mom! Age is just a number. Look how old dad is. Why have you locked him out of the room?"

"I wanted this time just for you and me."

"You're being selfish. He wants to spend this time with me, too. He says he's ready, but it is hard on him to let go, too."

"He won't even keep you on his team," she complained.

"I'm glad. If I were on his team he would never let me get my hands dirty. He'd be just like Uncle Justin is with Addison. He made a wimp out of that boy."

Jodi couldn't help but laugh. "Yeah, he did, didn't he?"

"But, Dad is helping make a man out of him. It

doesn't mean Dad doesn't love him, or won't protect him. It's easier to let go when it's someone else's son. My dad has put me with a team where everyone has 'Ultimate' Watchers' powers, Mom. He's given me as much cover as possible. He's done the right thing. You are the one that's wrong."

Adam was wise beyond his *year*. What he said made a lot of sense. Fathers feel as deeply as mothers do. Brock loved to hold his son. He rocked him to sleep, every night. He was going to miss those times, too. Shame on her. She was being selfish to Brock, again.

She blamed him for their son being a Watcher. But, she married a Watcher, didn't she? Twice. What had she expected? That her children would be human? She should be thankful that only *one* of them was a Watcher. She reached out to Brock, *"I'm sorry. I always get it wrong, don't I?"*

"Open this door, Jodi Mae. Right now!"

She heard the frustration in his voice. He was more than furious with her; he was *pissed!* She walked over and opened the door. "I'm sorry, Brock."

Brock didn't respond. He just took his son from her and walked in the bedroom.

She followed him; but he slammed the door in her face.

Oh Snap! She did *not* see that coming. She just stood there. Payback was a…*!*

§

"Don't be mad at mom."

"I'm furious with her."

"It's hard on her, Dad."

"It's hard on me, too. After tonight you won't need me anymore."

"I'll always need you, Dad. You and mom are tripping. It's not like I'm moving out of the house."

"But you won't be sleeping in here with us anymore."

"And truthfully I can't wait. You and mom are a little too frisky for me."

Brock laughed out loud. "Boy, you were supposed to be asleep."

"It's hard to sleep the way you guys carry on."

Brock laughed again. "It's more than time for you to get out of our room."

"By the way; don't you think it's time to stop getting my momma pregnant?"

"Boy! Mind your business."

Adam laughed. He already sounded just like his father. "From the moment I was conceived I've known that no other children would have better parents. You and mom are good parents. Elizabeth and Hannah think so, too. Aurellia is over the top for you guys. I heard her tell Deuce that even if her natural parents were alive, she'd want you both to be her parents. She said that when she

[5]

was little you used to protect her from her natural mother."

"She remembers that?"

Adam laughed. *"At first she didn't. She really believed that she'd never been spanked before. After the trip to the Island, it came back to her. She said she'd hide behind you, and peek at her mother from between your legs."*

"She was a brat."

"Still is. But she said you were always more of a father to her, than her natural father was."

"Her father had issues, but he was a good man."

"He drank too much, and left the child rearing up to her mother. But you and Mom do it together. And you do it well."

"Thank you, son."

"So open the door and let Mom in. It's almost time."

"Give me a few more minutes."

"Okay."

"You know why I assigned you to Doc and Akibeel, don't you?"

"Yeah. I just told mom it was the right decision. But, I also know you are worried."

"Yeah, I am."

"Don't be. I am as powerful as you are, Dad. Just like Samjaza gave you all that he was; you have done the

same for me."

That wasn't *actually* the truth, but Brock laughed. *"Does that mean that you are going to kill me one day?"*

"If you were like Samjaza I wouldn't think twice about it, but you're not. Thanks man, for giving me all you have."

"I'm not ready for this, Adam. I've given you powers that you don't know how to use. With this much power comes responsibilities, son. I feel like I've given a loaded gun to a baby."

Adam ignored the last two sentences. Of course he knew how to use his powers. *"Neither is Mom. Together, you guys will be able to handle it. Apart, you guys fall apart. Haven't you figured that out yet?"*

"I know that, but she was wrong."

"Yeah, but what's done is done. You could have easily come on in anyway. Why didn't you?"

"Because I knew she was upset."

"So were you. But you still put her needs first. That's what I mean...thanks, Dad."

"You know there's a party for you tonight."

"Yeah. My boy, Henry, put it together. I am looking forward to hanging with my cousins. Especially Henry, Sam and Matthew."

"So I've heard."

"Listen. You need to forgive Grandpa Hezekiah."

§

He and his men had given up their powers to fight in the preserves with the Walkers and their sons. While they were still human, Lightwings attacked him and Doc. He was still furious with H for his non-assistance in that attack. H had stood there and let Lightwings physically attack him. He even insinuated that Lightwings was right. That was bad enough, but he let Lightwings attack *Doc,* too. That really pissed him off. He beat Lightwings' ass, until he got an understanding. Then Baby Girl had a nervous breakdown. Snow Anna had to jump time to save her.

There were supposed to be only *five* people who knew about that event. And Adam wasn't one of them. Brock frowned. *"How do you know about that, Adam?"*

"I just do. Let Mom in, Dad."

Brock didn't get up. He reached out and opened the door.

§

Jodi was leaning with her hands and ear up against the door. She fell in and almost hit the floor.

§

Brock almost laughed. He was tempted to let her butt fall; but he wasn't *that* mad. He still loved her as much he did the day they met. If not more so.

Adam laughed. *"You better not had let her fall."*

"Hush, boy! Don't get too grown for your britches. Or I'll give you your first and last spanking."

[8]

§

Jodi walked over and sat next to them, but she didn't reach for her son. She'd selfishly held him for two days. She'd had her time, and now it was Brock's. "I am sorry, Boo."

"You better be glad I am still *disgustingly* in love with you, woman." He leaned over and kissed her.

§

Adam smiled. *"I've got the best looking parents in the world. And I don't care what everyone else thinks, Mom and Aunt Lillian do not look alike."*

"I agree with you, son."

"Y'all just have blinders on. Lillian and I are salt and pepper."

Brock laughed. *"Yeah, she can be a little salty, and you're hot!"*

He leaned over and kissed her eyelid. "Smokin!"

She caressed his bald head and shivered. That man of hers still drove her crazy. If she touched him, she wanted him.

"Cut that out!" Adam used his little hands and separated them. *"It's time."*

§

He transitioned into a fully grown man…sitting on Brock's lap.

§

Chapter 2

The family was in the yard, setting up for Adam's party. Henry had come up with the idea to celebrate, but he needed help. After seeing that Jodi was going to be useless, he solicited Symphony's help.

Everyone saw it as an olive branch, of sort; but not Henry, or Symphony. He'd said what he said, at the Island, and he was done with it. After he thought about it, her feelings towards Hope were *past tense*. But, it was the shock that she'd felt them, in the first place, that had pissed him off.

However, he believed criticism wasn't worth a damn, unless it was constructive. He decided to help his little cousin find her purpose.

She had put forth an effort, and started teaching the children how to sing. But, he could see she wasn't happy doing it. Just like Addis, with construction, that was *not* her niche. Bless her heart; she still needed to be the center of everyone's attention. And the children's singing stole the attention away from her. Everyone concentrated on how cute they sounded; not on the fact that she'd taught them.

He remembered the day he, and his cousins, came to live at the estate. She pranced around like she was the hostess. She was in her element. No request was too small, or too large. That got him to thinking…

He asked her to help him coordinate the party. And just like Addis' eyes, at the prospect of being an appraiser, her eyes lit up. She tackled the job with zeal, and left very little of the details for him to handle.

Everyone noticed the change in her. Smittie was the one to remind Floyd, "Before her attack, Symphony was on all the planning committees at church, Preacha."

Clyde co-signed, "That's true; she coordinated picnics, anniversaries and Christmas pageants. People came from miles around to her Easter plays, remember? At one point it was even televised. She could pull an event together at a moment's notice."

"Then those thugs attacked her; and stole my daughter's joy," Floyd responded. "But, you did good, Henry."

"I did *nothing*. Symphony pulled this together, all by herself," Henry replied.

"You did good by realizing *what* she's good at," Floyd corrected. "Look at her."

"You ain't seen the half of it, Unc. She came up with ideas I couldn't imagine." Henry smiled. "No doubt, Symphony is our 'Event Planner'."

Floyd nodded. "Indeed."

§

Symphony was all over the place; smiling and making sure things were in order. She was making sure everyone was comfortable, and not in need of anything.

[11]

The music was blasting, and excitement radiated across the yard. Colorful Chinese lanterns hung from the trees, just in case they partied into the night. Piñatas were strung for the children's enjoyment. Five twelve-foot steam-tables were in the middle of the yard; each filled with cuisines that represented the family's ethnicities: Soul food, Chinese, Polynesian, Indian, Jewish, Egyptian, German, Spanish, you name it. Coolers of water, soda and beer were strategically placed throughout the yard for everyone's convenience.

§

She invited the Ultimate Watchers to join the party. She turned it into not only a birthday party, but a meet and greet. All of them accepted the invitation. That is, all except Lightwings. He graciously declined, stating his inner-circle needed him.

§

The 'spirit' mates were happy to welcome more women into their sisterhood. Robyn introduced Jehoel's mate, Shelonda, to her parents.

"I am so glad things worked out for you. Robyn was distraught over your disappearance," Earlie told her.

"I didn't have Robyn's number. I didn't even have her last name. But, I thank God for her every day," Shelonda replied. "She saved my life."

§

Chaz introduced his cousin, Hasdiel, and his wife, to

his family. Hope liked Sonji, but she was more in line with Charity, Amanda and Lara's age group. She and Charity hit it off. Both of them had an unnatural elegance and grace about them; but neither was snooty.

"Where is Jodi?" Sonji asked.

"She and Brock are with Adam right now. They should be out shortly," Charity replied.

"They must be excited."

"I don't think so. I don't think Jodi is dealing with it very well."

"I wouldn't be either," Lara replied. "I loved *raising* my children. James still feels bad that I had to raise them alone. But I had a ball with my boys."

"You've never told him that?" Sonji asked.

"Of course not," Lara replied. "I didn't want James to think we didn't need him."

"How considerate," Sonji replied.

"Not really. I did need my husband." Lara laughed. "I just didn't need him to help raise our kids."

§

Kobabiel and his wife, Kiche, were right at home. Snow Anna, and her sisters-in-law, monopolized all of Kiche's time. They hadn't seen her since the last night the women were in the wolf-den.

"Where is my son?" Kiche asked Snow Anna. "He should be here by now."

"At the last minute he had a change of plans. He

said his new inner-team needed him, and he wouldn't be able to make it," she replied. Although, she knew that wasn't the reason. Wolf had barred him from the property. For the time being, she agreed with him.

§

Nate's 'spirit' mate, Layla, and Destiny hit it off. She was a beautiful African with skin as smooth as Ali's. Her eyes were coal black, but happy. She was full figured and...

Destiny smiled at Ali. *"Her butt is bigger than mine!"*

Ali squeaked. *"A black man's buffet, lil Darlin'."*

Knowing that Ali's uncle's wife was her size made her feel good. Nate seemed to be into Layla. He kept his hand on her lower back, just a breath away from her rear. Ali always did that to her, too. She gazed across the yard. Sure enough, even Donnell's brother had his hand close to his wife's rear. She still didn't understand it though.

Ali was listening to her thoughts and decided to bust her out. He squealed, "My lil Darlin' is perplexed why we brothas like big booties."

Destiny blushed. "ALI!"

Nate cracked up. "We do love our women thick."

Layla laughed. "That's a good thing for us, Destiny. Could you imagine being mated to a man who thought our butts were too big?"

They all laughed. Then Nate frowned. "Thank God

the decision wasn't left up to Michael. I'm sure he would have given me a flat-crack woman." He visibly trembled at the prospect. "It's bad enough he gave me a crazy mother-in-law."

Destiny and Ali stopped laughing. They couldn't believe he said that in front of Layla.

Layla laughed. "Nate is tripping. He knows my mother has a chemical imbalance. He talks a lot of crap, but he was the first one to seek help for her."

"You're lying?" Destiny replied.

Layla shook her head. "He insisted on getting her some help."

"Yeah, as far away from *me* as possible," Nate replied.

Layla hit him. "Stop it, Nate. That's not why you took her to Wisconsin."

Ali frowned. "What?"

"She's there because after all the research *he* did, it was the best place. They-"

"Wait just one damn minute!" Ali interrupted. "My uncle had me believing he tried to get the demons to kill your mother."

Layla hit Nate again, and laughed. "He did pull her in the middle of a battle."

"I told cha'." Nate laughed.

"But that was because he already knew demons are afraid of her. He and his team were outnumbered. He needed her help."

Ali hit him. "You punk!"

Nate laughed. "Man, my mother-in-law can scare a haint up a thorn tree."

"Did Nate tell you I'm going to visit her?" Ali asked her.

"Yes. He said you wanted to see if there was anything you could do for her. I appreciate that, Ali."

"I understand you had a rough childhood, because of her," Destiny said.

"It is terrible to love a person that has a mental illness. They don't realize what they are doing to you. I had no friends and no other relatives. Some days she was very coherent. But most days she rattled on foolishly. I was alone, until I met Nate. He loves me, so of course he loves my mother."

"No, I *don't*," Nate laughed. "I just want to make you happy, Laylo."

She smiled. He called her Laylo whenever he felt a depression coming on her. "You do make me happy."

Ali smiled. "So if you give me the information, I will visit her this week."

§

Justin was standing close enough to hear the conversation. "If you don't mind, I'd like to go with you."

Ali frowned. "Why?"

"Maybe I can help," he replied and walked away.

[16]

"That was strange," Layla replied. A tingle ran down her spine. He felt familiar to her. "Who *is* he?"

"That's Justin; my sister Amanda's husband. And you are right; that was strange." Destiny frowned.

"Hell, I'll take all of the help I can get with that crazy ass woman," Nate replied.

Everybody laughed.

§

Desiree was introducing her brother and sister-in-law to the nephews. She was beaming. She finally had family in the mix. "This is Ezeqeel and Dena. Zeek is Donnell's older brother."

Leroy extended his hand. "It's good to meet you, man."

"I can't believe how much Seraphiel's family has grown, since the wedding," Zeek replied.

"Yeah, we're pretty big. But you guys are a part of our family now," JR replied and shook his hand.

"You guys have got to come to our place and hang out," Zeek replied to both of them.

"No doubt," Leroy replied.

§

Chapter 3

Brock and Jodi were still in their suite, with Adam. They wanted some quiet time with their *now* grown son. Plus, Jodi had to pull herself together.

§

"Boy! You are too big. Get off my lap." Brock laughed, and stood up.

Adam jumped up before Brock dropped him on the floor. "I'm the same size as you, Dad."

"Like I said, you're too damn big to sit on my lap." Brock patted him on his back. His boy was a younger version of him. He looked like Akibeel.

His heart was about to jump out of his chest. He smiled, because for all practical purposes, he had three sons. Adam…Yomiel…Akibeel.

§

The thought of Yomiel and Akibeel brought sadness to his eyes and heart.

They loved Hezekiah, and thought of him as a father, too. But, he let them down. He let all of them down. Of course, he made sure that Akibeel didn't remember it. But he and Yomiel wore the scar like it had happened a minute ago.

§

H apologized, and Brock believed he was sincere. But it was *much* too little…*way* too late. Shoulda, coulda, woulda was just a song. It didn't fly in the real world.

Snow Anna jumped time and gave them a do over. But that was for Baby Girl's sanity. H and Lightwings had all but destroyed his daughter. He would never *forget* or *forgive* that.

Not to mention the fact that Lightwings had physically attacked Yomiel. Every time he thought about that shit, he wanted to beat his ass again.

Akibeel had been emotionally scarred by the whole incident. That added fire to his rage.

He quietly told Lightwings to get the hell out of dodge. He told him to use whatever excuse he wanted with his family. He further told him that unless there was a meeting with the Ultimate Watchers, he was *not* welcome back. Lightwings had bowed his head and teleported out with his new 'spirit' mate. And that was that!

§

Everyone knew something was going on between him and H, but they didn't know what it was. It was probably good that Jodi had been upset over Adam's impending adulthood. She was the only one that didn't have a clue. He liked it that way.

Snow Anna was frosty with H, too. She had a hard time hiding her emotions. Every time he said something to her, she snapped.

Yomiel stayed clear of the man. He wanted no part

of the so called 'father-son' relationship. He came right out and told H, *"Brock is my Pops; and don't you ever forget it!"*

§

"Dad!"

Brock was lost in thought and didn't realize he'd zoned out. "Yeah?"

"Where is your mind? What are you thinking about?" Adam asked out loud, but then whispered, *"Let it go, man."*

Brock looked at his son and smiled. His boy! Then he looked over at Jodi. She was a hot mess! He shook his head and hugged her. "We'll get through it, Dimples."

"You don't like me grown, Mom?" Adam asked.

She pouted her lips and sobbed. "No."

§

Brock and Adam knew it was going to take a minute for Jodi to get herself together. Adam put his arm around her and led her to the living room sofa. "We won't go out until you are ready, Mom."

"I ain't ever going to be ready," Jodi replied.

"Have you picked out a room yet, son?" Brock asked.

Jodi cried harder. It just hit her that he wouldn't be staying in the nursery anymore. The girls' twin beds, and his baby bed, were in there.

"No, but I figure it'll be in the single men's area,"

Adam replied. But he didn't plan on staying there very long. He had more than one destiny that was about to be fulfilled.

"That's too far away, Adam," Jodi sobbed.

"No, it's not," Brock replied. "He's right. He needs to be on the other end, Jodi. He's not a baby anymore."

"But nobody is on that end anymore. He'll be by himself."

"No, I won't. Caim and Balam are down there. So are Addison, Tim and Paul. Plus, there are always a couple of guys staying over."

"What?"

"Addis, Tim and Paul like living here, Jodi. More often than not they sleep inside the estate."

"I didn't know that," Jodi replied. "But still, with everyone having moved out, there are a lot of rooms available on this end, too. I want Adam on this end, Brock."

Adam and Brock looked at each other. That was not too much to ask. "Okay, Mom. I'll choose a room on this end."

"But not the nursery; and not next door to our suite," Brock stipulated. It was time to let go. It was understood he would live inside the estate; all of their children would. But he didn't want them within ear's reach. He didn't want them to hear him and Jodi, and he didn't want to hear them.

Even though the estate walls were soundproof; they weren't to him. He had to forcibly block the noise coming from all the rooms.

He never told his family that ditty; otherwise they'd sure enough call him nosey. He wasn't though. He couldn't stand all the sounds in his head.

It had taken years for him learn how to filter down what he did not want to hear.

Evidently, Adam had inherited that from him. He was going to have to spend some time training his boy. He had too much power that he didn't yet understand how to wield. If not properly trained he could get into a lot of trouble.

Not only that, but Brock sensed the arrogance radiating off of his son. He honestly believed that he was as powerful as Brock; but he wasn't. No one was.

Although it was true that Samjaza had given him all that he was; it was subjective. That only meant that everything Samjaza could do; he could too. If Samjaza walked like a duck, he could too…but not as well. No one would give all of their powers to another person; not even a son.

The only way he was *able* to defeat Samjaza was by splitting himself. Samjaza had been watching and thought he was still at the estate. In essence, he'd caught the bastard off guard. Not to mention Samjaza was still chained against the dungeon wall. If Samjaza had been loose…it may have been a different outcome.

He only had *ninety-nine* percent of Samjaza's powers; and Adam only had *fifty* percent of his. But fifty percent was nothing to sneeze at; because that was at the level of an Ultimate Watcher. And Adam still needed to be trained.

"Is that what you're wearing to the party, Jodi?"

"No." She wiped her eyes.

"You should get ready. Everybody is here already."

"Okay," Jodi replied, and wiped her eyes again.

She didn't want to go out there. That would mean no turning back. Although, there was *already* no turning back.

§

When Jodi went to take her shower, Brock smiled at Adam. "After the party, you and I need to talk."

"About what?"

Brock smacked his lips. "You're grown, and you are powerful. But you still need to be trained."

"Why?"

"I feel like I put a loaded gun in the hands of a baby. You are not ready for the powers you have inherited, Adam. I wasn't ready, and neither are you."

"But unlike you, I've had a father all along. I've watched every move you've made, Dad. I'm ready."

Brock closed his eyes and shook his head. "Not even close."

Then he told him about how he acted when he first realized how powerful he was. "I made a whole host of mistakes, Adam."

"I know everything you did, Dad. Trust me. I'm ready."

Brock had a sense of dread. Adam wasn't a baby anymore. He wasn't even a child. Brock couldn't send him to his room, like he did Aurellia when she was small.

Adam was a man, who thought he knew it all. But, it was just a thought. Brock stood up and walked towards the bedroom. He needed to get ready too; but he silently prayed, *'Lord help me…help my son.'*

He closed the door behind him and leaned up against it. His head was bowed and he whispered, *"He's not ready, and he won't listen, Dad."*

§

Michael appeared in the room. He smiled at Brock, *"And neither were you, son."*

Brock nodded. *"I know. I don't want my son to make the same mistakes I made."*

"If he does, you will clean it up for him…just like I did for you."

§

Chapter 4

Symphony was finishing up the last minute details. She was prancing around telling everyone where they needed to be.

The children were excited. They were going to play a major role in the celebration.

The male cousins all gathered around her to get the last minute instructions. "I haven't seen you this hyped in a long time, Spoiler," Mark told her.

"I just need everything to be perfect," she replied. "We get one chance and one chance only."

"Don't worry, Symphony." Henry smiled. "You've done more than I expected. Everything looks good." He hugged her, and kissed her cheek. "I'm proud of you, girl."

She smiled. Then her eyes watered. It was important that Henry approved. She'd never be to him what Dawn was, but it was still important that he approved.

He'd called her out on her flaws, but he didn't leave it there. He gave her the opportunity to *find* herself. He gave her the opportunity to show *everyone* her self-worth. She *had* to get this right. "Thank you, Henry. I really enjoyed this."

"I enjoyed working with you."

§

"I wonder what is taking them so long to come out," Sam asked.

"If I know Jodi, she's the hold up," Ditto replied. "She's not ready to let him go."

"I wouldn't be ready either," Symphony said. "I can't imagine Mary as a grown woman."

"We all feel the same way." Faith walked up. "And thank God we don't have to worry about it."

"Ain't that the truth?" Ditto agreed. "I want to experience my mini take his first steps."

Doc and Kwanita walked up. "It was awesome to see Abe take his," Doc told them.

"Lil man is walking?" Nantan asked.

"Yeah. He's already trying to run. Of course he bumps his head a lot." Doc laughed.

"That's what I want my shorty to experience," Arak said and smiled. "It'll make him tough."

"Hey, did you guys notice Tim and Paul?" Sam whispered.

"What?" Everyone asked.

"Look over my shoulder," Sam replied.

§

They were at the far end of the yard. Paul was holding hands with Mysia. Tim had his arm around Nikki's waist. No doubt it was more than casual.

"Well damn," Leroy laughed. "Aren't they our cousins?"

Henry smirked. "Oh please. That blood line is so thin, it doesn't matter."

"What number are they?" Deuce asked.

"Satariel said they are tenth. We're ninth. So who gives a damn?" Matthew asked.

Mark laughed. "Evidently they don't. Besides, must I tell you guys again, God is doing something?"

"You don't have to tell me," Nantan agreed.

"Besides, everyone is related one way or another; if you think about it. All of the Fallen were Michael's brothers, right," Eugene stated.

"That's true. So then all the Watchers are cousins, right?" Mark added.

"The demons are too for that matter," Eugene continued.

Everyone nodded their heads.

"That means that all of us are cousins. I'm not only related to Baraq, I'm related to Dawn, too. And Dawn is even related to Baraq."

"Damn, Eugene. That's right!" Mark responded.

Henry squealed, "That also means you and Nantan are related."

"Shut up, HENRY!" Eugene laughed.

"I'm just saying; you brought it up." Henry kept laughing.

But it was the truth. Everyone that was related to a Watcher was related to each other. What in the world was God doing?

§

Addison and Isabella were off by themselves. Her mother had finally gotten over being angry with her. But she warned her that she'd better not make a scene, or she was going to bring out her wooden spoon.

She grabbed his hand. "Let's sit in the garden, Addison."

He smiled. "Okay." He'd really missed her, and was glad she came. They talked every day, but her mother had put her on punishment for her behavior. Strangely enough, she liked her mother being mad at her. She said it meant she cared.

§

The garden was empty, but he wanted to go deep; just in case. He put his arm around her. "Let's go to the Chinese garden."

"Okay."

§

Once inside, before she could speak, he did. "Marry me, Issie."

She smiled. "That's not *fair!* I was supposed to ask you."

He caressed her cheek. "You were taking too long, girl."

"I'll marry you, Addison, but you need to ask Papa."

He kissed her. Man he missed her. She made *his* toes curl. "I already did."

"When?" she asked. He hadn't been alone with her father since they arrived.

"Yesterday." He reached in his pocket and pulled out a ring. "He said yes."

"Does momma know?"

"Yes. She agreed. But she said not tonight. Tonight is about Adam. I haven't told my parents yet."

"You don't have a house. Where will we live?"

"Uncle Brock said you and I can live in the estate."

"He did?"

He smiled. "He said all of our children will live in the estate, too."

§

Caim was so over waiting for Virginia to be ready. It wasn't like she had to make up her mind about them. They were a given. They'd been freaky and frisky, all along. She let him get to the edge and then stopped him. She knew they couldn't make love until he took her blood. So she denied him that. But he'd had his fill of kissing and groping. It would be insane for Adam to physically mate before him. Not to mention once everyone knew they were mates, they'd also know that Virginia held out.

Although, he suspected Brock and Yomiel already knew. If they saw Lightwings and Sharon; they saw them, too.

He wrapped his arms around her. "You are my 'spirit' mate, Virginia. It's time to let everyone know," he chided. "I'm tired of waiting. I love you. And I know you love me, too."

Virginia smiled. He was a beautiful man; and not just visually. When she looked at him, she wondered how she put up with Mitchell. Everyone thought she was mouthy and outspoken; and she was. But she held her emotions close to the vest. The words that came out of her mouth, were contradictory to her feelings.

The truth of the matter was she hadn't wanted to give her daughter away. She worried about her baby every day of her life. She hated that she died without knowing her mother really did love her.

Beneath the surface she was *always* afraid. She'd believed her aunt, Penny, when she told her she was ugly. She believed that still. That's why she'd slept with Mitchell, because he was ugly, too. But she hadn't loved him. And she really did pretend he was Clark Gable.

But Caim made her feel her worth. She was worth so much more than her outward appearance. He told her that if she still looked seventy-five, he'd age to catch up with her. He even told her that if she didn't want children, he was good with that. But she did want them. She'd always wanted more children.

She smiled. "Yes."

"Yes…?"

"I'm ready."

Caim stared at her, and slowly smiled. "You *are?*"

She nodded her head and kissed him. "Yes."

§

Balam looked at Grace. She was soft spoken and introverted. She'd been through a lot in her youth, and he tried to be patient. He didn't want to rush or push her, but damn. His impatience wasn't about the sex; although it was, in part.

She was the most gorgeous, gentle woman, he'd ever met. Her voice was like a whisper, echoing on the wind. And every time she said his name, he felt a gentle breeze up against his heart. After a night of battling, her voice soothed his spirit.

But the meat of his impatience was simple. He wanted everyone to know that she was his woman. He wanted to call her *Gorgeous* in public. He wanted to hold her hand and caress her lips, openly. He wanted her to mother all of his children.

Plus, his inner she-demon was getting restless. She wanted out.

Grace smiled. She loved Balam and bemoaned the years they'd lost. At first, she wondered why Michael hadn't assigned him, and his brother, to her father. That would have saved her, and her sister, years of heartache. But then she realized they ended up in Indiana; where

Balam, and Caim had been all along. Her life had played out, just like it was supposed to. Patricia, Patrice and Patience had to be born; for their husbands.

Her only regret was that she never knew her *daughter*. But she loved her granddaughters. And unlike the rest of the older human women, she wanted more children. She wanted Balam's children. "Virginia and I always do everything together, Balam."

His heart leaped. "Meaning...?"

"I'm ready, too. *I've* been ready from day one. Virginia made me wait on her." She laughed. "But we must tell Papa and Momma first."

He lifted her up in his arms. "Let's do it now, Gorgeous."

§

Adabiel and Gabriella walked into the rose garden. They had expected to be greeted by Addison and Isabella. But it wasn't them. Virginia and Grace were in there with Caim and Balam.

"What's going on?" Adabiel asked. Then he looked down and saw their hands. *"What?"*

"Virginia is my 'spirit' mate, Biel," Caim replied.

"And Grace is mine," Balam added.

§

Adabiel's eyes watered. He was a man who didn't mind showing his emotions. He never tried to control them; he couldn't. Happy, sad, angry, disappointment, whatever; he let them rip. His brothers hated that about him. Because whatever he felt...they felt, too.

He never thought his daughters would reach the point where they'd try love again. That had broken his heart. They lived too long to live alone. He wiped his eyes. "Sweet Jesus."

"You don't approve, Papa?" Grace asked.

He hugged her and sobbed. "I approve, more than you will ever know, Gracie."

He shook Caim and Balam's hand. Then he hugged them. "A man can never have too many sons."

§

Gabriella was beside herself, too. Her daughters were mated to Watchers. That guaranteed they would never leave her, again. They would stay until that Great Day of Judgment. "I am so happy." She hugged her girls and cried.

§

Addison and Isabella walked into the Rose Garden. "Why are you crying, Momma?"

Gabriella wiped her eyes. "Your sisters are 'spirit' mates to Caim and Balam."

"I already knew that."

"How did you know?"

"Addison told me."

Caim frowned. "How did *you* know?"

Addison smiled. "A wolf told me."

[33]

Isabella extended her hand so they could see her ring. "Addison asked me to marry him."

Virginia and Grace screamed, and hugged her. "You *little* brat!" Virginia said and swatted her butt. "You can't get married before me and Gracie. And you can't get married on the day we get married."

"Why?"

"Virginia and I are a twosome," Grace replied. "Three is a crowd."

Gabriella tried to soften the blow. "It would be fitting if our last child had her own day, Isabella. We will plan a big wedding for you. One like we had for Ana Luci."

Isabella and Addison smiled. "I'd like that, Momma."

§

Adabiel's heart was full. All of his daughters were mated to fine young men. He eased into Gracie and Virginia's mind. They wanted children. Yea! Soon enough, his house would be filled with grandchildren. He wiped his eyes again, because his cup runneth over. "We'd better get back outside before Adam comes out," he said and grabbed Gabbie's hand.

§

They made it to the front yard just in time.

§

[34]

Chapter 5

Adam walked out the front door, flanked by his parents. The boy had an arrogant swag. With his hair cut close to his head, he looked more like Akibeel, than Brock.

The family was outside, waiting. They'd strung a banner, *'Happy ?? Birthday, Adam!'* Then underneath those words it said, *'How old are you anyway?'*

§

The children started to sing Stevie Wonder's version of 'Happy birthday to Ya'. Jas was the leader. Even Justina, Elizabeth and Hannah were performing. They were clapping…off beat. But, they were on key and so cute.

§

When they finished, Symphony handed Floyd something to recite. She had instructed him to read it slowly and with purpose. He could do that.

"The steps of a good man are ordered by the Lord, and He delights in his way…"

Behind him, the nephews started to perform a 'step' dance. Those boys had some serious moves.

Floyd continued, "Though he falls, he shall not be utterly cast down; for the Lord upholds him with His hand."

Ditto was leading the step. He'd do his steps; then his cousins would mimic him. They were rocking the

[35]

yard!

Old Pastor Floyd got carried away. He added his own verse. "Thy word is a lamp unto my feet, and a light unto my path."

The nephews didn't miss a beat. They kept right on stepping.

Floyd raised his hand. "But if we walk in the light, as he is in the light, we have fellowship with one another, and the blood of Jesus, his Son, purifies."

Those boys kept right on stepping and Floyd kept right on preaching!!

§

Without a doubt, Symphony had outdone herself. She stood to the side with her arm around Ram. He kissed her cheek. "I can't believe you pulled this together, Precious."

"It's for Adam, Angel." She smiled. "Everyone wanted to be a part of this."

"What will the women do?"

She smiled. "You'll see."

§

As soon as the children and men finished, the music started. The nieces started to perform a praise dance to the instrumental of the song, 'Order my steps in your word, dear Lord'. Faith led the dance.

The nephews joined in. Every time one of the nieces attempted to step out of place, a nephew would gently guide her back in step. Every time one looked like they would fall, a nephew would lift her up.

No doubt they'd rehearsed this to perfection. Symphony's perfection. It was surreal.

§

Brock's eyes watered. That song told the story of his heart's desire for his son. He literally heard his friend, David's voice, *'The steps of a good man are ordered by God.'*

Floyd looked over at Henry. He felt like having some church. He mouthed, "WOW!"

Henry smiled. Symphony had most definitely outdone herself.

When the music stopped, the children released hundreds of balloons into the air.

§

The family made their way to Adam, one by one; starting with Aurellia and the twins.

"I guess we have to call you 'big' brother now," Aurellia said and hugged him.

"Yep!" he replied and hugged her. "I got cha back, Lil' bit."

Elizabeth and Hannah were jumping up and down laughing. "Me next."

His eyes lit up and he smiled. Then he picked them both up and kissed their cheeks. "Hey Squirts." He was going to love being all of his sisters' big brother.

ADAM - BEGINNINGS and REVELATIONS

§

Akibeel had never seen his nephew grown and was blown away. "You could be my twin."

Adam laughed and hugged him. "I figured since you think of my dad as your Pops, we should be around the same age."

Akibeel laughed. "So I guess you won't be calling me Uncle."

Adam smirked. "Don't count on it."

§

Doc was next. He hugged Adam. "You're with me."

"I look forward to it. And I ain't calling you Uncle either."

§

Hezekiah had the biggest dimples yet. "Don't think you are too grown to call me Grandpa, boy."

"I wouldn't think of it, Grandpa."

Snow Anna stood next to Hezekiah, crying. She opened her arms and Adam walked in. "Don't cry Grandma Cutie. Or is it Grandma Tiny Bit?" he teased.

"Grandma Cutie," she sobbed. "I'm going to miss holding you, Adam."

He kissed her cheek. "I'll sit on your lap whenever you want me to."

Sarah got her hug in, too. "You're a fine young man, Adam."

[38]

"Thanks, Grandma Sarah."

"Congrats, son," Satariel said and hugged him.

"Thanks, Satariel," Adam replied. He already knew Sat didn't like being called 'grandpa'.

Satariel smiled.

Kiche also hugged and kissed him. "You are as handsome as your father."

"Thanks, Grandma."

"I'd like to spend a little time with you, Adam," Kobabiel said and hugged him. "You've been imbued with a lot of power, son."

"I know, but I got this."

Kobabiel looked over at Brock. *'He is definitely your son, Seraphiel.'*

Brock frowned.

§

One by one his great uncles and aunts hugged, kissed and slobbered over him. The women cried and the men were proud.

§

Then the Watchers all gave him a fist bump and a one armed hugged. Chaz laughed and said, "No more diaper changes for this boy."

All the Watchers laughed and agreed. Adam laughed and said, "It's about time."

Jon and Jas ran up to him, and Jon said, "So, you not gon' be a baby ever again?"

Adam squatted down. "Nope. I'm your big cousin now."

"That's cool," Jas replied and hugged him. "I still like you."

§

All of the little girl cousins hugged him. They bombarded him with a lot of questions.

Sheila asked, "Can you read?" She read everything she got her hands on.

"Yep."

"Can you count?" Autumn asked. She loved math.

"Yep."

"Can you ride a bike?" Adriana asked.

Adam frowned. "I don't know. We'll have to see."

"If you can't, I'll teach you," Sylvia replied.

He smiled. "I'm going to hold you to that."

They were so innocent. They were asking questions the grownups hadn't even thought about.

Summer said, "Do you have grown people's teeth or baby teeth?"

Adam smiled and let her see his teeth. They were as pearly white and beautiful as his dad's. "They're grownup teeth."

"Man, you lucky." She smiled and let him see one of hers was still out.

He laughed.

"Can you tie your shoes?" Summer asked.

"Yes."

"Do you know your colors?" Sylvia asked.

"Yes."

She didn't believe him. "What color do I have on?"

"Blue. It's my favorite color."

She smiled. "Mine too."

"I love you, Adam." Justina smiled. "You pretty!"

He reached down and picked her up. "You're pretty, too. I guess since you're my little sisters' big sister, I'm your big brother, too."

She looked down at Elizabeth and Hannah and licked her tongue out. "I told y'all he was my brother, too." Then she hugged and kissed his neck. "Do you know your ABC's?"

"Yep!"

§

Next all of his aunts stood in line to welcome him. When it was Robyn's turn, he hugged her and whispered in her ear, "Thanks for working on Hope for me, Auntie."

"Now how you gon' call her Auntie, and not call me Uncle," Akibeel complained.

"It is what it is," Robyn replied and squeezed Adam's neck. "I love you, baby."

Hope was next. She smiled shyly. "I'm there."

"I know you are, Aunt Hope." He kissed her cheek.

When he hugged Kwanita, he gave Abe a high five. "My buddy."

Abe smiled and spoke to his mind. *"You are a lucky dog, man. I wish it was me."*

Adam laughed out loud. He sounded like his father. *"I wish you could come along with me, too."*

Brock and Doc knew they were talking, but they didn't snoop. In time, Abe would catch up with Adam.

§

Lillian stood off to the side. She was afraid Adam didn't like her, because of her negative influence on Hannah. He'd tried to warn her to get control of her mouth, but she hadn't. Then Hannah was spanked. Aurellia still wasn't *that* crazy about her. She was sure he didn't like her, either.

Adam was his father's son. He was snooping on her thoughts. He walked over and hugged her. "That's not true, Aunt Lillian. I love you, too."

She pouted her lips. "I'm so sorry, Adam."

He hugged her. "No worries, okay."

He lifted Symphony off the ground. "That was awesome!"

§

All of his male cousins slapped him a high-five. "We couldn't wait, man!" Ditto told him.

Mark hugged him. "Yeah, it took you long enough."

One by one they all welcomed him with excitement. Then it was Matthew and Sam's turn. The three of them hugged like they hadn't seen each other in years.

"Man, I've been counting down the days. I didn't sleep at all last night," Sam informed him.

"Me either," Matthew added. "It's good to finally have you grown."

"Word," Adam replied.

§

Henry smiled. Unlike Ditto he never had a 'male' best friend. Associates yeah, but nothing like Ditto had with Eugene. And even though he thought of that clown as his brother, too; he was Ditto's boy.

Dawn was, and always would be, his girl; but he looked forward to his bond with Adam. Sure, Sam and Matthew would be a part of their posse, but Adam was *his* boy.

He slapped him a high five and snapped his fingers. "My Dawg!"

Adam smiled. He had a love for Henry that trumped all of his other cousins; even Sam and Matthew. They'd all be tight, no doubt. But Henry was his boy. He hugged him and squeezed him tight. "I couldn't wait, man."

"Me neither."

"We gon' kick-it later?"

"For sho," Henry replied.

§

Jodi and Brock stood to the side and smiled. They still had a hard time, but the worst was over. He was grown now. They'd get used to it. Jodi rubbed her stomach. At least she'd be able to raise the baby she carried.

§

Adam looked over Henry's shoulder and smiled. He released him and walked through the crowd. All of his cousins fanned out.

At the end of the row, Mordiree stood alone. She never took her eyes off his. He was a *beautiful* man. Her *beautiful* man. Her eyes watered.

Adam arrogantly walked up to her. Then he stroked her cheek and wiped her tear. "Maude."

She smiled. "I waited for you, Adam."

"I knew you would," he replied. Then he leaned down and kissed her.

She wrapped her arms around his neck and caressed his head. "I love you."

He wrapped his arms around her and lifted her to his height. "I have *always* loved you, Maude. And I always will." Then he kissed her again…passionately. Proper!!

She straddled her legs around his waist. She'd waited a long time to do this. Her man was finally here. They both felt their hearts merge and moaned.

They knew they were making a spectacle of themselves, but didn't care. Whatever fallout there was; was going to be fallout, anyway.

And they both knew it was coming.

§

Their parents, aunts, uncles and grandparents' jaws *dropped*. They were all in a state of confusion. None of them had a clue. Not even daddy Brock or Grandma Snow.

They looked around and it was apparent the next generation *all* knew. They had stuck together and kept this secret. Why?

§

Clyde looked at Brock. It was obvious that he didn't know either. He thumped him on the back of his head. "You nosey ass bastard! How could you not see *this* shit?" That was his baby girl. "How the hell could you not know, man?"

§

Brock and Jodi were catatonic. Neither of them could say a word. This was too damn fast. And why hadn't Brock known?

Jodi wanted to cry. This was too soon. She sobbed, "My baby!"

"I'm still your baby, Mom," Adam whispered to her and Brock's minds. *"But Mordiree is my 'spirit' mate. She always has been."*

"Why did you hide this from me, son?" Brock asked. He had deliberately blocked Brock from reading his mind. And he didn't like that shit. Not one damn bit! That boy had a lot to learn.

"You weren't ready to let me grow up. I knew you wouldn't be ready for this. I didn't want you mistreating my mate, while I couldn't defend her."

"We'd never do that," Jodi responded.

He put Mordiree down, turned around and stared at his parents. *"Then why are you crying? I would like your support. But regardless, Mordiree is my future. Just like you and Dad were mated in the heavens; so were Maude and I."*

They realized that was why Mordiree never once held him. If Jodi came in a room carrying him, Mordiree left. She never went to the daycare. She never changed his diaper, fed him, or bathed him. She didn't want to *see* him as a baby, because she knew all along she was his…

Oh God! How could they not have known?

§

Mordiree was the only cousin that wasn't a *blood* cousin. She'd brought a date to Brock's birthday party, and Adam had had a fit in her womb. He'd kicked her all day long. He hadn't settled down until the man left.

Mordiree never went out on any dates after that. God! How could Brock not know?

In truth, Jodi thought she might be a lesbian. She even said as much to Amanda and Lara. She had wanted to tell her that it was okay, if she was. After all, Nantan and Eugene were gay and happy. She thought maybe Mordiree thought Clyde and Rebecca wouldn't accept it.

Was she ever wrong?

She wiped her eyes and walked between the onlookers. She stopped right in front of them. "You're right. I'm sorry."

Then she bawled like a baby.

Adam hugged her. "Don't cry, Mom."

§

Rebecca walked over to her daughter. "You should have told me, Mordiree."

"Does it make a difference, Mamma?"

"Well no. But it would have been less shocking."

She looked at Clyde. "Babbo?"

Clyde looked distraught. It wasn't that he had a problem with them. Not at all. But, Mordiree was his baby. She always talked to him about everything. "Why did you keep this from me?"

Hope spoke up. "It's because of me. I had a problem with the two of them. They kept quiet because they didn't want anyone else making them uncomfortable."

"You knew?" Brock asked. He knew she had a problem with Adam going from baby to grown. But no one told him about *this!* How was it possible that he hadn't gleaned it from any of their minds? He raised his brows. Damn! Adam had blocked *him!*

"We all knew," Chaz admitted. He wasn't going to let Hope take the blame. "Or at least Arak and I knew."

[47]

Brock looked from Chaz to Arak. Arak hunched his shoulders. "My bad!" Then he cracked up.

Brock knew it wasn't their story to tell, but he was still pissed at them. He reached out and squeezed their damn hearts.

"Ouch!" Chaz cried and grabbed his chest.

"Damn!" Arak grabbed his chest.

"Dad!" Adam shouted. "Don't blame them."

Brock grunted and released their hearts. He was warm. He stared at Chaz and Arak. "Don't ever keep anything, about *my* children, from me again!"

He turned and walked back in the house. His son was acting like his mother. Damn that boy! He may be his son, but he treasured his privacy, like his mother. He still had a lot to learn. As a Watcher nobody had total privacy. At least not from *him*. He hadn't tried to read Adam's mind because he didn't realize he needed to.

It hurt his feelings for his son to treat him like that. He wondered if that was how Samjaza felt. He could understand it if he was a bastard, but he wasn't. He just wanted to protect his family.

§

Chapter 6

The team couldn't believe that Brock had hurt Chaz and Arak. He'd promised to never do any of them harm. They were more than a little disappointed that he hadn't kept his word.

"This is bullshit." Ali took off behind him.

"Wait, Ali," Nantan called out. "Give me a minute with him."

"Just one. Then I'm coming in."

"We all are," Ram added.

"Okay, how about five."

"Not a second more," Dan replied.

"Fair enough," Nantan replied. Then he went in the house and closed the door.

§

Jodi didn't give a damn that it was Adam; nobody hurt her husband. She lit into him. "Look what you made your father do. He has *never* hurt his team members."

"I didn't *make* him do that."

"Yes, the hell, you did. You disrespected him, Adam. And made sure everyone else did." She knew Adam had blocked Brock from being able to see his relationship through his cousins' minds.

"I wasn't trying to disrespect Dad. You don't like his snooping, either."

"That has nothing to do with you, boy! That's

between me and your father. Besides how would you *know* that, unless you had snooped yourself?" she shouted at him.

He couldn't deny it because it was the truth. They never argued in front of him and the girls. While he blocked his thoughts from them, he listened to theirs. He needed to.

It was a part of his accelerated learning process. He not only got his strength from his father; but his knowledge, too. He learned how to dress, brush his teeth, shave, and yes even intimacy; from snooping.

He learned how to count, his colors, read and basic school knowledge from his mother.

He arrogantly thought his reasoning was more justified than his father's. He bowed his head. "I'm sorry."

"Nature shouldn't leap. You may know your colors, how to count and read; but you didn't know the fundamentals. Things like common courtesy and consideration of other people's feelings. Respect!" Jodi turned and walked away. She was more than a little pissed.

§

Henry leaned over and whispered to Adam, "You need to go and deal with your father, Dawg."

"Why?"

"Because if you don't he will never accept this

relationship."

"You think I was *wrong?*"

"That's irrelevant," Henry replied. "He's hurt, man. Don't ever leave bad feelings. Always try and work things out; especially with your *father.* A man always needs his father in his corner..." He raised his eyebrows. "...No matter what."

§

H was standing close enough to hear Henry's statement. He cringed. He hadn't been there for his boys; and it had cost him dearly. Not only had he lost his sons; he lost their *respect.*

The last five days had been the worst in his life. Even worse than when he thought he lost E. Even though he lost him, he knew E had died still respecting, and loving, him.

Neither Brock nor Yomiel had looked him square in the eye since that day. Yomiel no longer called him Dad. Like Akibeel, he now called Brock *Pops.* Damn if that didn't hurt.

"Henry is right, Adam. Don't let anything or anyone come between father and son."

"Yes sir," Adam replied.

He turned to Mordiree. "I'll be back."

She squeezed his hand. "I'm sorry. We should have handled this differently. It was too soon, Adam."

"No, it wasn't. It was twelve months too long." He

couldn't wait a minute longer, because of her. "If I hadn't needed his strength I would have come here as an adult." He leaned down and kissed her. "I'll be back."

She nodded.

§

Nantan did not knock on the door. He just barged in and asked, "What's *really* eating at you, man?"

Brock looked up from his desk. He hadn't gone back to his suite for fear Jodi would follow him. He couldn't believe the way this day was going. Hell, the whole damn week, for that matter.

"What are you talking about?"

Nantan sat across from him, and crossed his leg, ankle to knee. "Man, don't act like you don't know what I'm talking about. Talk to *me*."

Brock stared at Nantan. He was his sounding board, and he enjoyed their relationship. Even before this mess with H; he confided in Nantan, more than anyone else. He was impartial, but fair. Nantan helped him deal with the intricacies of humanity. He'd been on the earth for over five thousand years, and had dealt with his share of humans. But not like this. Not this many family members under one roof.

When the original Brocks lived here, he and his men lived apart from them. Sure it was the same house, but it wasn't really family living; not like now.

"You think I overreacted?"

"What I *think* is, your reaction had *nothing* to do with Adam. Or the fact that your team and, I might add *I* knew, about Adam and Mordiree. You've been in a mood for days, man. You won't look at H, or any of the Walkers, in the face. H looks like he's lost his best friend. Not to mention Doc is acting indifferent towards them, too. What happened?"

"Damn." Brock scowled. "Is it that obvious?"

"To me? Yes. Talk to me, Unc."

Brock leaned back, and closed his eyes. "It's bad, man."

"I figured that much."

Brock shook his head. "You don't understand. I mean earth shattering *bad*. I mean family destroying *bad*."

"But, we're all still here, aren't we?"

Brock was so used to sharing his inner most thoughts with Nantan, he blurted out, "That is only because Cutie jumped time, man."

"WHAT...?"

§

Brock and Nantan both looked up. They hadn't heard the door open. Or felt the teams come into the room.

"Aw Hell," Brock complained. "What are you guys doing in here?"

"I think you owe Chaz, and Arak, an apology," Ali replied. "For that matter, you owe all of us an apology."

Brock rubbed his face. He knew he was wrong

[53]

when he did it. He broke a promise to them. Even though he only physically hurt Chaz and Arak; he broke the promise to all of them.

"You're right. I am sorry," he replied.

"It didn't hurt that bad, Mi Amigo. But, what is going on with you," Chaz said, and sat down.

"You are the last person who would have a problem with predestination," Arak added, and sat next to Chaz.

"You owe us an explanation," Donnell said and sat down. "You owe us that much."

"I don't believe for a minute not knowing about Adam and Mordiree has put you in this bad of a mood. Plus, the fact that Chaz and Arak knew is no big deal, either. We all know things we don't share with you. It's called *nunya*. But at least we know you are not as big of a snoop as we all thought. Otherwise you would have known, right?" Ram said and took a deep breath. He sounded like Akibeel. That was a long statement, even for that boy. He sat down on Brock's right side.

"You promised us *'together we stand, man'*," Baraq added.

Batman smiled and said, "Semper Fidelis. Always Faithful! Always Loyal!" and took a seat.

"Word!" Dan said, and sat next to him.

"C'mon Pops, spill," Akibeel insisted. "What's wrong?"

Pretty soon they all were seated around the

conference table, even Caim and Balam.

Waiting.

§

Brock closed his eyes and shook his head. This was bad. He'd overreacted and drawn their interest. If he told them, he'd have to hold them back from attacking Lightwings, and the Walkers. But if he didn't tell them he'd lose their trust...their faith. He'd never let *that* happen. "Damn."

"Why did Cutie jump time, Brock?" Nantan asked.

He looked from Akibeel to Yomiel. Yomiel looked as concerned as he did, but he nodded his head.

"Lock the door, son."

Just as Yomiel went to lock it, Adam stepped in. He was a part of Doc's team now. He belonged in here, too. "Have a seat," Yomiel instructed him.

§

Brock looked at all of his men, and then Adam. "I'm sorry I overreacted, son."

"It's okay. I'm sorry I disappoint you," Adam replied.

Brock frowned. "Don't ever think that, Adam."

Then he looked back at his men. "For safety precautions, I've locked you all down. So don't even think about trying to teleport out."

"It's *that* bad?" Ali asked.

Brock didn't respond. He just opened up his mind.

§

Needless to say, they lost it. They destroyed the conference room. They viciously tore it apart...piece by angry piece. All of the fancy china...destroyed! Barstools...ripped to shreds! All of those nice chairs that Akibeel liked so much...broken to pieces.

Not one piece of debris hit Brock, Doc, Adam or Nantan.

§

Brock almost laughed. What was it about his boys that when they were upset, they lost common sense? Here they were having a fit about Lightwings attacking him, and Doc. They were so focused on the attack; they overlooked *how* he attacked them. They forgot they could, this very moment, attack Lightwings in that same manner.

Once again, they forgot that they could still reach out with their *minds* and take action. And again, Brock didn't remind them.

Once they had their fill of destruction, Brock put it back together. "You guys feel better?"

§

Nantan was the first to respond. He held his mouth and whispered, "Sweet Jesus. I can't believe E-du-di did that, man. I cannot believe he did that shit!"

Ram was next. "Baby girl!" His eyes were dripping with angry tears. Tearing up the room wasn't good enough. He was going to have to hurt *somebody*.

[56]

Ali was furious. "I'm going to kill that bastard! With my bare hands, ya heard!"

"No you are not, Ali. That is why I didn't want you guys to know. This is why I had Cutie jump time."

"If Cutie jumped time, does he remember doing that shit?" Caim asked.

Brock nodded. "It was important that he remembered. Otherwise I'd have to beat his ass, again."

"Well you damn sure did that!" Balam chuckled. "Good on ya!"

"No wonder he didn't show up today," Dan said. His vibration was jacking with all of their insides. "Punk ass coward. He ain't Watcher material, let alone Ultimate Watcher."

"Settle down, Dan," Brock commanded.

"What about H, and his brothers? Do they remember?" Donnell asked.

"H does, but the others don't."

§

Akibeel moved towards the door. His hand was all aglow. He was going to take out H first. That bastard had let Lightwings hurt his Pops and Yommy. Some father he turned out to be.

Brock yanked him back. "Don't go there, Akibeel!"

"I'll tell you what; that's the last time I give up my damn powers. If they want to fight us again, they will have to fight us with our powers. Otherwise, they can go to hell," Ram added.

"The bad part is we were down on the *women*, for taking us for granted. But in the end, they had our backs," Baraq said. "They were just as pissed as I am right now. Especially, SnowAnna and Lucinda."

"Snow Anna, hell," Ali squeaked. "Jodi and Kwanita were going to light his ass on fire." He looked at Brock and Doc. "You guys should have let them. His punk ass deserved it."

§

"I'd like to know, where the hell was Michael?" Batman asked. "He always seems to be too busy, when we need him the most."

"Ain't that the truth? Always, twenty-four hours late, and a hundred copper coins short," Chaz added.

"With a lame assed excuse," Arak agreed.

§

Chapter 7

Michael appeared in the room. "I was not late, nor do I have an excuse."

They all jumped, but Yomiel. He was *too* through with Michael, too. "Why didn't you answer me?"

"I put Seraphiel in charge of all the Watchers. He is the chain of command now. I will only answer his call. Or a human's. I heard you, but I assumed you were trying to by-step him. I assumed you were losing the fight in the preserve. It wasn't until I heard Hezekiah that I realized something was wrong."

"It was more than wrong, man," Ram spit out. "It was reprehensible!"

"Yes, it was. But, Lightwings didn't do anything that you, Ali, Chaz, Batman and even you, Akibeel, hadn't wanted to do to my son. That is a mystery to me. Why is it, when you guys find your mates, you attack the one person you *can't* defeat. It is like the spirit of *'insanity'* or *'stupidity'* overtakes you boys. Or maybe it is at that point, for a brief moment, you are totally human." Michael squinted and shook his head. "A total mystery to me."

"We *never*..." Batman started, and stopped.

Yeah, they did. They all had wanted a piece of Brock when their mates were in trouble. Each one of them thought back to that exact moment in their own lives. That moment when mutiny won the day; or their attempt at it,

[59]

anyway.

§

Ram remembered when he found out that Symphony had been raped. He was definitely gunning for Brock. It had taken the entire team to hold him back. He even broke Dan's jaw trying to get to the man. If they hadn't held him back, he would have acted as viciously as Lightwings.

§

Batman remembered when he found out who was behind Robyn getting shot. He had plans on lighting Brock's ass on fire. Ram had stood guard in front of Brock. Not to protect Brock; but to protect *him*.

§

Dan remembered he wanted a piece of him that day, too. Larry and Barry had sold Lilia into slavery. He wanted to find the bastards, but Brock wouldn't let him leave the building. He, Chaz and Batman had all wanted retribution. And a piece of Brock and each other.

§

Ali remembered the day he found out about Destiny's parentage. Brock had worked his last nerve. He was so angry he said some things he still couldn't get over. He'd gone to the conference room with the plan to throw down, and then sever all ties.

§

Akibeel remembered when Brock tried to stop him

from killing Maria's attackers. All of his life he'd been afraid of Brock, but not that day. At that point he would have tried to slice and dice Brock; with his glowing hand.

§

Chaz remembered that he had, in fact, got his hands on Brock. He teleported him, even though he knew it might hurt him. He wouldn't have stopped until Brock helped him.

§

Yomiel *would* have gone up against Brock the day he scared Kwanita. Kwanita snapped at Jodi, and pissed Brock off. Brock snapped at Kwanita, and pissed him off.

All of them had their team mates to thank for Brock not doing to them what he'd done to Lightwings.

§

Brock had warned them that *no one* would ever get the chance to hit him; like Ram had three thousand years ago. He all but promised a beat down would be eminent, if it ever happened again. He'd even put Ram in charge of making sure it never happened. But if by chance it did...

His actions with Lightwings confirmed that it was not an *idle* threat. He'd pulled out all the stops; and beat that old man's ass! Damn!

They all visibly shook.

§

Ali looked at Brock and frowned. "We damn sure did; didn't we? All of us, except Arak, Donnell and Baraq, wanted to hurt you." He looked at Michael and scowled. "What the *hell* happens to us, man?"

"It's a total mystery," Michael replied. "Unfortunately, Lightwings wanted a piece of him at the right time."

"More like the wrong time," Ram chuckled. Both teams laughed.

"Perhaps you are right, Ramiel. But, if memory serves..." He laughed. "...he will not make that mistake again." He looked at Brock. "Damn, son. You went, as they say, ape shit crazy on his ass! I actually felt sorry for his *arrogant* butt." He sat down, propped his legs up on the table, and bellowed.

§

"Raphael and Gabriel were having a ball. They were boxing their fists back and forth, shouting, *'Spank that ass, Seraphiel! Wax...that...ass!'* They made Father mad, because they were leaning over the balcony, cursing."

He wiped his twirling eyes and squeaked. "Raphael was acting like he was demonstratively spanking somebody. *'Tap that ass, Nephew! Show him who's the boss!'* They were hilarious!"

§

His eyes were glowing when he looked around the room. "Father said they had been hanging around *you guys* too much. They are on punishment and can't leave

Heaven for another week." He rolled. "Have you ever seen an Archangel on lockdown? They can only leave Heaven in an emergency."

He kept laughing and talking. "Right now, *Lucifer* has more freedom than they do.

"Oh man; they love Floyd's coffee. The three of us had coffee with him, every morning, in his office." He threw his head back and squealed, "They are going through withdrawal. Have you ever seen an angel in need of a *caffeine* fix?"

He was having way too much fun. He slapped his leg. "You boys are a bad influence on my little brothers."

§

None of them had ever heard Michael laugh so robustly. It made them laugh, too. The booming vibrato in his voice dissolved all the tension in the room.

§

Akibeel stopped laughing. "I am still upset with H and his brothers. Those bastards didn't try to help Yommy, and my Pops."

"I'm personally having a hard time with Elijah," Dan replied. "A *really* hard time. How could he encourage Lightwings after all Brock has done for his family?"

"He's done more for Elijah than he has for any of the others," Doc agreed. "But he's done a lot for all of them."

[63]

"They acted like Brock owed them an explanation," Arak added. "Like he answered to them."

"Yeah, they did," Batman agreed. "I wouldn't have told them a damn thing."

"Ya heard," Ali replied. "The only thing I would have told them was what Akibeel told them. Kiss my ass!"

"Since they don't remember, I'm going to tell them again," Akibeel promised.

"No the hell you are not, son," Brock replied. "You are going to keep your trap closed. Am I clear?"

"No!" Akibeel replied. "It's one thing to keep it from the women. I agree with that. But those bastards need to know. Otherwise they will do it again, Pops! Why are you protecting them?"

"I agree with him, Brock. At some point the Walkers need to be aware of what they did," Ali replied.

"Or didn't do," Ram corrected. "I agree too, Brock."

All of the Watchers were nodding their heads; including Doc. "I agree, Brock."

Brock was shaking his head. "No."

"Listen," Doc said. "I agree that their sons, daughters and wives, should remain in the dark. But, those men need to know. No one around this table will ever attempt to attack you, again. That's because we have seen what the fallout will be."

"That's not true," Ali said. "We will never attempt

to attack him, because we realized, even then, that he had our best interest at heart."

"But it don't hurt to know what will happen if we did." Dan laughed.

§

Michael nodded. "It is true, they did not help. But there is an understandable reason for that, too."

"What?" Akibeel asked.

"You have been deceived all of your life, Akibeel. You are just learning about loyalty, without waiver." He looked around the room. "In a sense, you all are. You have been with my son three thousand years. Why is it only now that you guys made a pledge to always be loyal and faithful?"

They all looked puzzled. Why had it taken that long to pledge an oath? Undoubtedly, Brock had always been committed to them. He stood in the gap every time, to protect them. That's why he didn't fight. His job was to make sure none of them were hurt. He watched them do their thing, even though he needed the tension release, too. And he went a little crazy when those mobsters hurt Batman; because that was his boy. They all were.

They thought they were committed to him; until their mates were in trouble. Then they wanted blood...his! Damn!

"What's your point?" Arak asked.

"You guys are committed to the Walker brothers;

and think of them as your fathers."

"We used to," Yomiel replied. "Not anymore. I have no use for them. I can barely stand the sight of them."

"I'm with you on that," Caim added. "I'm glad none of them are my father-in-law."

"Word!" Balam bumped his fist.

Michael looked across the room. "Is there anyone that could make you take sides against Brock, Akibeel?"

"No! My Pops can count on me."

"Why?"

"From the moment he rescued me from Hell, he has been there for me. If I call, he comes. No matter what." He looked at Brock and smiled. Then he looked at Adam. "I envy you, man. Pops is the *best* father a man can have."

Brock smiled. There was no need for him to envy Adam. In his heart, he had three sons. Akibeel was one of them.

"What about you, Yomiel. Can anyone make you turn against Seraphiel?"

"Not in this life."

"Why?"

"He has been more than a brother to me. He's been a friend, a confidant and yes, a father, too. In every way that counts, he is Akibeel's and my father."

"That's right," Akibeel agreed. "He's *my* Pops!"

"How about the rest of you guys?"

"Nope! Nada! No!"

"Is it because he has proven himself to all of you? Perhaps after your momentary 'stupidity', you realized he has *always* had your best interest at heart."

They all nodded. Even the wedding in Africa proved that point. It was to ease Ali's troubled spirit on his wedding day.

Even before they found their mates; the estate bore witness. He was looking ahead, not just for his mate, but all of theirs. He wanted a place where his team and their family would be safe. At the time he hadn't even known they were all related.

The sharing of his finances was a testament. None of them had thought beyond living in the moment. While he was amassing a sizable portfolio; they were spending every dime they had. Ram was buying a house for one woman after another. Before they settled down, the rest of them were wining and dining women. They went through money like it was water.

Brock was selfless and always put their needs first. Everything he did, he did with the team in mind. He not only made preparations for his 'spirit' mate, but theirs as well. He had the foresight to buy this estate, so there would be room for all the families.

They all placed their hands over their hearts and silently reaffirmed their pledge.

Brock smiled. They didn't realize that he'd done all

he did as penance. His treatment of his first team was *sinful*. He was not only emotionally abusive to them; but physically, as well. He pretty much told them they might as well be demons, because they were useless as Watchers. Even today, he couldn't believe Michael let him get away with that crap. Nate was right; their behavior was a direct result of his abusive treatment of them.

He used his powers against them on a daily basis. They all had been nineteen and twenty year olds; not much older than Yomiel and Akibeel. They'd gone from the abuse of their demon fathers, to his abuse. It was no wonder they acted out. They never had a role model. They'd never had anyone who treated them *right*. They didn't trust *anybody*; certainly not an Ultimate Watcher.

That's why Kobabiel recommended he walk in a human's shoes. He needed to feel how a weaker person felt. He needed to experience being bullied. It had worked, too. And now he worked overtime to treat these birds right.

Besides, they were devoted to him, too. Their actions time and time again, proved that. The way they loved Baby Girl was proof of that. They loved and protected her, because she was his. No amount of money could repay that devotion.

§

Michael nodded. "They were young men, when their father died. Hezekiah and Elijah were twenty-nine.

Floyd was only twenty-one, and newly engaged. It was a great loss for them. They were devastated, and not just because he was their father. He was their firm foundation. Their accountability partner, if you will. When he died, they lost their footing. Floyd was reckless and out of control; until MeiLi put her foot down."

He gazed at Brock. "Hezekiah stepped into the role of Patriarch, but he was grieving, too. He had a young family and six brothers depending on him. He had a mother who'd just lost her husband. She'd never worked a day in her life. Not to mention his community involvement. It was too heavy a load, for a young man to carry."

He looked across the table at Doc. "Who do you think stepped up to the plate, and *helped* him?"

He looked around the room. "Who do you guys think was there for *all* of them?"

No one responded, but they knew the answer. Those Walker boys thought of Lightwings as their father. When he killed his son, they surrounded him and lifted his spirits. They were all devastated they hadn't been there for him.

"Spirit Warrior took up the mantel and became their *surrogate* father. He never made a difference in them and his birth sons. As a matter of fact, he was closer to all those boys than he was to the son he killed. He never once wavered from his commitment to them; or their widowed mother. And when she passed on, he grieved her loss with them."

No one said a word. Lightwings had done for the Walker brothers what Brock had done for his own. He'd stood in the gap, and became what they needed the most. What every man needed. A *good* father.

"They are devoted to that old Indian. He was there when they needed him the most. And he has been there ever since."

Michael looked at Akibeel, and then Yomiel. "They are as devoted to him, as you boys are to Brock. They were bookended, Yomiel."

"How?" Akibeel asked.

"They were trapped between the father they love and the sons they love," Brock replied. That had never crossed his mind. Although truthfully, he still didn't understand it. He'd never let Michael attack any of his three sons. Even though he knew he couldn't win; he'd still fight to protect them. Just like he'd fought Samjaza.

§

Yomiel spoke what Brock had been thinking. "As much as I think of Brock as my father, I'd *never* let him hurt Abe."

"But Brock would never *try* to hurt your son, Yomiel. Brock was right when he said Watchers have a morality that humans do not. No one in this room would ever hurt the other's child; not physically anyway."

Everyone nodded their head.

"Damn straight," Ram voiced.

"But you are *not* human. Your emotions are guided by your heavenly genetics. Humans don't think like Angels, Ram."

"That's true," Nantan finally spoke up. "Remember, Howard was going to attack Mark. He loves him, but for a split second he forgot that." He chuckled. "Because of a *woman!*"

They looked at him and laughed. They wondered if he was gay because a woman led his father down the wrong road.

Nantan kept talking. "He would have hurt his brother's boy, because of his love for Lucinda."

"And Floyd was going to tap his ass for it too," Arak added. "That's what fathers do. Protect their children."

Everyone nodded.

"It doesn't change the fact that you all go crazy for your women," Michael responded. "That was a good analysis, Nantan. It is not just Watchers. Human men behave that way, too."

"I am still disappointed in E-du-di," Nantan added. "He had to know the position he was putting all of us in."

Brock smiled. "But I'll never forget that in my weakest hour, you boys stood with *me*." Brock offered his fist. "I'll never forget that, Nantan."

"We love you, Unc. We love all of you. And right now I don't care much for E-du-di." His eyes darkened.

"It opened up the wounds of my father attacking me."

"Time heals all wounds, Nantan," Michael replied. Then he looked at Brock. "Is that not what you told the keeper of my heart?"

Brock nodded.

§

"I agree with Seraphiel. No good will come out of letting the Walkers know. It would only burden them with the 'spirit' of guilt; and possible fear." He looked at Brock and chuckled. "I would have preferred that Hezekiah didn't know either. But, it wasn't my call. I am going to ease all of your spirits, and remove the spirit of resentment," Michael told them. "I want you to allow Spirit Warrior to come back to his family, Seraphiel."

Brock may understand why the Walkers acted the way they did. He even understood why Lightwings did what he did. But, damn if he'd forget. He didn't want that bastard on his property. He scowled. "Why?"

"It is the right thing to do. Besides, it will be harder on him to come back than it will be for you to let him. He feels remorse and shame." He laughed again. "You put a hurtin' on that boy."

Everyone laughed. Michael didn't realize he said *hurtin'* instead of *hurting*. Or that he was now using conjunctions; like *don't* instead of *do not*. He was becoming humanized, too. He just didn't realize it.

"And don't worry; I have buried all of your

memories so that your 'spirit' mates..." He looked at Nantan, "...and mate will never know."

"What about Baby Girl?" Ram asked. "Will she be okay?" His heart clinched. Seeing her fall apart had been the worst part. He was thankful Cutie could do what she did.

Michael frowned. "My granddaughter will be *fine.*" He kept frowning. "That is the only part of this that I am not happy about. I did not realize she was so fragile. You did *right* in asking Snow Anna to jump time, Seraphiel."

Brock nodded. There wasn't anything he wouldn't do, no chance he wouldn't take, for his *human* daughter. His baby girl.

§

Chapter 8

When they walked back outside, Brock went straight to H. He looked him square in the eye, and smiled. "It's all good, Old Man."

H wanted to cry. Seraphiel smiled; but it didn't reach his eyes. H's lips trembled. "I'm sorry, son."

Brock wasn't ready to hug him, not yet. Michael removed the resentment, but not the memory. He was no longer angry, but he was still hurt.

He extended his hand. "Don't say that too loud. Others will want to know what you are sorry for."

H looked at Brock's extended hand. Normally, Brock would have hugged him. Yeah, things had changed for all times. He nodded and accepted his hand. It was a start. Then he whispered, "I'll never let you down again."

"I know."

"Do you think you can help me out with Snow Anna?"

Brock grunted. "You're on your own with that bossy lady."

"She's locked me out of the bedroom. I've been sleeping on the couch for the last damn week. My back hurts."

"So *that's* where Jodi gets that crap from." Brock grunted, again. He reached out and removed H's back pain. "That's the best I can do."

[74]

§

Lightwings, and his family, appeared in the yard. Snow Anna did not speak to her father, but she hugged Sharon. Then she pulled her, and her nephews, away from him. "C'mon, let me introduce you guys to Adam."

§

Lightwings walked over to Brock and H. "Thank you for allowing me to be a part of this celebration, Wolf."

Brock did not hug him or shake his hand. "You are a part of this family, Lightwings. It was wrong of me to bar you from coming here. You are welcome to visit your family, any time."

Lightwings felt humbled. "That's kind of you."

"It's the right thing," Brock replied. "Excuse me. I need to speak with my future daughter-in-law."

Hezekiah, and Lightwings watched him walk away from them. Both of their hearts were heavy. "How are we going to fix this, Lightwings?"

"I don't know."

"I can't believe I allowed you to attack my son."

"I can't believe I did it. Wolf is a good man. I knew there *had* to be an extenuating reason for him to do that. I should have asked."

"If I coulda, shoulda."

"Yeah."

§

Ram went straight to Aurellia. She was talking with

Mordiree, Dee and Symphony. He put his arm around her neck, like he used to. "Excuse us, ladies," he said and walked away with her.

"What's up, Ram?"

"You know what I've missed?"

"What?"

"Us," he replied. "When is the last time we spent any time together? Just the *two* of us?"

Her words haunted him. *'I hate all of y'all.'* Cutie may have jumped time, but she'd said them, nonetheless. Too much had happened; both good and bad. Her once secure world had been turned upside down.

He feared the next argument, or catastrophe, would be the one to take her over the edge. Even if she didn't say it; she needed some of her old life back.

"Not since you found Precious." Aurellia smiled. "You put me down after that."

"We need to fix that, don't we?"

She wrapped her arm around his waist. "I've missed you too, Ram."

She would never say it out loud, but she missed the good old days. Those days when the two of them would sneak away had been a treasure. She missed the peace and quiet of the estate. She missed the days when demons weren't bold enough to attack. She longed for those days when she and Chef would stay up all night watching movies and eating popcorn.

She loved Deuce, her mother, her sisters and brother. But she missed the days when it was just her and her daddy. The days when she'd lay in the bed with him, and they'd talk for hours. Just the two of them. She missed the days when she didn't have *fear*. She'd taken those days for granted, and now they were gone. Forever.

He heard her thoughts, and his heart clinched. "I think we should take, at least, two days a month to hangout. We can leave Symphony and Deuce behind." He leaned in and kissed her cheek.

He was on the verge of real tears. The thought of her having a nervous breakdown scared him. He wouldn't be able to handle it, if it ever happened again. His eyes watered.

She squeezed his side. "It's a date."

§

The team had been snooping on her thoughts, too. They all made a bee-line to her and Ram.

"Doesn't this remind you guys of the old day?" Ali asked.

"Yeah. Ram and Baby Girl plotting." Dan smiled.

"What's up?" Arak asked. "How y'all gon' leave us out."

Chaz decided to make her say out loud, what she was thinking. It was always better to voice your desires. "I miss the days when it was just us," he said. "But don't tell Princess."

"I do, too. There are a lot of people here now, ain't it? Don't get me wrong I love all of them. But I miss the good old days," Aurellia admitted.

"We all do, Baby Girl. It doesn't mean that we don't love the life we have. It's just overwhelming sometimes," Ali told her.

She smiled, because they all understood. "Ram and I just made a date. We're going to leave all these people behind; and take a day just for us."

"Let's all go out to dinner tomorrow night. Just us and Baby Girl," Batman suggested.

Brock walked up, and pulled her away from Ram. He squeezed her a little too tightly. "Let's make it a fish fry, at Jodi's house. We'll leave Doc, and his team, in charge here. It'll be just the old crew."

They felt Aurellia's heart leap. She really *did* need this. They were all ashamed that they hadn't realized it before.

Chef appeared. He'd heard it too and wanted to cry. "With lots of Aurellia's favorites."

Everyone said at the same time, "Hush puppies!"

She smiled, and licked her lips. "With big ole wedgie fries, right, Chaz?"

He smiled. He loved wedgie fries. "You know it."

Ram kissed her cheek. "It's a date."

§

Brock walked over to Mordiree, Dee and

Symphony. He kissed Symphony's check. "You did an excellent job, Symphony. Everything was perfect. I'm proud of you."

"I was just telling her that," Dee added. "I could not believe how much fun it was."

"Me either," Mordiree added.

Symphony smiled. "Thanks, Brock. Is everything okay, though?"

"Yeah; everything's good. Can you, and Dee, give me a minute alone with Mordiree?"

"Sure," they both said and walked away together.

§

Mordiree looked nervous. Was Brock going to tell her to stay away from his son? She couldn't and she really hoped he understood that. They were 'spirit' mates, just like he and Jodi. She could no more turn her back on Adam, than he could to Jodi. Some things didn't have to make sense. They just were.

Brock smiled at her. "I am sorry for my behavior. I overreacted, and had no right."

She breathed a sigh of relief. "You're not mad?"

"Not about you and Adam. He couldn't have done better."

Her eyes lit up. "Really?"

He felt Maria, Akibeel and Jodi walking towards them. He winked. "If I can put up with that tactless Maria; you'll be a breeze."

[79]

"I heard that!" Maria shouted.

Brock and Mordiree laughed. She really was a beautiful girl. His problem with Adam had nothing to do with her. It was that boy's *cockiness.* It was a reminder of his younger self. One he did not like, and had hoped his son wouldn't inherit. But, just like Samjaza had given him his arrogance; he'd passed it on to *his* progeny.

He turned and looked at Maria. "Oops. Did I say that out loud?"

"Keep it up 'Pops'." She laughed and leaned up to kiss his cheek.

He popped her on the back of her head. "I got your Pops!"

Mordiree, Jodi and Akibeel laughed. Brock and Maria were quite a combination. He teased her, because she had no verbal filter. If she thought it, she said it. But he appreciated that. He always liked straight forward honesty. She was a perfect match for Akibeel. He was certainly honest, and frank, to a fault.

§

Mordiree sighed. "I'm sorry, Jodi."

"For what? You don't have anything to be sorry for, Mordiree," Jodi replied. "I don't like the way you and Adam handled your relationship; but I understand."

"You do?"

"Yeah. When I first met Brock, I was afraid for my family to know what he really was."

Brock wrapped his arm around her neck. "Oh *please*! You were afraid for them to know you were living with me." He kissed the top of her head. "My woman was afraid they wouldn't approve."

"Y'all *lived* together before marriage?" Maria asked. She looked genuinely shocked. "I'm ashamed of you, Jodi Mae."

Jodi looked at Brock. "She's as tactless as ever, ain't she?"

Brock shook his head. "She missed the whole point, didn't she? Besides, if I'm not mistaken she and my boy were shacked up, too. And right under her parents' noses."

"But I was healing, so nothing was going on," Maria replied. "Don't tell me you and Brock was abstaining?" Then she turned her nose up at the thought. "EWWW! Never mind. TMI."

Akibeel laughed. "Santa Maria!"

"What? They're old, Akibeel."

Brock and Jodi shook their heads. Maria was a trip. But both were more than willing to change the subject.

Jodi wanted to smack Maria, but instead, she smacked her lips. "Anyway, like I said; I'm not upset with you, Mordiree."

"I know what you're saying, Jodi. But, I'm still sorry. This was a nice party; and Adam and I ruined it."

§

"No, *we* didn't, Maude," Adam replied, as he

walked up. He reached for her hand. "I did."

"Let's not worry about it," Brock said. He leaned over and kissed Mordiree's cheek. "You are a beautiful young lady. I am glad to have you as my future daughter-in-law." He looked at Maria and laughed. "It kind of softens the blow of being stuck with this one."

"You know you love me, Pops," Maria replied.

He leaned over and kissed her cheek, too. "I do indeed."

He reached for Jodi's hand and they walked away.

§

"What I don't understand is, you've shared everything with me but this, Santa Maria." Akibeel looked almost offended. "Why would you keep this from me?"

Maria laughed. "I knew you'd tell Pops."

"I probably would have, but what's the big deal?"

As always, he didn't have a clue. He looked at it from the simplistic point of view. Adam is a Watcher. Therefore, he could be what age he wanted to be. Plus, spirits never got older; they just were. It was only the physical bodies that changed. Once the body was grown, and the decision was mutual, it was no one's business who loved whom.

"I'll explain it to you later, baby," Maria replied.

§

"What's going on with Aurellia, Brock?" Jodi asked.

[82]

"She's just a little overwhelmed. She misses the old days, Jodi."

"She does?"

"Yeah. The family has grown quite a bit, in the last four years."

"Can we do anything?"

"The guys, and I, are going to take her to your house for a fish fry. Get her away for a while."

"When?"

"In the next couple of days. Are you okay with that?"

"I know how you feel about our daughter's emotional state, Brock. You made that perfectly clear to me, remember?" she teased. "I'm six degrees away from giving a good damn."

He flinched. "I'm sorry, Jodi. I didn't mean that."

"Yes, you did. And you were right. Baby Girl is human. You should always put her needs first. If she needs this, do it."

"You sure?"

She put her arm around his waist. "I'm more than okay with it. I love her, too."

§

Chapter 9

There was a grumbling in the dungeons of Hell. It could be heard from one end to the other. The Fallen were on the warpath.

Several dozen, lower level demons headed toward the noise. They also had a gripe.

§

The original Fallen were all up in arms. "This is not fair, Lucifer!" one of his servants complained.

"When have you known that Man to ever be fair?" Lucifer replied.

"I'm not talking about Him! We followed you because you told us we could overpower Him. We've been stuck down here for eons. You are a liar!" another challenged.

"I did *not* lie to any of you. If we'd gotten enough to join our cause, we would have overthrown the Kingdom."

"The sad part of that statement is you believe it," another one said, under his breath.

§

His name was Araciel. He realized the error of his decision just before he came face to face with Michael. He was remorseful, of spirit, for what he'd done to those poor women. But he was not remorseful about his sons. He loved them. Still did.

He had apologized to both of his sons for the way he'd treated them. He told them that he loved them and wanted better for them, than this place. He knew he was doomed, but they did not have to be. He secretly told both of his boys to accept Michael's offer. And they had.

The fact that they listened to him, meant they had accepted his apology. He could live with his fate, because it was not theirs.

Periodically he visually checked in on them. Both were fathers now, and happy. What joy he had, came vicariously through their happiness. What decent father wouldn't want better for his sons than he had.

§

Lucifer scowled. "Did you say something, Araciel?"

"I believe you heard me."

"Yeah, I did. Speak loud so everyone can hear your insolence."

"I *said* you are a liar and the truth ain't in you. You are a deceiver, and the scum of the underworld. Was that loud enough, Lucifer?"

The other Fallen gasped. None of them had the nerve to be that outspoken to their leader.

He kept talking. "You make promises that you know you can't keep. You are the leader of an army of fools."

He looked around at all of the Fallen then back at Lucifer. "Where is your power? You are trapped in the God forsaken dungeon, just like your followers."

One by one, the Fallen started to nod their heads. "He does have a valid point."

Araciel laughed. "Lucifer conveniently forgets that the Archangels were not the ones that banished us. He refuses to acknowledge that the *true* Master kicked all of our butts, out of Heaven. All...by...himself! In fact, he has blocked out the fact that you guys didn't fight against an army of Archangels. Big brother, Michael, locked all of you down here; singlehandedly. Ain't that right, Lucifer? Go ahead, tell the truth, and shame *yourself*."

§

Lucifer had to get control of his army. He would not tolerate outbursts from any one of them. He shot a fire laden power ball towards Araciel. "Silence!"

Araciel, casually, lifted his hand up and the power ball bounced back. Lucifer flinched when it hit the pointy fingers of his chair; and demolished them. Araciel smirked and challenged him, "You want to have at it, *boy?* I am not afraid of you, or your puny army."

The demons gasped again. No one had ever challenged Lucifer. He was the most powerful of them all.

§

Lucifer was in a bind. He had to show them how powerful he was. He always knew he couldn't defeat

[86]

Araciel, in a hand to hand. Hell, Araciel was his big brother. He still found it hard to believe that he'd gone along with his plan.

Araciel, Raphael and Gabriel had been best friends. He thought if Araciel went along with it, so would Raphael and Gabriel. Araciel had thought the same thing. But they hadn't. By then the word had already spread throughout Heaven who was involved. Araciel could not turn back.

Now Araciel was challenging him. Lucifer stood up and extended his arms. His devoted servants stood up and reached for them. They helped him down the stone stairs.

Araciel smirked. "Bow down and kiss his pathetic ass, while you're at it."

"If he so chose, I would," one of the servants replied.

Lucifer was tempted to take him up on his offer, just to prove a point. His warriors were devoted to him, no matter what. He walked over and stood in Araciel's face.

Araciel didn't flinch. He was pushing Lucifer to reveal how *powerless* he was. Lucifer wouldn't dare strike him, because he knew better.

Lucifer smiled. "I have more power than you think, brother. If it had been my will, I would have released you eons ago."

The other demons gasped again. "You can set us free?" one asked.

"Why have we been down here, all of this time, if

you had that kind of power?" another asked.

Araciel laughed. "Your highness...and I do mean *your*...is Prince of the Air." He laughed again. "That's because he's full of it. But, in the air, he can't have fools bowing down to him. Those creatures, that he so defiantly hates, have more power than he does. He doesn't want you guys to see what happens when they resist his deceptive voice."

"What happens?" one of the demons asked.

"Do you want to tell them, little brother? Or shall I?" he arrogantly antagonized him.

"Quiet!" Lucifer shouted.

Araciel chuckled. "He flees from them. He *cowardly* runs." He kept going. "Tell them what happens when they call His *begotten* son's name?"

"I said shut up!"

"He trembles. He literally *quakes* in his boots." To prove he wasn't lying, he whispered, "Jesus."

Lucifer visibly shook.

He said it louder, "Jesus!"

Lucifer trembled.

He laughed and said, "Jesus...Jesus...Jesus!"

Lucifer looked like he was having a spasm.

"See." Araciel laughed. "You fools follow a coward!"

"Yet you are here, too!" Lucifer shouted.

"Indeed. I was a fool. But, I emphasize *'was'*. I

made my bed. But I won't follow or bow down to you; you pompous ass."

§

"Release us, Lucifer! We want out of here!" one of the Fallen shouted.

"He won't let you go; otherwise he'll have a kingdom with no servants. A worthless throne, with no one to bow down to him. If you jerks weren't here, he'd look foolish sitting his ass on that hard bench. Wouldn't you, brother?"

Lucifer was pissed. He'd never been challenged by his followers. What in the hell had gotten into Araciel? He was pushing him farther than he wanted to go.

He was right, if he let them out who would worship him. He wanted to slap the hell out of Araciel. And he would, except Araciel would hit him back. That bastard had been in a bad mood since day one. What in the hell was he going to do?

But, this may work out after all. Unfortunately his foot soldiers had been locked down so tight, he couldn't release them. "I'll release you on one condition."

"What?" Wrath asked.

"You have to come back, and you have to do what I tell you to do."

"What do you want us to do?" Fear asked.

"We'll do anything to please you, Master," Apathy added.

"Not you. You can't go," Lucifer replied. "Not this time."

§

Araciel shook his head. Lucifer was a self-serving fool. He was never going to stop. No matter how many times he got his ass kicked; he was still going to try. Why couldn't he accept the fact that the battle was over. He lost. They all had.

§

When Lucifer finished with his instructions, Araciel frowned. "Just keep one thing in mind."

"What?" the excited demons asked.

"Get near *my* sons and I will destroy you." He turned and walked out of the dungeon.

§

Chapter 10

Adam and Mordiree were visited by all of the cousins and their spouses. Each of them offered their support.

The male cousins wanted to teach him how to shoot pool. "He has never seen the den," Mark stated. "All women and children were banned."

"That's right," Eugene replied. "How about it, Adam?"

Adam squeezed Mordiree's hand. "Maybe tomorrow night."

"It's a date," Eugene replied.

"No, it's *not*," Adam laughed.

Everyone else laughed, too.

Eugene cracked up. "You know what I mean, fool."

"How did it go with your father?" Henry asked

"It went good. He's not angry at me."

"Then what was that all about?"

Adam paused. He didn't want to lie to his best friend, but he had to. "Well, he *was* angry. But after the team talked with him, he realized he overreacted."

"How about Jodi?"

"She's another story. She says she's okay, but I can feel how distraught she is. Man, I don't get it. They knew all along that I'd be a man today."

"It's one thing to know. It's another thing to be emotionally ready. It'll just take her a little time to get used to the idea."

"Henry is right, Adam," Mark responded. "We were all ready, because we've partied with you and Mordiree. We've seen you guys together."

"Not only are you no longer a baby; but you already have your future wife. That all happened in a matter of minutes, Adam. You gotta give Jodi time to come to grips with it," Symphony added. "I would be nowhere near ready, if it was Mary."

"Me either," Faith admitted.

All of the female cousins nodded their heads. None of them wanted to be in Jodi's shoes. They wanted their babies to stay babies.

Adam frowned. "So, ya'll think I handled it wrong, too?"

"Truthfully, yes. But then again, I handled introducing Candace wrong, too," Mark replied.

Ditto flinched. "Damn, man. Why did you have to bring *that* shit up?"

"I'm just saying, I could have forewarned Aunt Lucinda. And Adam *should have* let his parents know."

"You're right, Mark, but what's done is done," Adam replied. Then he looked at Mordiree. "Want to take a walk?"

She squeezed his hand. "Yeah."

She didn't want to spend the day rehashing the mistake they'd made. She wanted a few minutes alone.

§

They knew they were being watched, as they walked out the gate. The preserve was the best place for privacy. It wasn't as though they were ready to jump each other's bones. They just wanted to be alone; to truly talk and get to know each other. In a sense, he was like his Uncle Ali. He wanted to date Mordiree.

And although he wasn't all knowing, he knew enough. He knew when and where they would make love, for the first time. It wouldn't be today, or even next month, for that matter. He knew exactly when their sons would be born. And what their names would be; all seven of them. He knew his daughter was as beautiful as her mother.

But for right now he just wanted out of the view of prying eyes.

§

They were deep in the preserve, sitting on a fallen branch, when Mordiree asked, "So do you want a do over?"

"Nope." He laughed. "You and I both know time wouldn't change anything. My mom will always see me as her baby."

"Yeah, my father, too. But, I could hardly wait, Adam. I know they all think it's weird, but I don't. We live in the paranormal. What's the difference in you choosing to be thirty and your father choosing to be late forties?"

"None; except he's over five thousand years old." He looked down at her, and smiled. "In their eyes...I'm *one!*"

They both laughed.

"You're one alright; my *one* and only," she replied and kissed him.

It wasn't as though they hadn't kissed before. They'd done plenty of that, the night of Henry's wedding.

But that night they'd both been timid. Maybe it was because they were sneaking. They had both been afraid of what their cousins would think. Hope's attitude hadn't helped.

Plus, they were afraid of being caught by their parents. After the ceremony, Adam teleported back to the nursery, because he couldn't, openly, be with her.

Thank God, those days were over. Everyone finally knew about them. Whether they liked it or not, they knew. Now, they could relax; because they weren't having a clandestine meeting. They were a legitimate couple. A couple that was *madly* in love.

This kiss was different from those that night. It was more passionate and more desperate. Adam was a man, with manly desires.

§

He caressed her cheek. "Twelve months was too long, Maude."

"But you are here now, Adam." She stroked his bottom lip and kissed him again. She could do this until the rapture.

Adam looked like his father, but she didn't think of Brock as sexy. Like Maria, she thought of him as *old*. Maybe it was the gray 'stache and goatee he sported. Ew! She didn't see Akibeel as sexy either, and he and Adam looked *exactly* alike; except their eye color. They both even claimed the same age.

But Adam was the sexiest man she'd ever met. Some nights when she felt lonely and left out, he'd whisper in her ear, *'Hold on, I'm coming. Wait for me, Maude'*. Other nights he'd sing her to sleep, with love ballads. He romanced her all along, with his voice.

No one knew it, but he blinded her to him, as a baby. He didn't want her to get twisted up. Whenever Jodi or Brock would come in a room with him, she could only see them. But he'd whisper to her, *'Leave the room, Maude'*. If the family was gathered outside, she could see the other children, but not him. It still amazed her that he could be visible to everyone, but her.

Adam smiled. "I'm listening to your thoughts, Maude."

"We pulled it off, didn't we?"

"For sure."

§

Adam cranked some music in the preserve, that only they could hear. They were slow dancing to Rance Allen's 'I belong to you.' Adam kissed her ear. "I've always loved you, Maude."

"I love you too, Adam." She felt their hearts beating together, as one. "I'm glad you're finally here. I'm glad you're finally mine."

"I've always been yours."

§

When the music stopped he looked in her eyes. "Tell me something I don't know about you."

"You already know the important things."

He kissed her cheek. "Tell me again."

"Mamma and Babbo adopted me when I was thirteen."

"Why?"

"My birth parents died."

"Like Aurellia's parents."

"Yes."

"Tell me the things you don't like."

"I don't like heights. I'm afraid of it."

He already knew that. She'd told him a dozen times what her fears were. "What if you were with me? Would you still be afraid?"

"Yes."

"You wouldn't trust me to keep you safe?"

"Yes, but…"

"Look down."

"What?"

"Look down, Maude."

She did and panicked. He'd levitated them up between the trees. "I'm scared, Adam. Put me down!"

He slowly started to descend. "Don't you trust me? Don't you know I'd never let anything happen to you?"

"I know that."

"But do you believe it?"

"Yes."

He paused mid descent. He started the music again. This time it was the O'Jays' 'Stairway to Heaven'. He started to sing, "Here we go, climbing the stairway to heaven."

She relaxed. Like his father, he had a beautiful baritone voice. It was hypnotic. She stared in his eyes, while he took them higher and higher.

"Are you afraid now?"

"No."

He leaned in and kissed her. "This is how I feel. Like my life with you will be a stairway. Together you and I can do anything…" He started to sing again. 'Step by step, together…'

She'd been afraid of heights since the day her parents died. But she didn't feel any of that fear now. Not in Adam's arms. But, she was glad she had on pants.

Plus, she kept her eyes on him. "How do you know all of these old songs?"

"That's the only thing my parents listen to."

He was listening to her thoughts again. He pointed with his head. "Look over there."

She looked in the direction his head had pointed. She could see the entire front yard. The family had settled down. They were laughing and eating. "They've evidently forgotten about us."

"That's good, ain't it?"

"Yeah. I was starting to feel like a freak show."

He laughed. "Me too. You want to go a little higher?"

"Yeah." It actually felt alright. "Just don't let me go."

"Never gonna happen."

§

They were laughing and talking; and getting to know each other. It was heavenly, indeed.

But, they weren't paying attention and had ascended ten thousand feet up, in the air.

And all hell broke loose!

§

Mordiree screamed, "ADAM!"

Out of nowhere, Adam found himself surrounded by a legion of demons. And not just any old demons. These were the original Fallen!

§

"Thank you for bringing her to us, boy!" Wrath said.

"Like hell!" Adam replied.

Hundreds of demons swarmed closer, and tried to take her out of his arms. "She's ours!" Fear shouted.

Mordiree screamed when the demon got too close. "Adam!"

Adam encompassed them in a ring of fire. The demons jumped back. "Give her to us and we'll let you live!" Wrath shouted. "Release her now!"

§

Adam was as powerful as his father, but not as skilled. It took years to develop the level of power he'd inherited. But, he didn't have years. He didn't even have *minutes.*

He regretted that he had blocked his father from snooping on him and Mordiree. He was his mother's son, and hadn't appreciated the difference in snooping and watching.

Now he needed his father's help, like yesterday. But no worries; he was definitely going to let him snoop now!

He opened his mind and let him see, and feel, his rage.

§

Chapter 11

Lightning flashed and clapped so sharply, the sky looked like Armageddon. It danced over the grounds of the estate and blasted holes in the landscaping. Thunder responded with rolling vibrato. The ground beneath the estate shook, violently.

Everyone jumped and ducked their heads. Even Batman and Jehoel jumped.

The residents of the estate had experienced that level of rage from Mother Nature only a few times in the past. Those times had been in response to Brock's emotional state of being. But he was standing in the yard laughing, and talking, with Ram.

§

Everyone looked up and an ominous scene unfolded right before their eyes. Mother Nature's rage was not in response to Brock's rage.

The Watchers instantly realized why the territories had been combined.

§

Hundreds of Fallen hovered, in a circle, around their targeted victims.

The demons had one goal in mind. Destroy Seraphiel's son.

This was going to be the battle to beat all battles.

§

[100]

Jodi screamed, "MY BABY!!!"

§

Seraphiel jumped his ugly ass out, and roared... "*MY* SON!!!" He took off in an all-out run. He moved at whirlwind speed, away from the family. Tree branches snapped in the wake of his rage. Patio furniture was caught up in his wind tunnel; and tossed across the yard.

When he was far enough away from the family, he hoisted his fiery *wings*. They spanned eighteen feet, *tip to tip*.

He shot straight up in the air in a blaze of fury; with a double-edged sword in both of his fiery claws.

§

The back draft of wind, embers and smoke caused the family to lose their footing.

Everyone gasped. Not even Brock's team knew he could fly; or that he had *wings! They* sure as hell couldn't! And didn't! Sure, they could *levitate*; but they couldn't *fly*. And they damn sure didn't have wings. They were witnessing the *real* Seraphiel...

Unedited!
Uncut!
Unrestrained!

§

Everyone had the same thought. It's *not* a myth! Brock is the *Phoenix*. And they all just witnessed the *rising*.

[101]

BEGINNINGS and REVELATIONS

§

Seraphiel shot through the sky like a meteorite going in the wrong direction. With every flap of his fiery wings, embers fell and scorched the earth. Birds in flight cawed and gave him a wide breach. Even the Bald Eagle flew out of his way.

The menacing growl coming from his fiery laden mouth caused the attacking demons to pause. They trembled, but held their position. "Grab her quickly!" Wrath ordered.

None of them were willing to cross the fiery line. "You grab her!" Fear demanded.

"Somebody do something! We can't go back without her!" Wrath shouted.

"When the battle starts, the fire will go out. We'll grab her then," Fear rationalized.

§

Although not as strong as Seraphiel, *physically*; intellectually Kobabiel was superior. He believed in self-examination. Will your actions lift up or tear down.

While Seraphiel's mind was solely on his son's safety; *his* was on humanity's. That was their commission. *Protect God's so-loved.*

Right now, Seraphiel was more of a threat to them, than any demon could ever be.

§

He jumped into damage control mode. He sent a

shout out to all of the Ultimate Watchers, across the globe. *"Force an Eclipse. NOW!"*

§

Then he reached out and destroyed the cameras on the satellites suspended in space. No doubt big brother was watching. He wiped the memories of all the employees of those satellites, who had already seen too much.

He shouted, *"Put up a blinding shield!"*

§

Doc, Satariel and Hasdiel immediately complied; as did Ultimate Watchers all around the world. Kobabiel was right. If any humans saw this battle, there would be mayhem in the streets. They'd think the end of the world had most definitely come. People around the world would flock to the nearest churches, temples, mosques and synagogues. Although, that might not be a bad thing.

§

Kobabiel reached across the world and destroyed all cameras and binoculars. He destroyed every telescope. Every Observatory went *black*. All memory chips and film *destroyed*. He destroyed system servers, including the one at the estate. Sorry!

He destroyed cell phones camera, internet and social media. No doubt there would still be mayhem, but everyone would believe it was due to the satellites malfunctioning.

Nuclear power grids shut down all over the world. Emergency generators all failed to start. Alkaline batteries corroded.

Air traffic control screens went snowy. Airplane screens went green. No communication could be had between the towers and the pilots.

Yeah, mayhem was starting.

§

As prolific as Seraphiel was physically, Kobabiel was equally prolific, *intellectually*. His mind was calm but deliberate.

"Send forth some of your field Watchers to guide airplanes to a safe landing spot," he commanded.

All across the world, Watchers took to the skies. Through no help of the pilots, planes safely and smoothly touched ground.

"Guide ships to the nearest port," he instructed.

Another group of Watchers took to the waters.

"Bring sub-marines to the surface," he added.

Another group of Watchers hit the waters.

"Check for swimmers and mountain hikers. Guide them to safety."

Two more groups of Watchers took off.

"Cover patients at hospitals, clinics and nursing homes. Unless you see Sammael, don't lose a single soul."

Three more groups of Watchers took off.

"Rescue anyone trapped in an elevator."

Hundreds of Watchers descended on skyscrapers.

"Cover prisons and jails. Let no one escape."

Thousands, upon thousands, of alley guards hit the skies.

§

Street lights went out on every continent. The sound of car horns vibrated and nervous human voices resounded, across the horizon.

"Send Watchers to direct traffic," he calmly commanded. *"Be sure to cover all bridges."*

Mass numbers of Watchers complied.

"Don't let any wild animals, in captivity, escape."

Watchers landed at every Zoo and Wildlife preserve.

"Kill any demon trying to take advantage of this situation."

"Gladly Sir!" they all shouted.

§

Mayhem was a *happy* spirit. He was wreaking havoc all over the world; including on the estate grounds.

§

Not only had the sky gone black, but none of children had ever seen *'Seraphiel'*. Not even Elizabeth and Hannah. They'd all just seen him turn into a ball of fire. They were screaming and running to their fathers. Elizabeth and Hannah were screaming, "Daddy!!"

Hezekiah grabbed them up in his own trembling arms. "Oh Lord!"

Justina screamed and ran. "Monsters! Monsters!" Celia tried to grab her, but she ran to Adrian. All children believed their fathers could protect them. She jumped up in his arms. "I skid, daddy!" she screamed. "Monsters!!"

Adriana was holding on to his forearm, screaming and trying to climb up his body. Celia picked her up and the two of them tried to comfort their children. However, they were shaking themselves.

Sam caught Sylvia and Sheila up in his arms. They were afraid and crying but did not say a word. Celina wrapped her arms around her daughters and the four of them looked up at the battle in the sky.

Autumn and Summer were too afraid to move from where they stood. They screamed, "Daddy! Daddy!"

Chef ran to his daughters. "Here I am!" He picked them up in his arms. "You're alright." He kissed their cheeks. Lorraine was holding little Elijah, and was just as afraid as her girls.

Jon and Jas took off running. It was pitch black so they couldn't see their father and were shouting, "Dad!! Dad!!"

Chaz dropped down to his knees and grabbed his on-the-run sons. Hope was trying to calm a screaming Ruben and Ruth.

§

It wasn't just the children that were afraid. Dee had never seen '*Seraphiel*', either. She was as frightened as the children. Her bladder dropped, but she didn't notice or care. Plus, hers wasn't the only one. She was squeezing Aden's neck and screaming.

Nikkita was shocked speechless. Satariel had told them about Seraphiel, but she hadn't imagined this. She was squeezing Tim's hand so tight she almost broke his fingers. Her hand was trembling and her mouth was open; but she could neither speak nor hear. She was virtually a deaf mute.

Even though it was new moon dark, Mysia had Watcher's eyes and could see clearly. She realized her sister was in trouble and screamed, "Nikki!" She and Paul ran towards her. They got there just as Nikkita grabbed her chest and passed out.

Sarah screamed, "She's having a heart attack! Help my daughter, Satariel!"

Satariel reached out and caught her heart rate. He brought it back down to normal and eased her spirit. He would never allow Sarah to grieve for *another* child. "She's okay now, Mon Chéri."

§

Ali and Destiny had been on the ground playing with Eve and Alyni. The minute Seraphiel jumped out he put a shield over their eyes.

But they heard the commotion and were frightened and crying, nonetheless. Lara reached for Eve and held her face to her breast.

§

Batman and Robyn were both grateful that Joy loved to nibble on her father's face. She had been busy gumming Batman's chin and didn't see Seraphiel's spectacle.

However she was crying because all of the other children were crying. And when she cried, she wanted her mommy. Robyn took her from Batman and rocked her. "It's okay, baby."

Shelonda and Jehoel were trying to quiet their little ones, too.

§

Little Henry Eugene was screaming his lungs off. He was fighting Naomi, Eugene and Henry. He didn't want anyone to touch him but his daddy.

Ditto took his son from Henry. "I got cha, son." He rubbed his protective hand up and down his boy's back. "Daddy's got cha!"

§

Mary had been asleep in MeiLi's arms. All the crying woke her up. She woke up screaming and slapping MeiLi. Ram took his daughter. "Ssh." She went right back to sleep. Then he reached out and lit all the Chinese lanterns in the yard. At least they'd have some light, for the humans.

§

Petra had seen the entire thing. That boy was *not*

afraid. He was clapping his hands, and pointing up in the sky. "Ooooo, Big Bird!"

Dan had to laugh at his tough little man. But, Lillian was freaking out.

§

Abe was unaffected also. No doubt he and Adam were in constant communication. He spoke to Kwanita's mind. *"Those demons want Mordiree."*

However Kwanita's four little nephews wet their pants. They wanted to go home! So did their parents.

§

"Wipe all the children's memories!" Justin shouted. His granddaughters were screaming uncontrollably. Adrian and Celia were having a hard time calming them down. Thank God Amanda had had the mindset to cover Kiah's face. But, she was still crying because all the children were. "Do it now!"

§

Arak had instantly put Smittie to sleep. He felt bad because he hadn't thought about anybody's child but his own. Now all of the babies and children were screaming. No doubt these children would be afraid of Brock, unless they did something.

He reached out across the yard and put all the children to sleep. Some fell where they stood, others slumped in their parents' arms. "Wipe your children's memories before they wake back up," he instructed. "I'll help Adrian, Ditto and Sam with theirs."

Dee was still choking the crap out of Aden. He shouted, "Put Dee down too, Arak!"

§

Aurellia knew her father and brother couldn't handle all of those Fallen by themselves. She also knew they would have no help from the teams; they weren't strong enough. There was only one person that *could* help. She screamed, "Grandpa Michael! Help!"

§

In the midst of the blackened sky, they all saw a window into Heaven. They heard and glimpsed...

§

Chapter 12

Gabriel and Raphael stopped mid-stride and scowled. "Where did that Eclipse come from?" Gabriel asked.

Before Raphael could respond, they saw Michael barreling towards them. "What?"

"ADAM!!!" Michael replied and leaped over the balcony of Heaven.

Gabriel and Raphael did a somersault right behind him. They looked like they dove off of a diving board. They kept their wings in check, to allow them velocity. With swords in hand, their descent was at the speed of light.

Their battle started before they could get to the boy.

§

Hundreds of Fallen shot up to block their path. Their instructions were to keep these Archangels away from the battle to destroy the new ADAM.

§

Although frightened, the family felt privileged. Of course they knew about the Great War in Heaven. They even knew of Michael's reported fighting abilities. But, to bear witness was breathtaking.

It was no wonder Akibeel had been afraid. That Archangel wielded his ancient sword with merciless precision.

They heard him shout, "FOOLS!"

§

The Ultimate Watchers realized it was going to take a minute for Michael and his boys to fight their own battle. They were going to be of no assistance to Seraphiel and Adam.

"Get the family to the shelter," Kobabiel commanded, as he and Adabiel took flight. They also had wings.

The two of them were the second and third Nephilim to be born. Although not as powerful as Seraphiel, they were powerful enough. Or at least they hoped they were.

"NO!" Jodi shouted. "Don't touch me! That's my baby!"

"You pull yourself together and see after your daughters, Jodi Mae!" Snow Anna snapped at her. "Wolf will take care of Adam! Elizabeth, Hannah and Aurellia need you!"

Jodi knew her mother was right. She hugged a trembling Aurellia. Then she took the twins from Hezekiah's arms. They were asleep but were trembling and whimpering. The minute she wrapped her arms around them they settled down. Somehow, she was able to pull Aurellia into her arms, too. She sighed and kissed their cheeks. "Momma's got all of her girls."

§

Kwanita looked around. "Has anyone seen

Mordiree?"

"Oh God!" Rebecca screamed. "Where is Mordiree?"

Clyde looked up and squinted. His legs buckled under the weight of fear. "She's up there! With Adam!"

Rebecca looked up and screamed. "Get my daughter!" she shouted at the Watchers. "Somebody get my child!"

Everybody looked up...*helplessly.*

§

Seraphiel looked like a dragon, as he blew fire from his nostrils and blasted those bastards away from his son. Adam was holding them at bay, as best he could. He'd wrapped a shield of fire around him and Mordiree, to keep the demons from getting to her. But, he was too inexperienced to do battle with the Fallen, and shield her, too.

§

Mordiree was screaming her bloody head off. Not only was she afraid of these creatures and heights; she was afraid of *fire.*

In her mind she was thirteen again; trapped on the top floor of her burning home. This time her Babbo would not be able to rescue her.

§

Seraphiel yanked her out of Adam's arms and wrapped her in a ball of fire. Then he tossed her straight down and shouted, "LEILAZEB!"

§

Everybody on the ground saw her tumbling down, in a ball of fire. They could hear her terrified screams.

Dawn, Rebecca and Maria screamed. Embry, Lamar and Clyde shouted, "MORDIREE!"

Dawn was hysterical. She screamed, "My sister is burning up!"

§

"I GOT HER!" Leilazeb replied and caught her.

§

Several of the Fallen attempted to follow her, but stopped abruptly. Seraphiel had turned the sky into a gulf of fire, just below them.

§

He twirled his fiery swords backwards and forward and speared both those demons in the throat. Then he sliced side to side and took their heads. "NOBODY TOUCHES MY SON!!" he roared. They fell into his lake of fire.

§

The family watched, in horror, as four more demons attacked and overpowered him. One struck out and clipped his fiery wing. They all knew if you clip a bird's wing it couldn't fly. They cringed when Seraphiel staggered backwards and hugged his wounded wing up against his fiery breasts.

§

They screamed and shouted when another stabbed him in the back. A third one viciously pierced him in his chest. They held their mouths when Seraphiel faltered.

He dropped down into his *own* lake of fire!

§

Like billows, sorrow and despair rolled across the estate. They knew, beyond a doubt, Seraphiel had just perished...in the sky.

§

Jodi and Aurellia were screaming, "Brock! Daddy! Brock! Daddy!"

§

"They killed my son!" Hezekiah openly sobbed. His brothers tried to comfort him but couldn't. He was a hot mess. So was Snow Anna.

Lucinda was weeping uncontrollably. "My brother's gone."

Henry and Ditto were in just as bad a shape. All the nephews and nieces were. There wasn't a soul in that yard who wasn't crying. All for their beloved Seraphiel...Brock...Pops...Wolf...Brother...Boo...Daddy ...Uncle Brock!

§

Addison wiped his eye and shouted, "LOOK!"

Everyone gasped when Brock shot back up, out of the flames. He had split himself into two birds. They remembered what happened when he split himself before. They all feared the fallout, when this was over. If he survived.

"He's going to destroy himself up there!" Elijah shouted.

"Ease yourselves. That's *not* Brock," Doc informed them.

"What?" Hezekiah asked.

"That's Seraphiel. Seraphiel can split himself, without causing Brock harm."

"What?" everybody asked.

"Long story," Doc replied and everyone looked back up at the sky.

§

They all heard him roar, "I AM SERAPHIEL! THE SEED OF SAMJAZA!"

They watched as the two of him decapitated the four demons.

But, six more attacked…

§

The two of him fanned their fiery wings and sent all six flying across the galaxy. "ALL THAT SAMJAZA WAS… " The both of him flexed their fiery wings and roared, "…*I AM!*"

§

Even though he won that battle; his family still didn't relax. There were too many damn Fallen up there.

ADAM - BEGINNINGS and REVELATIONS

Even though Kobabiel and Adabiel were on their way to assist; they were still outnumbered by dozens.

Aurellia screamed, "PLEASE HURRY, GRANDPA MICHAEL!"

But Michael, Gabriel and Raphael were still in their own battles. The Fallen were keeping them busy, so they could not get to Seraphiel and Adam.

§

Another dozen demons charged both of his beings. Adabiel and Kobabiel intercepted four of them. Up here in the heavens, amongst the stars, their powers had increased to the *nth* degree. But it was still too many of them. How in the world did they escape?

Kobabiel was fighting his own father. "You again!" he shouted and swung his battle axe.

"You caught me off guard the last time, son," his father replied and jumped out of the way. "You're no match for me face to fa-"

While he was concentrating on the battle axe; Kobabiel cut his head off with his other 'scissored' hand. "Where *is* your face?" he calmly asked.

§

Adabiel saw one of the Seraphiels take his father's head. "Damn! I burnt his ass up, how is he here, Seraphiel!"

§

Seraphiel was mad as hell, and didn't respond. It

[117]

was bad enough that these bastards had attacked his son. But, to add insult to injury, they were forcing him to reveal all that he was to his family. His next move was going to scare the hell out of them. But, he had no choice...

One of his beings morphed into a Prehistoric Monster.

§

Everyone, including the Watchers, screamed. If they hadn't been screaming, they would have heard Adam screaming, too!

"Shit!" Baraq complained. He wet his pants! He wasn't the only one.

Adabiel and Kobabiel dropped down a few feet. "Cut that shit out, Seraphiel!" Adabiel shouted. "I hate that creature!"

Kobabiel looked at the front of Adabiel's pants and laughed. "Is that rain?"

"Screw you!" Adabiel replied.

§

The demons stopped in their tracks. Seraphiel was no longer human. He wasn't a bird, either. He was a *snake*. A constrictor, but not your run of the mill *Boa*. He was a gargantuan 'Titanoboa'.

At forty-eight feet long, and weighing a ton, this monster had been long extinct. History records that the Titanoboa was more powerful and dangerous than the Dino and the Rex.

They attacked and stabbed him; but he didn't feel it. He zigged and zagged until he coiled his humongous body around three dozen demons. Then he applied over four hundred pounds of constrictive pressure on those birds.

The demons could no longer fight, because their hands were trapped. They extended their fangs and bit down. A dozen more jumped on him. They were stabbing him and drawing blood, but it didn't faze Seraphiel. He slithered across the sky, right into his lake of fire.

§

The family was praying that he would emerge as a human. Hell, they'd be happy if he was a bird again. Anything but that damn snake! No doubt there'd be requests for memory swipes when this shit was over.

§

Seraphiel emerged as Brock, just long enough to settle his family's nerves. He immediately switched back to Seraphiel. Not the bird. The *ugly* one. But he still had wings.

With his swords in his hands he continued to fight.

"Don't do that shit again!" Adabiel demanded, as he flew back up and fought next to Seraphiel.

"My bad!" Seraphiel replied.

§

"Bunk this!" Doc shouted. His nerves were rattled. That was a big ass snake. "We need to get this shit over with. No telling who or what else that bastard will turn into next."

He reached for his battle axe. Then he and Akibeel took wingless flight. Satariel, Jehoel, Lightwings, Nate, Ezeqeel and Hasdiel were right behind them.

§

Both teams tried to take flight, but they were all locked down. Damn! Truthfully, they knew they'd be in the way anyway. None of them were powerful enough to defeat an original Fallen; even if they did have ultimate powers. Only Brock/Seraphiel had *that* power. They all silently prayed that the other Watchers would not be hurt.

§

Several demons charged Adam. He shot a fire ball at one, but the other ran his claws through his arm. He screamed from the pain and lost control of his gravity. He and the demon were tumbling downward, out of control.

§

Jodie screamed, "A.D.A.M!" Unlike when she'd come to Aurellia's rescue; she was helpless. Her baby was being attacked...in the sky! "SOMEBODY HELP MY BABY!"

§

Doc roared and threw his battle axe. It sliced off the demon's hand. He grabbed the demon by the throat and yanked him away from his nephew. He punched the bastard in the face, and knocked him back. Then he slung his battle axe with such force that it was permanently embedded in the bastard's chest.

The demon dropped in the lake of fire. He and the battle axe both destroyed.

No worries though. Doc stretched his arm and called forth another one. This battle was long from being over!

§

Adam was still spiralling downward, towards the lake of fire. "STEADY YOURSELF, ADAM!" Brock shouted.

As another demon shot down to attack him, Adam did a backwards flip and righted himself. Then he yanked the demon's claws out of his arm and slung the hand across the cosmos.

He pulled himself up and ascended back toward his battle station. On his way back up, he bent his knees and kicked out. The demon flew backwards across the sky.

Like father, like son. Adam extended, and flapped, *his* wings. "I AM SERAPHIEL'S SON!" he arrogantly boasted, and rapidly shot fireballs, at the bastard.

The demon screamed and staggered backwards; right into Akibeel's glowing hand.

"AND MY NEPHEW!" he shouted. He ran his entire arm straight through the demon, and pushed his heart out of his chest. The heart caught fire and disintegrated in the sky. He threw the bastard's useless body into the fire.

§

Maria screamed, when two demons accosted Akibeel from behind. "NO!"

Charity wrapped her arm around her terrified sister, and they watched.

Smittie and Leevearne were standing behind their daughters. Smittie whispered, "Lord save my son. Be all the strength he needs."

§

Akibeel clapped his hands, and the damndest thing happened. Not just one, but both of his hands lit up like roman candles. They were shaped like a pirate's hook.

He reached over his shoulders and hooked them around his attacker's neck. They slid through like they were slicing air. The demons' headless bodies dropped and burned in the atmosphere. Their heads were right behind them.

"Go Baby!" Maria shouted, through her tears.

§

Kwanita screamed, "YOMIEL!"

§

Doc was surrounded by a drove of Fallen. There were way too many for him to defeat alone. He wasn't as powerful as Seraphiel, but was just as resourceful. With one knee bent, he shot up one thousand feet. Then he stretched out his arms and beckoned the *stars*.

As the demons rose to catch him, he shot them one

by one…with the celestial lights.

Light was light, right? Wrong. These were the sisters to the lights that imbued all of their battle axes.

They were the first line of defense to keep the Fallen out of Heaven. When humans saw a star twinkle it was because the Fallen were testing the defensive line for a weak point. When they saw a star fall, it was because the star was escorting the scourge back to the underworld.

§

Everyone on the ground watched as the demon exploded, from the inside out. They all saw the stars twinkle and return to their post, behind the Eclipse.

§

Floyd dropped to his knees and raised his arms. "The Heaven's *declare* the Glory of God!"

§

Chapter 13

Leilazeb appeared in the yard, with Mordiree in his/her arms. He/she allowed everyone to see him/her. Not even Destiny noticed that he/she looked exactly like her. They were just grateful to him/her for delivering Mordiree safely.

Clyde grabbed his frightened daughter up in his arms. He was sobbing like a baby, "Thank you!"

"It was my pleasure."

Mordiree was screaming, "They wanted me, Babbo! They wanted *meeee!* Adam wouldn't let them get me!"

"Ssh." Clyde rocked her back and forth. "Babbo's got cha, baby." She was neither flesh of his flesh, nor bone of his bone; but she was his *baby*. She always had been.

He was there the day she entered this world. Rebecca was the mid-wife who had delivered her. Once she was born, he'd held her before either of her birthparents had.

A week later, she was baptized as his goddaughter. He promised her and her parents that he would always take care of her. She was the one who started all of his other children to calling him 'Babbo'.

Then on her thirteenth birthday, her and her parents' home caught fire. She was trapped on the second floor. He drove a bulldozer up close to the house and lifted its bucket. Then he climbed in the bucket and knocked the window out. He crawled through the broken glass and rescued his baby. *"Babbo's here, baby!"* She was afraid and wrapped her trembling arms around his neck. He passed her out the window into the bucket and then he joined her. Embry jumped into the driver's seat and backed them away from the burning house.

Then he ran into the fiery building to rescue her parents; but collapsed from the smoke. Embry and Lamar pulled him out.

He had saved her, but her parents perished. Their bodies were later found on the stairs. They were trying to get to her, but died from smoke inhalation.

A month after their funeral, he and Rebecca legally adopted her. But, she'd always been his baby. He *loved* his youngest daughter. "Damn demons!" he sobbed. "Babbo's got cha."

Dawn, Rebecca and Maria were crying and hugging her from the back. "Ree!" Dawn sobbed. "My Ree!"

Embry and Lamar wrapped their trembling arms around their mother and sisters. All the male cousins formed a complete circle around them all. The Walkers surrounded that circle.

James did not object when his four sons took a defensive stance, alongside him. He knew like Lara knew...all bets were off! If those demons wanted Mordiree, they would have to come through the whole damn family.

§

Ali extended his trembling hand. "Thank you, Leilazeb."

"My team and I will watch over the women and children. I recommend you and your team keep watch outside. Let the guards monitor the preserve."

"You think they will come here?" Chaz asked.

"Of course they will come here. The demons can see the fight in the sky. They believe that you all will join the battle. That would leave your human family unprotected."

"We would've followed them, except Brock locked us down," Dan replied.

"Not Brock."

They all frowned. "Who?" Dan asked.

"I locked you all down."

"WHY?" Arak shouted.

"You guys *can't* defeat the Fallen. Your best bet is to stay here and protect the family."

"What about Doc and Akibeel?" Baraq asked.

"They are *Samjaza's* sons. Add that to the fact that Michael gave them both something extra. Although not as powerful as Seraphiel, they are powerful enough."

"Have our defenses been compromised?" Batman asked. Lightning bolts were jumping all around him. That man was pissed!

"You can never be sure. But, for Joy's sake, it's better to be safe than sorry. Wouldn't you agree?"

Batman trembled and nodded.

"Plus..." Leilazeb looked over at Mordiree. "They still want *her*."

"Why?" Embry asked.

"Yeah, Why!" Lamar echoed.

"Your sister and Adam will usher in a new race. All of their sons, and their son's sons, for generations to come, will be *born* 'un-cursed' Watchers. That makes her enemy number one."

They all remembered what Akibeel had told them. The battle was between demon and women. Clyde squeezed his daughter closer to his chest. "Damn!"

§

"They can come if they want to!" Baraq declared. His eyes were glowing red like neon signs.

Everyone turned around and looked at him. His hands were flowing like a waterfall. A *holy* Waterfall.

"Saturate the preserve, Dawg!" Ram instructed.

"Oh, I'm so there," he replied angrily. "I'm also covering the houses."

"Leave the preserve be; and just cover the houses. I need to work off some steam," Ali demanded. He wasn't about to hide behind Baraq.

Everyone agreed. Baraq sent showers over the estate and sub-division.

"How far can your hands reach, Donnell?" Arak asked.

"As far as they need to reach," Donnell replied.

"Send them forth," Ram commanded. "Give our boys up there a hand or two."

They watched as Donnell's hands flew through the sky. Other than James; the humans didn't know he could do that. It freaked the hell out of them. All of Walker brothers' minds went to the handwriting on the wall, in the Old Testament. WOW!

Eugene frowned and stared at Donnell. "What in the hell?"

Floyd and Donnell both recited, "Mene Mene Tekel Upharsin!"

§

Ram took control. "Call in the guards," he instructed Donnell.

"They are on their way," Donnell replied.

"Get the women and children inside," he commanded. "They do not need to *witness* this. Addison, you go too."

"NO! That's my uncle and cousin up there. I'm not going any damn where." He'd long gotten over his fear of anything. Seraphiel was like a father to him. He was going to stay right there and bear witness to this unimaginable battle.

§

[128]

All of the mothers moved towards the house, as Ram instructed. He was right, the babies were all asleep but they were fretting. All of them were twitching in their mothers' arms. God only knew if they were having nightmares.

§

"We need a plan in case they show up here," Dan suggested.

"First thing is to get all the humans inside the house," Ram replied. "Make sure they have light, Leilazeb."

"Will do."

"I'm not leaving yet. So long as my sons and grandson are up there doing battle; I'm planted right here," Hezekiah informed them.

"Same here," all the men agreed.

"If they come you all will distract us. We can't protect you guys and fight them!" Ram ranted.

"We won't need your help," Ditto responded. Then he looked at his boys. "Let's do this."

They all ran in the house.

"Teleport Dee to the shelter, Chef," Aden requested. Chef wasn't a fighter so he agreed.

"Where are they going?" Smittie asked.

"They prepared for this battle some time ago," Baraq informed them.

"How?"

"You'll see," Baraq responded.

"This is not the time, Dawg," Ali replied. "See what?"

Before Baraq could respond, a battle erupted in the preserve.

§

"You women get in the house! Lock yourselves in the shelter! Now!" Ram shouted.

All the women ran inside.

§

Chapter 14

The nephews ran out the house armed with a multitude of automatic rifles. They tossed them at their fathers and uncles.

"Those won't stop the dem-" Ram started to object but a slew of demons burst through their defenses.

Smittie jumped. "Shit! We're compromised!"

§

The Watchers all teleported to the fence and fought the demons. They were trying to move them back out of the gate but there were just too many of them.

They decided the humans had two choices. Run their asses in the house, or fight as best they could. All of their minds were on their 'spirit' mates and children.

Arak shouted at Baraq, "Keep the house covered, Dawg. Don't let them get to the women and children."

"I'm on it," Baraq responded. He teleported to the roof of the house and let his holy water encompass the estate and sub-division.

§

Chaz was snatching hearts out of those bastards at a rapid speed, but they kept coming.

Batman's lightning was stronger and sharper than ever. Evidently once they received Ultimate powers, their gifts increased, too.

Ram tried what he'd seen Akibeel do. He clapped

his hands and sure enough both his fists were solid as concrete.

Caim and Balam hadn't wanted to display their gifts in front of all the other Watchers, but what the hell. They had a group of demons salivating and trying to get to them. They moved swiftly into the preserve knowing the demons would follow them.

Donnell dispatched two more sets of his hands. He worked with the twins. He ripped the hearts out of the demons and their cohorts never even noticed.

Ali had a group of them puking their guts out. Only he hadn't called on bacteria. He filled their stomachs with plain old table salt. Their insides were dissolving.

Dan created sonic waves in the pits of their stomachs. The slightest move they made caused them to catch fire. From the inside out.

Arak dispatched the bodies of the demons that succumbed to Ali and Dan's treatment. His battle axe was bloody and more powerful than it had ever been.

As prolific as they were, some still got through the gate. They were set on getting Mordiree, at all cost.

§

"DROP!" Lara shouted, from the doorway.

The men hit the ground. Mrs. Lara Goldberg aimed her shotgun and lit those bastards up.

Her aim was dead on. In her mind there wasn't any difference in these demons and Destiny's father. They were coming for her babies; and she'd be damned if they could have them. She continued to shoot as she walked down the steps. She looked like Anne Oakley.

She stepped into the yard and walked just past her husband, sons, father, uncles and nephews. She gave them the cover they needed, to get their act together.

They all rose up on one knee and James shouted, "Fall back, Lola!"

She kept shooting, as she was walking backwards. When she got even with her men, she dropped to one knee, too.

§

One after another demon exploded into a brilliant light and vanished. The Walker brothers were surprised, but grateful. "What the hell kind of bullets are in these guns!" Hezekiah shouted over the gun fire.

All the nephews responded, "Holy Water capsules!"

From the moment they found out that Baraq could produce Holy Water, they'd put their plan in motion. Every day they set aside a couple of hours and filled hundreds of shotgun shells with holy water capsules.

"Do we have enough?"

"Let's hope so," Mark replied. "We've got over a hundred thousand stockpiled so far."

"You boys make me proud to know ya," Smittie said and then laughed. "I just hate I didn't think of it. Some strategist I turned out to be."

They were all laughing and blowing those demons back to Hell.

§

"Let's spread out and form a half moon!" Floyd instructed.

He said that just in time, because demons appeared to the left and right of them.

"What about the back yard!" Clyde shouted over the gun fire.

"Baraq has the backyard covered, along with the estate and sub-division," Henry replied.

"What about the seniors?" Sal asked.

"Arak put them to sleep. They won't hear or see anything," Ditto replied.

§

Floyd rose up off his knee. "I only bow to the Master." The man was a preacher and sharpshooter. "Let's finish this."

He was walking, shooting and reciting verse. "His truth shall be my shield and buckler!"

Everyone else followed suit. They moved away from the house out into the yard.

"What is his truth, Preacha?" Smittie shouted over the gun fire.

"No weapon formed against me shall prosper," Floyd responded.

"Why not, Reverend?" Howard asked.

"He has given his Angel charge over me..." Floyd responded.

"For what, Dad?" Mark asked.

"To keep me in all my ways," Floyd responded.

"How will he keep you, Dad?" Matthew asked.

"He shall cover me with his feathers and under his wings shall I trust," Floyd responded.

"Do you really trust him, man?" Sal asked.

"With all my heart, mind and soul," Floyd responded.

§

They could actually feel the spirit of the Lord moving over them. They felt emboldened. They kept on walking and shooting and quoting verse.

The demons were falling by the wayside, but not one of them had been hurt.

§

"Are you afraid, Walker?" Aden asked.

"Not of the terror by night or of the arrow that flies by day."

"Why?" Henry asked.

"Because greater is he that is in me, than these scourges. With my eyes I will behold and see the reward of the wicked," Floyd replied.

"What is their reward?" Sam asked.

"They shall be trampled under his feet," Floyd replied.

"What else did he promise, Sonny Man?" Elijah asked.

"Ten thousand shall fall at my feet, but it shall not harm me," Floyd replied.

"Why not?" Addison asked.

"Because he knows *my* name!" Floyd replied.

"What does he want you to do in return, Floyd?" Clyde asked.

"Honor him!" Floyd replied. Then he stopped. "I will bless the Lord at all time..." He fired one last shot.

Hezekiah shot one last shot and shouted, "... His praise shall continuously be in my mouth."

They pulled their half-moon close together and lit up the yard. They had the demons on the run. The few that were inside the gate, turned and high-tailed it back into the preserve.

Luther commanded, "Lift up your head, oh ye gate."

All the men shouted, "Be ye ever lifted up!" They fired one last shot.

Lara very calmly said, "And the King Of Glory Shall Come in."

§

They were proud of themselves. They were hugging and kissing each other's cheek. They had killed all the demons in the yard and moved the ones at the gate back out into the preserve.

§

"From now on, we will all take a little time every day to make these capsules," Hezekiah instructed.

"Let's set up a work schedule. Plus, we need a link between all of us," Ditto agreed.

"We'll store them in our homes. I don't believe they will need them in the main house," Henry added. "Plus, we need to teach our wives how to shoot."

"That's a good idea. I don't want to live constantly under Baraq's holy showers. I want my girls to be able to play outside," Sam added.

"Plus, I don't want my children living in fear. They have to be confident that both their parents can protect them," Adrian agreed.

"You old dudes need to start spending time in the gym, too," Mark replied. He wasn't being funny or smart mouthed. "Brock gave you guys your youth, but you're not in shape. All of us need to get and stay in shape."

"You guys see us women working out every day. We understood the importance of staying in shape."

Floyd hugged Lara. "You're alright, niece. I'm proud of the way you covered us, until we could get situated."

She was the only woman out there and was as capable as the men. James had been right; Lara was some kind of marksman.

"What about me!" Addison asked. "I didn't run. Did I?"

Justin hugged his baby boy. "I'm proud of you, son."

"It's about time he grew up," Aden said and then blew on his neck.

Addison screamed and beat his neck. He thought it was a demon. Then he realized it was only Aden. "Stop that!"

Everyone laughed.

§

They stayed in the yard with their weapons ready. Mark had been right when he said they needed to learn how to fight collectively. This was a three pronged battle and this was *their* battlefield. And they were good soldiers. From this day forth they'd do battle with demon and human enemy, alike. They kept their eyes on the gate.

This was the newly woven fabric of their lives. Mordiree was in as much danger as Elizabeth and Hannah.

Demons wanted the twins, because of their wombs and bloodline. As Nephilim, they would be able to survive procreating with demons. They'd be able to produce an army of demons with Samjaza's blood. On the other hand; they would also produce more powerful Nephilim, males and females.

Mordiree, on the other hand, was the *mother* of the next generation of Watcher. No doubt they'd be as strong as Seraphiel and Adam.

"They've been after my baby since she was

thirteen." Clyde spoke what they all were feeling. They all surmised that that's what the fire had been about. Destroy the 'Vessel'.

"I'll always remember we were supposed to be in Indiana the day of the fire," Lamar replied.

"We were disappointed that we couldn't afford the trip that year. Then when you rescued Mordiree I was grateful," Embry added.

"That's why you trust not your own understanding," Floyd replied. "God can see down the road that isn't even in our view."

"But, thank God for his promise, Preacha," Smittie replied. "No weapon formed against this family, shall succeed."

Aden raised his hands and replied, "That'll preach, Walker."

§

Chapter 15

The battle in the sky continued. One Seraphiel and Adam were fighting back to back. The other Seraphiel was a short distance away. They were fending off a half a dozen demons. "Are you good, son?" Seraphiel asked.

"I got your back, Dad, if you got mine."

This was exhilarating to him. These punk assed Fallen bastards were no match for him and his dad. "Thanks for coming."

"I don't appreciate your arrogance, son. You could have gotten Mordiree killed."

"I was trying to help her get over her fear of heights."

That pissed Brock off more than anything. "By bringing her up here?" He turned and faced his son. "What the hell kind of sense does that make? It was immature and unthoughtful. It's your job to protect her and keep her safe. Not *put* her in the line of fire! You may look and think you're grown, but your actions prove otherwise!"

"Look out, Dad!"

Brock shoved his blade backwards and caught the approaching demon in the heart. "We will discuss your behavior later," he reprimanded.

"Yes sir." Adam felt his father's anger. He didn't mean to hurt him or make him mad. That was the last thing in the world he'd ever do. He was so proud to be the son of Seraphiel; he guessed he was a little arrogant. Well, not a little. "I'm sorry, Dad."

"Enough talking, let's finish this."

§

Doc was fighting three of the Fallen. He was outnumbered but not out powered. He turned his feet into sharp blades. With as much speed as he could muster, he contorted his body into a circular blade. He zoomed in and sliced the three across their stomachs. Their guts spilled and caught fire. He zigzagged across their necks. They were dead!

§

Nate was awesome! Even though that boy was on a mission; he still had jokes. He needed to rally as many in his direction as possible. His niche was his voice. "COME TO ME!"

It was so hypnotic that for a minute even the Ultimates started his way. "NOT YOU DUMB ASS BIRDS!" he shouted.

§

Hasdiel shook his head and laughed. "Damn, Nate!"

§

A couple dozen Fallen marched towards him. They looked like they were in a trance, or were zombies. But, it wasn't enough.

"I SAID...COME TO ME!" he shouted again.

"NOW!"

In obedience to his command, two more dozen flew across the sky. They stopped at his feet. Their eyes were dead, as they patiently waited for his next command.

§

Ezeqeel frowned. "That's cheating, man. What's the matter, scared to get your hands dirty?"

"Punk ass!" Hasdiel laughed. "He's scared to get too close to them."

Lightwings flinched. That's what he had done to Seraphiel. He stood at a distance and attacked their leader. He was *still* ashamed of himself.

"*Please,*" Nate laughed. "Destiny just gave me a fantastic manicure. I ain't trying to mess that up, okay!"

They got quiet and listened for his next command.

§

"ADABIEL!" he shouted. "Give it up, man."

§

Seraphiel was the first born and the most physically powerful. Kobabiel was the second born and most intellectually powerful. Adabiel was the third born and...

§

He blasted those demons with gut-wrenching emotions so painful, they started to cry. They were boo-hooing!

§

Satariel looked at Nate. "That's why Michael don't

like your ass. You play too much. Here we are in the battle of our lives and you are still having fun."

§

The rest of the Ultimates cracked up. There in the sky, badass demons were crying like babies. They were wiping their eyes and *bawling!*

§

None of them particularly cared for Adabiel's gift. He could fill your heart with unthinkable joy or unimaginable grief. If he chose to, he could make you wet your pants, with laughter. Or drown in sorrow.

§

Nate was squeaking. He loved his job. There were no blueprints on how to perform his duties. So long as at the end of the day demons were dead.

When he had his fill, he roared, "YOUR BROTHER MADE YOU CRY…KILL *HIM!*"

§

Those demons started to fight each other. All because Nate told them to. With their claws extended they were slinging orange and black colored blood all over the atmosphere. And crying all the while.

§

"TOSS THAT BASTARD IN THE *FIRE!*" Nate commanded.

§

The demons started to push each other toward

Seraphiel's lake of fire. Each demon was trying to throw his opponent in. Before long all four dozen were in the fire.

§

"I believe my work is done," Nate boasted.

"There's still a lot up here, man," Hasdiel reminded him.

"Four dozen is my maximum daily fix." Nate laughed. "Otherwise it's no fun."

Satariel laughed. "You just want to get out of town before Michael gets here."

Nate flipped him the bird, and descended back toward the earth.

It was the truth, though. Michael made him nervous. The man was a hard-ass. He didn't take Nate serious, even though he was.

Nate believed that if you commit to a job, you should enjoy doing it. And he did enjoy taking those bastards out. He just didn't believe you had to wear a frown to do it.

He had only found his 'spirit' mate ten years ago. Prior to finding her, his life had been empty; devoid of joy. He was stuck fighting a war with no end in sight. He lost his nephew, Ali, to Seraphiel. Thanks to Michael. He was alone and stuck in 'bush' country. He had an inner-circle that couldn't stand him…and the feeling was mutual.

He didn't like sex, because the women's blood

didn't taste right. It tasted like wasteland, bush meat or some unwholesome shit. Even his stomach rejected it. For a while he thought maybe he was supposed to be a demon. None of the other Watchers seemed to have a problem with it. But, it wasn't right for him. He didn't like the taste of alcohol, either. His life was desolate.

He complained to his friend, King David. David's reply was so profound that he still held onto it; even today. David said, 'Nate...I encourage *myself!*'

That's when he realized that he couldn't look to others, or circumstances, to make him happy. He had to find his own joy. And he did, through *laughter.*

He found it to be good for his soul. His ability to laugh and make the demons laugh was what kept him going for five thousand years.

After he found his 'spirit' mate, Layla, he realized she was worth the wait. Having her in his life made him enjoy laughing all the more.

The only downfall to their union was her crazy ass *mother!* Man, he resented that sick chick. She deprived him of fatherhood. He envied Ali, so much. Alyni was the cutest baby he'd seen, since Ali was a baby. He wanted one that looked just like her. Like his beloved sister.

He secretly hoped Ali could get to the bottom of that crazy woman's craziness. Then it would just be the matter of convincing Layla. But, that would be a breeze.

§

He landed back at the estate just as Michael entered the fray in the sky. He swaggered towards the Walkers and wiped his brows. "Damn. That was close!"

The Walkers laughed at him. That boy was serious. He and Michael did *not* get along. "I don't get it, man. What is it with you and Michael?" James asked.

"That tightwad has a bur up his ass," he responded and smiled. "He thinks I put it there."

They all laughed. Nate was *too* funny. They liked the idea that he was now a part of their family. He really should have been a standup comedian, though. Evidently that's where Ali got his sense of humor from.

§

Like his brother, Jehoel wielded lightning. Except his was more intense and even stranger. Batman made his lightning bolts dance. Jehoel's was like tentacles. And he had hundreds of them. You couldn't see him for all the bolts.

They shot out across the sky, like fishing lines; and hooked into the chests of those demons. Once inside, the lightning wrapped itself around the demons' hearts. Then he reeled his lightning home. Each bolt had a heart in its grip. The demons dropped into the lake of fire. The hearts burned in the cosmos.

Another group attacked him head on. It was too many. Lightwings and Zeek tried to help, but *damn*. Hasdiel and Satariel joined in the fight, but they were still outnumbered.

They had the strangest feeling that these demons were specifically gunning for Jehoel.

§

Lightning shot *up* out of the bowels of Hell. The sizzling and crackling sounds were deafening. Out of the lightning, they heard a roar. "I *WARNED* YOU!"

§

Batman stopped fighting, on the ground, and looked up. His heart started to race. He never thought he'd see... "How?"

The demons in the preserve vanished. That was one Fallen they did *not* want to come up against. They ran for their lives.

§

Lightwings and Zeek jumped out of the lightning's way. All of the aggressive demons backed up.

Jehoel did not budge. He frowned. *"Father?"*

"Son," Araciel replied.

He *was* lightning. That was the reason Lucifer wouldn't challenge him. But, he'd only given his sons a smidget of his powers. He was about to correct that mistake.

"You will both need this." He stretched one hand toward Jehoel and the other down to Batman; and gave them *all* that he was. His sons would be second, only to Seraphiel! *Damn!*

[147]

Jehoel and Batman lit up like roman candles. The power they were receiving was unbelievable.

"I love you, Father."

"And I you, son," Araciel replied.

Then he wrapped himself around all the demons that had attacked his boys; both in the sky and the preserve. "Be well, my sons."

He shot back down to Hell and dropped his crispy cargo at Lucifer's feet. "If you don't want me to destroy any more of your followers, you had better call them off. *Now!*" He turned and walked away.

§

Michael, Raphael and Gabriel finally entered the fray. Those Archangels were vicious. Michael's voice boomed and shook the constellation. "HOW DID YOU ESCAPE?" It was a rhetorical question. It didn't matter how they escaped. It was his pleasure to send them back to the dungeons.

He chopped the head off the demon before he could respond.

§

Lucifer had failed, once again. Not only did Adam have the support of his Father and the Ultimate Watchers; he had the support of Michael, Gabriel and Raphael.

Not to mention the regular Watchers had destroyed his troupes on the ground. His plan had been so clear. He just knew the Watchers would join Seraphiel in the sky.

That would allow his warriors to grab that woman.

Those Walker brothers, and their sons, had developed a new bullet. They, and that female, had dropped his warriors, coming and going.

Plus, they could not get close to Adam's woman, because of those she/he spirits hanging around the estate. Lucifer shouted, "RETREAT!"

They would have to try again in a couple of weeks. By then they would have a fool proof plan; because now Seraphiel knew the deal. If only they could get his brothers out of that block of ice!

§

Not to mention he needed a way to get around Araciel. He had not released him; so how did he get *out*?

He was not afraid of his brother, but he wondered why he was even in Hell. Evidently he could leave whenever he chose to. That had to mean…

§

Chapter 16

That had been the longest battle yet. Needless to say, everyone was wiped out and not in the mood to celebrate.

Kobabiel sent a shout out and reversed everything he'd done.

The Eclipse was gone. Technology rebooted. Street lights came back on. Everything was back to normal; but people *would* remember.

Brock gave one final command: "Wipe everyone's memory of this night."

Across the world Watchers performed the cleanup.

§

"Check on your families. Then meet me in the conference room in ninety minutes," Brock instructed all the Watchers, including the Ultimates.

He looked at his nephews and the Walkers. "You guys did real good."

Finally he looked at Adam. "Go check on Mordiree. Then meet me in my office, in an hour."

He turned and walked into the house. He needed to check on Aurellia. For the first time in his life he wanted to hit a child of his. He wanted to smack some sense into that arrogant boy.

§

Adam knew Mordiree was in the ICU. He also

knew she was traumatized.

When he reached the door, Clyde stepped out. "Desiree gave her a strong sedative. She won't wake up tonight."

"May I sit with her for a while?"

"Come talk with me first," Clyde requested. "Let's go into the chapel."

You would've had to be blind not to see that Clyde was not happy. "Yes sir," Adam replied and followed him into the chapel.

§

Once they were inside the chapel, Clyde unleashed. "What the *hell* were you thinking?"

Adam was very respectful. "I'm sorry. I was just trying to help her overcome her fear of heights. My father has already reprimanded me for my behavior."

Clyde frowned. "Do you even know *why* she's afraid?"

"No sir."

Clyde told him what happened to her and her birth parents. "Not only did you endanger her; you made her relive her worst nightmare, son. You made her relive the day she lost her parents."

"I'm sorry, I did not know," Adam replied. Man he felt like a real jerk. His father was right, sometimes you needed to snoop. If he had, he would have known.

"I have no problem with you and Mordiree, as a

couple. But, I do have a problem with you taking foolish and unnecessary risks with my daughter. It's bad enough that she'll be the target of demons for the rest of her life. I don't need you helping them out."

Adam frowned. "What do you mean she'll be the target?"

Clyde told Adam what had been told to him. For the first time, Adam looked frightened. He had not seen that four-one-one coming. "What?"

He jumped up. "I need to see my dad." He shot out of the chapel, like a bat out of Hell.

§

Brock found Aurellia in his suite, with Jodi. Baby Girl was shaking uncontrollably. This was the worst battle yet. He hugged her and calmed her nerves. "It's over, Aurellia."

"Is Adam okay, Daddy?"

"He's fine, baby. How are you?"

"Scared," she replied. "Where's James?"

§

Deuce walked in the room. She ran into his opened arms. "James!" She started to cry.

"It's okay, Rellia," James said and hugged her. He was worried about her, because she was going through a rough patch. He needed to talk with her parents about it. "Let's go to our room."

§

[152]

The twins were asleep, but Brock still had to ease their spirits. He jumped into their dreams and let them see him. It quieted the storm. They both sighed and began to sleep restfully.

§

Jodi was a mess. She was scared for her son. "I told you I didn't want him fighting demons, Brock. Look what happened."

"I told you I'll never let any of them hurt our son, Dimples. He's not hurt; neither is Mordiree. Although, I'd *like* to hurt him."

Jodi paused. "Why?"

"He was showing off and took her up there. She's afraid of heights. He claimed to want to help her overcome her fear."

"He did that on purpose?"

"Yeah."

Jodi recited the same story Clyde had just told Adam about the house fire.

Brock's jaws were jumping. He could not believe that his son was that foolish.

"Take his powers, Brock," Jodi demanded.

"I can't do that, Dimples."

"Why not?"

"Like it or not; he *is* a Watcher. Demons know he's a Watcher. If I took his powers, it would put him in greater danger."

She knew Brock was right. If the demons knew he was a Watcher without powers, he'd be targeted again. "He's not ready."

§

Adam burst through the door. "DAD!"

Brock heard the fright in his son's voice. He reached out to Mordiree. She was asleep in the ICU. He checked the yard. All was quiet. "What is it, Adam?"

"Did you know?"

Brock read his mind. "Damn! No I didn't."

"Know what?" Jodi asked.

"It appears our son and Mordiree are enemy number one. All of their sons will be Watchers, Jodi. And their sons' sons. Our son will usher in a new race of people."

"Oh God!"

Adam frowned. "You read my *mind*?"

Brock laughed and not in a comical way. "I always *could*. I just didn't know I *needed* to."

"But...?"

"But nothing. As you boldly proclaimed, you are Seraphiel's son. Not *Seraphiel!*" Brock frowned at the boy. "I don't snoop unless I'm given cause to. Don't ever forget that."

"What are we going to do, Brock?" Jodi asked.

Brock hugged her. "I promise you it will be okay. I will never let anyone hurt my children, Jodi."

Then he turned to Adam. "Go to the conference

[154]

room, now."

Adam turned and walked out of the room, with his head cast down. He was in *so* much trouble. He longed for his diaper days. Hell; that was just yesterday.

§

"He's too arrogant, Brock. Can't you do anything?" Jodi asked.

God he hated to answer her question. She was going to be pissed off. "He falls under Yomiel's command. Any reprimand will have to come from him."

"WHAT!" Jodi shouted. "I know you're not going to *leave* him with Doc, Brock."

"Yes, I am. If I brought him onto my team, one of two things will happen. Either, his ego will get bigger; or he'll feel like he's being punished. Not to mention I would be stepping on Doc's toes. He has the right to be the leader of the team he chooses."

"Michael changed teams *all* of the time."

"Not arbitrarily, he didn't. He put us in the vicinity of our mates, Jodi. Adam already knows who his mate is."

"I don't like it," Jodi complained. "He's out of control."

"I can't argue that."

§

When Adam walked into the conference room, Doc was already there. He did not look pleased, at all. Neither of them said a word to each other. It was more uncomfortable than being surrounded by the Fallen. He bowed his head and sat down.

Silence…

Silence…

Silence…

Annnnd… silence.

§

Brock finally came through the door. He sat at the head of the table. Then he looked at Adam. Again, he was reading that boy's mind. He almost laughed. Doc was giving him the quiet treatment.

He looked over at Doc and smiled. "State your position."

"You are under my leadership. You will follow my direction from now until that Great Day of Judgment. Am I clear?"

Adam didn't look up. "Yes sir."

Brock burst out laughing. He was listening to that boy's thoughts. *'Come ooooon diaper!'*

Adam blushed. "I know I was wrong, okay. I won't make that mistake again."

"You damn right, you won't," Doc replied. "As of right now you are in training. You will not fight any battles, until I say so. You understand?"

Adam looked up. "What?"

"You heard me. If we are under attack, you are to go in the shelter with the humans."

"Dad!"

"You heard him. He is your *boss*."

"This sucks!"

"So does your attitude."

§

Brock's entire team walked through the door. They all had worrisome looks on their faces.

Ali sat down next to Adam. "You are not ready for battle, son."

"Yes I am!" Adam replied. "I fought next to my dad!"

"You *mimicked* your father!" Arak replied. "You don't know the first thing about fighting."

"If you had been *ready* you would have teleported back to the yard," Chaz added.

Adam frowned. "I didn't think of it."

"That's because you're not ready," Dan replied. "You froze, son."

"The minute you saw your woman was in danger, you should have teleported *home*. Her needs come first, understand? Never leave her in the line of fire. That is your first responsibility," Ram said.

"Never mind the fact that you frightened all of the humans, with your arrogant display of alarm," Doc added. "The children were traumatized. Plus, we had to jack with nature to cover up your crap."

"We were all in the yard. They never would have

set foot on the estate grounds, Adam," Batman added. "They are princes of the air. Our air *was* hollowed."

"Your actions put our family in danger. The children, the Walkers, and the women," Chaz informed him.

Baraq spoke with his mind. *"All you had to do was reach out to your father, just like I'm doing to you, now."*

"Because of your actions, the demons were able to break through our defenses," Doc informed him.

"The Walkers, and Lara, I might add, had to battle demons."

"What?" Adam frowned. "Aunt Lara had to fight?"

Everyone nodded their angry heads.

§

"So until I say otherwise, these birds are going to be on your ass, twenty-four seven. Is that clear?"

"Yes sir."

"And Adam?"

Adam looked up at his Uncle. "Yes?"

"Your father is not the only one who can read your mind. Don't even think about sneaking away. Even if you want to go on a date; you will be chaperoned. Is that clear?"

"That's not *fair!*"

"It's high time for you to learn that life never is." Doc stood up and walked towards the door. "I'm disappointed in you. Not only did you put your woman in danger. You put all of ours in danger, as well. That includes your mother and sisters. You put Abe in danger, son. Count yourself lucky that your father doesn't take your powers."

§

Adam looked at his father pleadingly. Brock smiled. "Ya heard."

Adam frowned. "Being grown sucks!"

Ali squeaked.

§

Doc opened the door. "You may leave now. Do not leave the building."

"Everyone else stay put. We need to have a meeting," Brock instructed.

"Shouldn't I be in the meeting?" Adam asked.

Doc pointed out the door. "Go!"

Adam stood up and walked out.

§

Brock had allowed Jodi to listen in on the meeting. She smiled. *"My poor baby."* But, she was pleased with Doc's instructions. *"Not only will he not be fighting...but no sex, either! Yea!!!"*

Brock laughed. *"You are sick, Dimples."*

"That's how you felt about Aurellia, on her wedding night, Boo."

"True that. But he will, one day, Jodi."

"Not today." Jodi laughed. *"I'm going to tell Doc*

to keep him locked down for eighteen years."

"You're a mess."

§

Chapter 17

Adam walked out of the conference room with his tail tucked. He wished he was one year old. He'd screwed up royally. Now all the Watchers were going to treat him like a kid. He might as well have stayed one year old. The only thing missing was the diaper. He'd welcome that right about now.

His buddies were waiting on him. "Don't say it. I already know I screwed up."

"It's cool," Henry replied. "We didn't come to brow-beat you."

"That's right," Sam added. "But turn around."

Adam turned around, and looked over his shoulder. "Why?"

"We just wanted to see how big of a bite they took out of your ass!" Matthew said, and burst out laughing.

They all did, even Adam.

Henry patted him on his back. "Let's go. The guys are waiting in the den."

"I need to check on Maude first."

"We'll wait."

§

When Adam walked into the ICU, Clyde was still in there. He looked up and scowled, and then smiled. Adam felt like an even bigger jerk. "I'm sorry to interrupt you. I just wanted to sit with her a while."

Clyde looked back down at his daughter. "She stole my heart the first time I saw her. There has never been a time that I didn't think of her as my daughter."

Adam didn't respond. He just sat next to him. The man evidently needed to make a point. He'd earned the right to express himself; to state his claim. To vent, if he needed to.

"Her birth mother was Rebecca's first cousin. They were decent people. I tried to save them too."

"What happened?"

"Living on the farm they, like most farmers, had a propane tank. It supplied gas for the tractors and other vehicles. I advised them not to place the thing so close to the house. But, her father didn't listen. Some kind of a way the tank was punctured. Nobody knows when or how. They had invited us over for dinner. When we got there the house was ablaze."

"What happened?"

"When she turned on the stove the house blew. Evidently the fumes from the tank..." He shook his head. "The thing is; her father never left the keys to the tractor in it. He did that day," Clyde said and stood. "She's always been my daughter. I'll be watching." He walked out the room.

§

Adam reached for Mordiree's hand. He kissed her fingers. "I'm sorry, Maude. I messed up. Being grown is harder than I imagined."

He held her hand with both of his and bowed his head. Then he poured out his heart's desires. "Everyone is mad at me. Your father, mine. My uncles. My mother. I am officially in training. I can't fight. I can't leave the property." He kissed her fingers. "If I didn't love you so much, I'd go back to being a baby. Thirty years was too long for you to wait on me. Thirty years was too long for *me* to wait."

He reached up and brushed her hair. "I didn't mean to hurt you. I won't ever do that to you again. I promise. Don't give up on me, Maude. I'll get it right."

He leaned over to kiss her but felt her twitch. He frowned. She was having a nightmare. He eased into her mind. She was in that damn fire!

"DAD!"

"What is it, son?"

"I need you!"

Brock appeared in the ICU. "What's the matter?"

"She's in the fire. I can't help her."

Brock eased into her mind. She was trapped on the second floor of her house. Her heart was racing and she was screaming. She was thirteen. She wouldn't know him. Damn!

He reached out and eased her heart rate. *"Mordiree, can you see me."*

§

Mordiree jumped. She'd never seen a man that big in her life. *"Are you an Angel? Am I dead?"*

"You're not dead, Sweetheart. You are having a nightmare."

"I'm dreaming?"

"Yes. Take my hand, okay?"

"Why?"

"I'm going to lead you out of this nightmare, Honey."

"How?"

He smiled. *"I'm going to walk with you through the fire."*

"I'll get burned."

"Not as long as you are with me you won't."

"Who are you?"

"I'm Brock. I'm your future father-in-law."

"I'm only thirteen. I don't even have a boyfriend."

"You are thirteen in this nightmare. You are much older in real life."

"Are you real?"

"Yes. Take my hand, please. I can help you."

§

She hesitated. But, anything was better than burning up. She reached for his hand. It felt comforting...and familiar. He felt familiar. Safe. Strong. She *knew* him, but she didn't know how. She trusted him. *"Can you help my parents?"*

"This is just a dream, Mordiree. I can only walk you out of it."

§

With great care, Brock walked her back into present day. It felt like she was fast forwarding on a movie. She saw her Babbo rescue her and try to save her parents. She saw their funeral. She saw her Babbo and Momma adopt her. She saw all the mischief her and Dawn got into over the years. She laughed.

"You girls were something else." Brock laughed.

"If Babbo knew he'd have a fit."

"It'll be our secret, okay?"

"Okay."

§

Finally she saw herself surrounded by demons and all that fire! She trembled. *"You wrapped me in a ball of fire!!"* She tried to pull her hand away. *"I'm afraid of fire!"*

"I didn't know that at the time. I am sorry I frightened you, even more than you already were."

"How did you do that?"

"I can control fire. It bends to my will."

"How?"

"I am an Angel, Mordiree."

"And you are my future father- in-law?"

"Yes. Don't you remember my son, Adam?"

She frowned. *"Oh God! Adam. Is he alright?"*

"Yes. He is fine."

"He didn't know I was afraid of fire. He was trying to protect me from those demons. Oh God! Those demons wanted me!"

"I am aware of that. But he acted foolishly. He should have never taken you up into the atmosphere. And those demons will never get their hands on you. I promise."

"Where is he?"

"He's sitting beside your hospital bed." Brock laughed. *"Drowning in his tears."*

"He's crying!"

"In a manner of speaking."

"Why?"

"Let's just say he's on punishment."

She laughed. *"Isn't he grown today?"*

"Yep."

"How do you put a grown man on punishment?"

"He's lucky I don't take his powers. That man is too cocky."

"He just wants to be like you, Uncle Brock."

"You remember me now?"

"Yeah. And you had better not be mean to Adam."

Brock laughed. *"I'm going to box him upside his arrogant head."*

"Since you command fire, can you fix it so that I'm not afraid of it anymore?"

"I can remove your fear. But keep in mind, fire is still dangerous. The only reason it didn't burn you was because I changed its composition while you were wrapped in it."

"That's deep and way too cool!"

Brock laughed again. *"Cool, indeed."*

"Can I wake up now?"

"I'm not sure. Desiree gave you a strong sedative to help you sleep. I think you should continue in your slumber."

"I want to speak with Adam. He must been feeling guilty."

"Yeah he is. But, that's a good thing. If he wasn't feeling remorseful he wouldn't learn his lesson. Then I'd really have to box his head."

"You wouldn't hit him. You don't believe in hitting your children."

"Shush. Don't tell him that. I need to keep my bluff up."

"The big bad wolf, right?"

"Yep!" Brock released her hand. *"You feel better?"*

"Yes." She took a deep comforting breath. *"Much. Where is Babbo?"*

"He just left to give Adam some time alone with you. He'll be back, I'm sure."

"Is he mad at Adam?"

"I say yes, because I can't think of a stronger word for his feelings."

"It's that bad?"

"The only reason he didn't kill my son is because he knew I'd slowly torture him." Brock laughed.

"He wants to kill Adam!"

"I'm teasing. He is quite angry with him though."

"I need to wake up, Brock."

"No. Sleep. Morning will be here soon enough."

§

Brock sat down next to his son. "She's alright now."

"Thanks, Dad. I really screwed up didn't I?"

"Yes, you did. But, it was a good life lesson. You were right when you said you won't make *that* mistake again." He turned and looked at his son. "But you will make others, Adam."

"I just wanted to be like you. I thought I was as powerful as you are. I couldn't even jump in her dream."

"You could only take what I gave you, Adam. There was no way I was going to unleash all that I am to you. That would have been foolish on my part. It would have been like giving you a loaded gun, without first training you how to use it. There's great danger in too much undisciplined power, son. You look like you are in your late twenties; but, practically, you are only one year old. When I feel like you are ready to handle the power, I will give it to you."

"But I thought I only had twelve months to get it."

"You had twelve months to *take* it. I have a lifetime to *give* it. Think of it as an inheritance."

Adam grunted. "More like an allowance. If I behave, you'll increase it."

Brock laughed. "Yep. Good analysis."

"So what does Mom say?"

"She's tickled pink." Brock laughed. "She said no sex for that boy!" Brock rolled.

Adam blushed. "Dad!"

"Listen, I need to get back to my meeting. Come on out and hang with your boys. She won't wake up."

"Yes sir."

§

Chapter 18

Brock returned to his meeting. Both teams were there; as well as all the Ultimate Watchers.

"Is she okay?" Baraq asked.

"She's fine. She was having a nightmare and was trapped at age thirteen. Adam couldn't bring her out."

"Why?"

"Because, he's not powerful enough yet."

"I thought he was as powerful as you are," Dan stated.

"Not even close. Not yet at least. When he's ready I'll give it to him."

"Speaking of giving it to him," Hasdiel said and looked at Jehoel. "Man, your father was awesome. I can't believe a demon bastard helped us."

"He's a demon, but not a bastard," Jehoel corrected. "In the end, he loved me and Batman."

"Yeah, so watch your damn mouth," Batman added.

"Excuse me. My bad," Hasdiel replied.

"I can't believe he gave you boys more of his powers," Satariel said.

"He said we'll need it. So evidently the battle isn't over," Jehoel told them.

"It's too bad your father can't be saved," Lightwings replied. "He seemed like a good enough guy."

Kobabiel shook his head. "He doesn't need to be

saved. At least, not in the sense you are talking about."

Everyone turned and looked at him. "What?" Batman asked.

"His imprisonment is self-imposed,"Kobabiel replied. "He's in Hell because *he* can't forgive *himself.*"

"What?" Jehoel and Batman said at the same time.

"Michael didn't kill him."

"Say what?" everybody said.

"Michael did not *kill* him. He was so distraught over what he'd done, he sentenced himself."

Batman jumped. "He what!"

Kobabiel nodded his head. "He walked himself into Hell. And he has been there ever since."

"He's not a Fallen?"

"Oh, he fell from grace, alright. But, he realized the error of his ways. He had a contrite spirit."

"If he's not a demon, how did our mothers die?" Jehoel asked.

"Humans can't survive a union with an Archangel; Fallen or not."

"We gotta get him out," Jehoel demanded.

"We *can't.* He has free will," Kobabiel replied.

§

Brock was not aware of that. He sat there frowning and listening. "How do you know this, Kobabiel?"

"I was there. Michael was trying to convince him to come home. He said the Master had forgiven him. Araciel wouldn't hear of it. He wanted Michael to send him to the underworld. Michael refused. So he sent himself."

"He's alive down there?" Akibeel asked.

Kobabiel nodded his head. "Yes."

"Those demons don't attack him, like they did me."

"And me," Ram added. Those thirty days had been hell. He fought day and night with those bastards. Then all of a sudden they left him alone. He frowned. He'd forgotten all about that.

Kobabiel smiled. He was listening to Ram's thoughts. "That's right. They stopped because Araciel threatened to fry them."

"Damn!"

"The only two demons stronger than him are Samjaza and Azazel. They are both chained. So, the others knew to back the hell off you, Ramiel."

"What about Lucifer? He's stronger than him," Akibeel reminded him.

Kobabiel laughed. "No, he's not."

"Say what?" Batman asked. "He's the top of the demon power structure."

"Yeah!" all of the Watchers, including Brock, said.

"Lucifer's powers are strictly *persuasive*."

"What does that mean?" Akibeel asked.

"He's like a used car salesman. He can sell anything; including a thought."

The Watchers thought about Henry and how they

called him the blue eyed devil. They needed to stop that.

"He's a deceiver. He has no physical powers. His powers are his ability to make *you* believe he is powerful. The true hierarchy, based on strength is Azazel, Samjaza and then Araciel. Except you really can't count Araciel, because he isn't a demon." Kobabiel frowned. "He's just an arrogant Archangel who thinks his sins are bigger than forgiveness."

"Can we help him?" Brock asked. He felt Batman and Jehoel's angst. They loved their father. The man must have been better to them, than most.

"You can't make a mule drink water," Kobabiel replied.

Batman looked at Brock. His leader and the one man he trusted above all, including his brother. "We gotta try." His eyes watered. "He saved us tonight, man. We gotta try."

Brock nodded. He didn't know how they could, but maybe...

"Michael?"

§

Michael appeared in the room. He looked from Brock to Lightwings and back at Brock. He chuckled. "You called?"

"Yeah," Jehoel answered. "We want to get our father out of Hell!"

Michael was tempted to be hardnosed. He wanted

[173]

to say, *'I was not speaking to you, Jehoel.'* But the man looked distraught. "What would you like me to do? Make him come home?"

"Yes! That's exactly what we would like," Batman snapped. "He doesn't belong in Hell!"

"I know that better than you, Batariel. I have tried on numerous occasions. My little brother is stubborn."

"Does he even know he has grandchildren?" Jehoel asked.

"Of course. He has kept an eye on you boys, all along."

"How could you not tell us, Michael?" Batman asked.

"What good would it have done? He refuses to leave his cave."

"We can convince him," Jehoel replied. "We're his sons. He'll listen to us."

"I doubt it. He will not listen to his father; or his brothers."

"We are his sons. He'll listen," Batman replied.

§

"What is his problem, anyway?" Akibeel said then sheepishly smiled. "I couldn't wait to get out of Hell!"

Brock smiled at him. If only Adam could be as humbled as Akibeel. And Yomiel for that matter. But, they weren't his sons. Adam was. And he'd been cocky at that same age.

[174]

"His problem is he killed his children's mothers. Innocent humans that we are charged to protect," Michael replied.

"I can't stand the thought of him down there, Brock," Batman reiterated.

"Maybe I can help. I killed innocent women, too," Akibeel offered.

They all turned and stared at him. They could not believe him. Doc's mind went back to a question he'd asked himself, just days ago. *'Could a Watcher have a ministry?'*

They all, including Michael, said at the same time, "Damn!"

Akibeel misunderstood. He frowned. "I'm not bragging, y'all. I resent what I did. But, I've learned to live with the guilt."

§

"We know that, son," Brock assured him. "And I think it's a good idea."

"Man, I swear you are the answer," Doc replied.

"They may be right, Akibeel," Michael agreed. "But, are you ready to revisit Hell again?"

Akibeel's Adam's apple jumped. He swallowed so loudly, they heard it. "I thought you could bring him here." He smiled.

They all smiled.

"Okay, I'll go; if my Pops goes with me."

[175]

Brock smiled. "I wouldn't think of sending you alone, son."

"I want to go too," Jehoel said.

"I *am* going," Batman stated.

Michael stood up. "I shall accompany you all." He smiled. "I like to jack with Lucifer every now and again."

Then he decided to mess with Nate. He looked at him sternly and said, "Would *you* care to accompany us?"

Nate did not verbally respond. He shrunk down in his chair and shook his head.

Everyone in the room quietly laughed. Poor Nate didn't realize Michael was playing with him. They all wondered what in the world happened between those two.

§

Brock stood up. "Okay, the rest of you guys, stay here and keep an eye out."

"Nate and I need to take care of some business, Brock. I'll keep an ear posted, but I really need to look into this business."

"I'm going with you, Ali," Doc informed them.

Brock knew where they were going. It was just as important as what he was about to do. "Okay. But everyone else, stay here. Ali, keep me posted."

"Will do," he replied.

He, Doc and Nate immediately walked out of the conference room.

Brock, and his crew, teleported to the bowels of

Hell.

§

Chapter 19

Adam walked into the den. He had only seen it in his father's mind. All of his male cousins were in there. They looked at him and smiled.

"He doesn't look any worse for wear," Nantan said.

"Just his ego." Ditto laughed.

"Hey man." Adam laughed. "It's not funny."

"How is Mordiree?" Embry asked.

"She's sleeping. I'm sorry I did that to your sister."

"It's cool," Embry replied.

"What's even cooler, is my future nephews," Lamar stated and slapped Adam a high five. "Man, that is tight!"

"No doubt," Mark replied. "That's why there are double teams surrounding us. It is for your and Mordiree's protection."

"And their future children," Eugene added. "Hey, can I be the Godfather?"

"Get that damn thought out of your mind, clown," Henry responded. "I let you be little HE's Godfather. Ain't no way in hell you are claiming even one of Adam's sons as yours."

"Damn straight," Sam agreed. "Henry, Matthew and I have that covered. You understand?"

"So back the hell off!" Matthew added.

"You never know," Eugene replied. "He might find I'm a better role model."

"In what damn universe?" Henry asked.

"No doubt my boys get first dibs. But, I am in so much trouble, I wouldn't look for that to happen anytime soon," Adam told them.

"What happened?"

"They locked my ass down! The only thing I can do alone is go to the bathroom."

"What?" they all said.

"Man, I don't think they will even let me shower alone."

Baraq appeared in the den. "You got that right." He laughed. "I got first watch.

"Aw Man!" Adam complained.

His cousins cracked up.

"Twenty-four-seven, my man," Baraq said and laughed again.

"Oh well. I asked for it." Adam laughed.

"It's almost like Spoiler knew; isn't it?" Mark said to no one.

"What?" Matthew asked.

"Remember the scripture she had dad read?"

They all frowned and focused on the same part of the verse.

'Though he fall, he shall not be utterly cast down; for the Lord upholds him with His hand.'

"She said she had discernment," Henry finally said. "Damn!"

[179]

"No kidding," Aden replied. "I didn't see it coming, that's for sure."

"That's because you can't keep your mind off of Dee," Adrian teased him.

"Yep!" Aden laughed.

"How is she, man?"

"Desiree gave her a sedative. Man, she was freaked the hell out." He laughed. "That woman damn near choked me to *death*."

Addison laughed. "You shouted, *'Put Dee dooowwnn!'* like she was a rabid dog, or something."

Everybody laughed, except Adam. He looked stricken. "I'm sorry, Aden. I didn't mean to do that to your wife."

"You didn't. Your ugly ass father did. That bastard shot up in the air, engulfed in fire."

"Yeah, but if I'd been prepared I would have just teleported back to the yard."

"True that."

"They said, that alone tells them that I'm not ready for battle."

"Oh please," Henry replied. "If that's the case, why didn't Brock just teleport you guys back?"

"That's right!" Eugene said. "NOOOO he had to put on a big spectacle too!"

"And what was up with that damn snake?" Sam asked. "I damn near crapped in my pants."

"You guys better stop," Baraq said. "Don't encourage him. Adam was wrong and he *knows* that. Brock didn't teleport them, because the battle was eminent. The Fallen were already there. Although truthfully, that snake was a jacked up move."

"Baraq is right. It was my fault. That's why I'll have a babysitter until I'm thirty, in real time."

Everybody cracked up, but him.

Chaz walked in. "At least you don't have the diaper."

"The meeting's over?" Adam asked. He had wanted to be in there. He should have been in there. He was a Watcher too, wasn't he?

"Yeah," Chaz responded. "Let's shoot some pool."

§

Ali, Doc, Nate and Justin appeared in the ward where Nate's mother-in-law was staying. She was sitting by the window, gazing out.

"Man, I hate this woman," Nate said.

Ali frowned. "No, you don't. You just hate what she's done to your life. You want her to get better, and you know it."

Nate didn't respond.

"I can feel it, man. You are hoping we find an answer."

"What is her name?" Justin asked.

"Loretta."

"Call out to her," Justin asked.

"HEY, LO...RET...TA!" Nate shouted.

Ali laughed. "Why are you shouting, man? Is she deaf?"

"No." Nate laughed. "Just crazy."

§

She was a beautiful African woman. She looked like Layla; or rather Layla looked like her. But her eyes were lost; sunken. Tormented.

"Who dat?"

Nate didn't answer. He just stood back. Justin walked over and knelt down beside her chair. "My name is Justin. I am a friend of your daughter's."

Out of nowhere her eyes focused and she smiled. "You're like my Layla, aren't you?"

"I believe so." Justin reached for her hand. "I've come to help you."

"No one can help me, son. I'm trapped."

§

Nate's eyes were about to pop out of his head. He'd never seen her so calm or talk so lucid.

Ali was equally surprised. "What does she mean that you are like her Layla, Justin?"

"I can't read her mind. Can you, Ali?" Doc asked.

"No," Ali replied.

"Have you ever tried, Nate?"

"Hell no. I wasn't trying to get trapped in there,

[182]

with her."

Ali squeaked. "You sick!"

§

Justin rubbed her hand. He could not believe he'd met someone like him. All of his life he kept it a secret. Even when he moved in with the Watchers, he still didn't say anything.

His childhood had all but destroyed him. Amanda had been a savior for him, but he still kept quiet. Now was his opportunity to help someone. It would make up a lot for what he wasn't able to do when he was a child.

"Justin," Ali asked again. "What does she mean?"

Justin looked over his shoulder. "Can we take her to the estate?"

"I don't know, man. Brock is not there," Ali replied.

"We have too many women and children. We need to figure out what's wrong with her, first," Doc insisted.

"When will Brock be back?"

"Hopefully soon."

Justin looked back at Loretta. "I believe I can help you. Can you hold on until tomorrow?"

"No one can help me. I'm trapped."

"What does she mean?" Nate asked. "Why is she talking like she has sense?"

Justin kissed her hand. "I promise I'll be back tomorrow. I won't leave you here, okay."

Loretta smiled. "Okay. You're a good boy, Justin. Better than my...no good...thinks he's funny... son-in-law. Did he tell you he tried to get some demons to kill me?"

"What?" Justin asked and looked over at Nate. There was unmeasured resentment in his eyes. "You did what?"

"Don't worry; you know demons can't hurt me." Loretta smiled. "Don't you?"

"I wasn't aware of that. But, he still should not have done that to you," Justin replied and kissed her hand.

She laughed. "He knows they couldn't hurt me, too. He just doesn't know *why* they can't hurt me." She laughed again. "I wouldn't tell him our secret. I'll tell you when he's not in the room."

Then she frowned. "He, and my Layla, think I'm crazy because of all the drugs I've taken over the years. But, you know better, don't you?"

"Yes ma'am."

She rubbed Justin's cheek. "How did she deal with all the voices?"

For the first time, Justin frowned. "She didn't."

"Was he mean to her?"

"Yes."

"Her who?" Ali asked.

"He who?" Nate asked.

They ignored both of them.

[184]

"Do you have children, Justin?"

"I have three sons and one daughter."

"Are they like you and my Layla?"

"I believe so."

"Do they know?"

"No ma'am. I've never told a soul."

"You were afraid no one would believe you?"

He smiled. "Yes ma'am."

For the first time, Loretta looked sad, too. "Layla, and that, not so funny husband of hers, don't want children. They are afraid they'll be like me. They don't understand that they'll be like Layla...*not me.*"

"I know."

"Maybe you can help them understand. My Layla is a good girl. She deserves a family of her own. It's just too bad my...not so funny...son-in-law will be the father. I wonder what Michael was thinking giving my baby to him."

§

Nate's heart raced. How in the hell did that crazy woman know about Michael? He looked over at Ali. He was frowning, too. *"What the hell is going on, Ali? Who is Justin?"*

"I don't know, man. But, your mother-in-law doesn't sound crazy to me. As a matter of fact, she's got your number."

"I don't know about that. I am funny. But, you are

right; I do want her to get better."

"I know that. Everyone knows that. And not just for Layla's sake."

"It's like Justin has stabilized her emotions. I wonder if he'd consider coming to live with us. If he would, I'd take that crazy woman home...today!"

"I doubt it. Plus, Brock would never let that happen."

"Something's gotta give, man. I want my own little Alyni."

Ali smiled at his uncle. *"You'd be great at it, man. Look at how I turned out. For all intents and purposes, you were my father."*

Nate smiled. *"I did raise a pretty decent kid, didn't I? And I did it all...by...myself,"* he boasted.

§

Justin stood up. "I'm going to go now, okay? But, I'll be back tomorrow."

"Promise?"

He leaned down and kissed her cheek. "I promise."

"You're a good boy. Not like that no good son-in-law of mine."

§

He walked back over to Nate. "That was low, man." Then he looked at Ali. "Let's go."

They teleported back to the estate.

§

"What the hell was that, Justin?" Nate asked. "How are you like my Layla? What does that even mean?"

"I will tell you after I speak with Brock. We need to get her out of that ward. She is *not* crazy," Justin said and walked away.

"What is she?" Ali asked.

"I need to speak with my family, first. They should know first," he said and walked away.

§

Ali was just as perplexed as Nate. He could read Justin's mind, but for some strange reason, he didn't want to. This was big!

Doc did read his mind and frowned.

Ali sent a shout out to Brock.

"Brock?"

"What's wrong, Ali?"

"We've got a situation here. How long are you going to be?"

"We're on our way."

§

Justin was anxious. He wanted Loretta out of that place. He gathered his wife and children up for a private family meeting. "I need to share something with you guys."

"What?" Amanda asked. She saw how nervous her husband was. "What's wrong, Justin?"

His sons saw it, too. "What's wrong, Dad?" Adrian

[187]

asked.

"I want Floyd in this meeting."

"He's in his office," Aden told them.

§

Justin knocked on Floyd's office door and poked his head in. "You got a minute?"

"Yeah; Come on in," Floyd replied. He noticed and felt Justin's distress. His brows were bunched and he had a scowl on his face. His entire family looked nervous. Something was definitely wrong. "What's the matter, son?"

They all sat down. Justin rubbed his forehead. It just seemed right to speak with Floyd first. Not that he had anything to confess, but it just felt like the right place to start.

"I let you guys see what my childhood was like."

"Yes. It was deplorable. I'm sorry we did not know. We would have changed things for you."

"My mother killed herself, when I was eight years old."

"What?" his sons all said. He'd *never* told them that.

Amanda rubbed his hand. She knew that much. He'd told her when they were little kids. He was always so sad. It became her mission to help him. She made up her mind to find a way to make him laugh. And she did. After that, she made him laugh every day. That's how they became friends. Boyfriend and girlfriend. Husband and wife. Then Lovers. Parents. Grandparents. But, above all...friends.

Floyd shook his head. "I'm sorry, I didn't know that."

"She had been in and out of mental wards for all of my life. They said she was a Schizophrenic."

"What?" Aden asked. "Schizophrenic!"

"I wasn't aware of that. I'm sorry."

"We lived in the same neighborhood, man. You don't remember my mother?"

"I vaguely remember. But I never met her."

"She was always doing crazy things. I thought the entire neighborhood knew."

"I heard rumors of things going on, but I never listen to rumors. No one ever came to me seeking my Pastoral help."

"My father was cruel to her. He locked her in a room, for days on end. I could hear her screaming and talking to herself."

"It must have been traumatic for you."

"It was. My father moved his girlfriend in the house, while my mother was still alive."

Floyd frowned. "What?"

"What?" Amanda echoed. She did *not* know that.

"My mother was locked in a room, and my father and his girlfriend acted like she wasn't even there."

"Lord, have mercy."

"One day I found the key and went in the room." He frowned. "There was no bathroom in there."

"What?" Floyd frowned again.

Justin nodded his head. "Waste was all over the place. I brought her out and tried to help her get cleaned up. That was the first time my step-mother attacked me."

"Because you tried to help your mother?" Addison asked.

"That and the fact that she thought I was cursed. That was why she beat me every single day of my youth. My father just stood there and let her. My mother kicked both of their asses."

"Go grandma!" Adrian said. "I wish it had've been me."

"I wonder if your stepmother is still alive," Aden asked. "I'd like to meet her."

§

Justin kept talking. "After my mother kicked their asses, she grabbed my hand and we ran."

"Where did you go?" Aden asked.

"Into the woods. We stayed there all night, talking. She talked and I listened. Then, I fell asleep. When I woke up she was dead. Hanging from a tree."

"Oh, my God?"

"To this day, I believe my father found us, and killed her."

"But you couldn't prove it."

"No; but here's the thing. My mother told me something that I've never told another living soul."

"What?"

Justin rubbed his face. And for the first time in his life he told his...*her* story. Somebody, other than him, needed to know his mother was important. They needed to know she wasn't crazy. They needed to know the cross she had to bear.

§

It felt so good to have someone else know. It felt good to finally tell his family. Justin felt like crying. Burdens are heaviest when you have to carry them alone.

"Why didn't you tell us, Dad?" Aden asked.

"I didn't think anyone would believe me."

§

Amanda rubbed her husband's hand. "You could have told me. I would have believed you."

He smiled at her. "I never knew happiness, until you walked up to me at the playground."

"What are you going to do?"

"I'm going to tell my mother's story to everyone here. It will help Nate and Layla deal with her mother."

"If you need me, I'm here for you, son." Floyd smiled. "Just say the word."

"Thanks," Justin replied.

Adrian reached over and grabbed his father's hand.

"We're all here for you, Dad."

§

Chapter 20

Brock and his crew arrived in the dungeon, where Araciel lived. It didn't look like Hell. As a matter of fact, Araciel had a nice chair, sofa, and a library that rivaled the one at the estate. He even had a bed and a closet. The room wasn't even hot.

He looked up the minute they landed. "I knew you'd come," he said and looked back down at his book.

"Are you not pleased to see us?" Jehoel asked.

"No."

"Why?" Batman asked and moved forward.

"I never wanted my sons down here. Not even for a visit. You boys are *too* good for this place."

"So are you," Brock responded.

"Seraphiel." Araciel smiled. "I should thank you for taking care of my son."

"I doubt that's accurate," Brock replied. "He's more than capable of handling himself."

"Yes, but I saw what happened when he was shot. I saw what you did to his attackers. Trust me; I finished what you started, once they arrived."

"Why do you choose to live here, Father?" Jehoel asked. "We need you."

"Even if I didn't live here, I would not live with you. I am an Archangel, son. I would be confined to Heaven. I'd have to look in the faces of everyone who

[193]

knows what I did."

"No one judges you, but you, brother," Michael replied.

"I imagine that is true. But some sins are unforgivable."

"Only to you," Akibeel said.

Araciel looked over at him. "Akibeel, right?"

"Yes."

Araciel nodded. "The Watcher who thought he was a demon."

"That's me."

"How are you fairing?"

"My family's support has helped to heal the terror of my memories."

"That's good. You are a good boy."

Akibeel walked over to him. "May I sit?"

"How rude of me. By all means, you all may have a seat."

§

Akibeel, Jehoel and Batman took a seat. Brock and Michael hung around the door. Their only reason for being there was to secure Akibeel's safety. Not to mention Akibeel, Jehoel and Batman could not teleport to Hell.

"This doesn't make any sense, Father," Batman said. "All of this time, you let us believe you were a demon. Why?"

"It was better that way."

"Why? So we wouldn't realize you *chose* to leave us," Jehoel replied. "You willfully left your young sons in a world full of demons."

"I knew you'd be fine, Jehoel. I knew you'd be an Ultimate Watcher. No demon can defeat you." He looked at Batman. "I requested my brother assign you to Seraphiel."

"What? Why?"

"You weren't as strong as your brother. He couldn't do his job and protect you. Only one Watcher could do that. Seraphiel was a better fit. A safer fit."

"So, not only did you not want me; you didn't want me to be with my brother, either?" Batman asked.

"It was the right thing to do. Can you honestly say you don't want to be on Seraphiel's team of elite fighters?"

Batman looked down. "No."

"See. Father knows best."

"That is such bullshit!" Jehoel replied. "If father knows best, he would get up and get his ass out of here. You have three grandchildren, man. How could you not want them to know you? Not want to know them?"

"They are beautiful little girls. So are your 'spirit' mates."

"You've *seen* them?" Batman asked.

"Of course. I take a look, from time to time."

"That's cowardly, man," Akibeel stated. "You can't get over your guilt, until you face those you sinned against.

I know. I had to walk back in the house I broke into. I had to look everyone in the face that I'd planned to hurt. I had to look at the mother of the children my brothers planned to rape. I did it. I looked every one of them in the eye and apologized. Every single day, I try to be the person I know I *can* be. The person I *know* I am. I shower those little girls with love and protection…every single day. You know why?"

"Why?"

"I'm *not* a demon…I never was. I am a Watcher. I am *not* Seraphiel's *enemy.*" He looked over at Brock and his eyes glazed. "I am his *son.*"

§

Brock nodded and smiled. Akibeel was Akibeel. He was going to talk until somebody listened.

§

"And you are not a demon. You are an Archangel. You are *not* Batman and Jehoel's enemy. You are their father." His eyes crested. "Even five thousand year old men *need* their father."

"But, you didn't kill your children's mothers," Araciel said remorsefully.

"I killed somebody's mother. Five of them, to be exact."

"You don't have to *see* their faces, Akibeel."

"I wish that I could. I'd lay prostrate, at their feet, and beg for their forgiveness. I'd spend the rest of my life making sure their lives were easier. You have an opportunity I don't have. You can make it up to your sons. You are not a jackass, like my father. He raped thirty one women. How many did you rape?"

Araciel flinched. "Two."

"Why just two?"

"It was wrong. I couldn't do it again." Araciel looked at his sons. "In the beginning, I was ruthless to you boys, but it was my guilt. You were a constant reminder of my sins. But, the first moment I saw your faces; you owned my heart. I loved you from the start. I still do." His eyes teared. "I always will."

He squared his shoulders. "But I *cannot* go to back to Heaven. That's too much to ask."

§

Michael lifted his head and closed his eyes. It was obvious he was getting a message. His twirling eyes lit up. "Father says he has forgiven you. Your place is in Heaven, and he wants you *home*."

Araciel shook his head.

"But, he says until you are ready, you may reside on earth. Lucifer will send more demons for your sons."

"What?" Jehoel and Batman both asked.

"Those demons that attacked Jehoel did so at Lucifer's instruction. You embarrassed him, by not yielding to his authority. He can't defeat you; but he can defeat your sons."

Michael looked at Brock. "He is also trying to find a way to recover your brothers from the ice block."

"Why?"

"He wants Mordiree. He knows his warriors can't defeat you, and Yomiel; or any of the Ultimate Watchers. But he thinks your brothers can."

"Let them come!" Akibeel spit out. "We're ready for them. Ain't that right, Pops?"

Brock smiled. "We're ready, son."

§

Araciel stood up, tall and erect and authoritative. He swaggered towards the door. There was nothing insecure about that man's disposition. It had an air of ruthlessness to it. "I'll deal with Lucifer."

Michael stopped him. "Father says do not touch him, Araciel. He says not one hair on his head should be out of place."

"Why?"

"He has a plan for Lucifer, in the final days."

"Come home with me, Father. Get to know your sons, your daughters-in-law and your grandchildren," Jehoel begged. "If you love us; fight with us. Fight for us. Let us fight at your side. As a family."

"Please," Batman pleaded. "I forgive you for what you did. My mother is happy in Paradise. It was her time."

"You do not *know* that."

"Yes he does, and so do you. No one dies before they are supposed to, Araciel. You are an Archangel, and you know that is the truth," Michael replied.

§

"You stubborn bastard!"

Everyone looked around. Gabriel and Raphael had arrived.

"You are the only Archangel with a family. What I wouldn't give to have my own *sons*," Gabriel told him.

"Yeah and Father will spank that ass too!" Raphael laughed.

Michael laughed. "Did you not get in trouble for cursing?"

Raphael put his hand over his mouth. "Do you think he's listening?"

They felt the dungeon shake. They all laughed and said, "Yep!"

"Listen up, boy. If I'm in trouble again, it better be for a good cause," Raphael told Araciel. "Akibeel is right. Isolation is not penance; it is cowardice. You can be productive at the service of your family. It will help you overcome your guilt. Then one day you will be ready to come home."

"Besides, if Raphael is in trouble I'll need someone to hang around with." Gabriel laughed, and then nodded towards Michael. "Big brother here has no sense of humor."

"What do you say, Father? Come home with me."

§

They all heard…

"Brock?"

"What's wrong, Ali?"

"We've got a situation here. How long are you going to be?"

Brock looked at Araciel. "What do you say?"

§

Araciel looked at his sons. They looked back at him. Their eyes were pleading; almost desperately begging. He didn't see the strong warriors; but the young sons he'd left behind. His eyes watered. He'd hurt them enough to last a lifetime. Damn Michael for bringing them here. He nodded at them, and whispered, *"For my* sons; I'll give it a try."

Batman and Jehoel hugged their father.

"We're on our way."

"Thanks."

§

Akibeel took a big sniff. "I got one question to ask you, man."

"What?"

"Why don't you stink?"

Brock hit him in the back of his head. "Shut your motor mouth *up!*"

§

Everyone teleported out…laughing.

§

Chapter 21

Adam felt it the minute his father returned. Good. He was fixin' to get these birds off his ass. Baraq was acting like they were conjoined at the hip. "I'll be back."

"Where are *we* going?" Baraq asked.

Everyone in the den laughed.

"My dad's back, man. Do you think I can talk with him, alone?" Adam said sarcastically. "Good grief!"

"No prob, man. As soon as I hand you off to him, I'll leave."

Everyone cracked up.

Adam was not amused. He smirked. "He who laughs last…"

"Handle your business, boy," Henry said and laughed. He and Adam were two peas. Both of them could win a battle, without throwing a punch. He wished he could be there to *see* it go down.

§

The first thing Brock did was reach out, to find his son. He burst out laughing. His boy was catching hell. He turned towards Araciel and shook his hand. "Welcome to my home. I'll see you guys later. My son needs me." He laughed again, and vanished.

§

"What was that about?" Araciel asked his sons.

"I don't know," Jehoel replied.

Batman laughed. "Adam is a little cocky. His team has been charged with knocking him down a peg or two."

"Oh," Araciel replied. "Good luck with that."

§

Brock appeared outside the den. Adam almost bumped into him. "Hey son."

"Dad!" Adam hugged him. Then he turned to Baraq. "You can get off my back now."

Baraq laughed. "No prob," he replied and walked back into the den.

Brock laughed again. "What's wrong?"

"Man, I can't even exhale, without Baraq recycling it through his own lungs."

Brock laughed. "That's a good one, son."

"Can't you get them off my back?"

Brock shook his head. "You fall under Doc's leadership. Baraq is doing what your boss told him to do."

"But, Dad-"

"You are going to have to prove yourself, son."

Adam frowned. He thought for sure he'd be able to make his father understand. "I might as well still be a baby."

"I can make it so," Brock replied.

"NO!" Adam jumped. "I'm just venting."

"Well, let me give you something else to vent about." Brock smiled. "According to your boss's instruction; you have to sleep in the nursery."

"Aw, c'mon man!"

Brock laughed. When Doc suggested that, he'd almost wet his pants laughing. "You've got to earn his trust, son."

"Alright," Adam replied. Then he smirked. "Just remember, I'll hear everything going on in *your* bedroom. Boo!"

Brock frowned. Hell, this shit just backfired on *him*. He couldn't put a cone of silence up, because the twins would be blocked out. Not to mention he wouldn't be able to hear Adam, either. Putting up the cone of silence would defeat the purpose of him sleeping in the nursery.

Plus, he needed to hear in case Lucifer's demons tried to attack again. "Now hold up. Let me see if I can get Doc to change his mind."

Adam showed his pearly whites. "I thought you'd see it my way."

§

Doc appeared in front of them. "What's up, "Brock?"

"Adam is *not* sleeping in the nursery, man."

"You agreed."

"I changed my mind. Let him sleep in *your* suite."

"That's cool. I just thought Jodi would feel better if he was with you guys. But, he can sleep in the room with Abe."

"I'm good with that." Adam smirked again. "I'll be

able to hear you and Aunt Kwanita, too. I might even let Abe hear."

"Hear what?" Doc asked.

Adam caressed his chest and mimicked Kwanita's voice. "Ooooo, *Yomiel*…make it last…*for…ever!!*"

Brock rubbed his face and squealed.

Doc blushed. Damn that boy! He'd had one too many sleepovers with Abraham.

§

They both forgot that he wasn't just Samjaza's grandson. Kobabiel, the most powerful '*mind*' Watcher, was also his grandfather. He inherited both physical and intellectual superiority. When the power of his fists wouldn't work, the power of the mind would.

He stretched, put his fist up to his mouth…and yawned. "I'm sleepy. Let's go to bed. Try and keep it under two hours, Unc. I start training tomorrow."

Brock howled. Damn! No wonder he and Henry were so tight. They were both *devils!*

"Oh hell nawl!" Doc replied. "This mannish boy *cannot* stay in my suite, Brock."

Brock squealed. Adam was like the *plague.* He was jacking with them coming and going. None of the other Watchers would want him either, once he jacked with them. And to get his way, he would.

"I can't?" Adam asked innocently. "Where *ever* am I going to sleep, *Uncle Boss Man?*" Then he squinted and added, "Keep in mind; I can hear *every damn body*. Baraq and Dawn. Akibeel and Maria. Donnell and Desiree." He raised his eyebrows. "Caim, Balam…all of them."

Damn if that boy wasn't blackmailing them. No doubt he'd pull the same crap on H and Cutie; and all the humans. Brock looked at Doc. "What is your recommendation?"

"He can sleep in *this* wing," Doc relented and vanished.

Adam chuckled.

§

"Listen. Don't push it too far, son. You won this battle, but don't make us regret it. You stay your ass inside the estate, you hear me? If you get out of line, or manipulate us again, I will take *all* of your powers. You understand?"

"Yes sir," Adam replied. "Actually, I just want to sleep in the ICU with Mordiree. I want to be there when she wakes up. I need to apologize to her for what I did."

"Why didn't you just say that, in the first place, Adam?"

"Because if I had, Baraq would be sleeping in there, too. I know I messed up. I promised you guys I wouldn't do that again. And I won't. I know I need to learn how to fight. I'm stoked to be properly trained. I'm willing to follow Doc's leadership, to the letter. Including hiding in the shelter and not fighting, until he says I can."

He squinted again. "But, I am *not* willing to be treated like a juvenile delinquent. If Doc does this to me; the entire team will treat me like I'm a snot-nosed kid. I'm thirty years old, *man*; and too old for a truancy officer. I may not know much; but I know the difference in right and wrong. I know it's *wrong* for everyone to treat me like I'm untrustworthy."

"No one said you weren't trustworthy, son."

"What do you call saying I have to prove myself? What would you call dogging my every step? I can't hang in the den with my cousins, without a chaperone. According to Baraq, I can't even take a shower by myself. What kind of *crap* is that, Dad? I may not have all of your *powers*, but I do have your integrity. And Mom's too, for that matter. My word is as good as my parents', man."

Brock nodded. Adam was right. He wasn't some rogue hothead Watcher; like his first team had been. Adam was *his* son. That came with a multitude of advantages. Integrity was just the tip of the iceberg. Sure, he wasn't humble yet; but neither had he been.

At first he swung too far to the right; and alienated everyone. Then too far the left; and no one listened. Eventually, he leveled off. Right down the center of the road.

In time, Adam would do the same thing. But they couldn't overly yoke him. Otherwise, he'd never develop his own style. "You're right, Adam. I'll talk with Doc."

Adam extended his fist and Brock met it with his own. "Thanks, man," Adam replied, and walked back into the den.

§

Adam looked at Henry, and smiled. "Told cha."

Henry laughed. Adam had let him hear the entire conversation. He was going to like hanging around with this dude. He slapped Adam a high five; and they both snapped their fingers. Then they bumped chests. "Woof! Bow wow!"

§

Baraq frowned. "I don't know what you did or said. But I am free to go."

Adam didn't even look at him. "Don't let the door hit cha."

"Cocky bastard." Baraq laughed. He and Chaz walked out the den.

§

They remained quiet; until Baraq and Chaz were sufficiently out of earshot. Then they all looked at Adam. He was showing all of his pearly whites.

"What happened?" Sam asked.

"I didn't like being backed into a corner. If there's a way into trouble…there's a way out." He laughed.

"So, what did you do?" Mark asked.

§

Adam told them; both verbally and *demonstratively*.

[208]

He reached out and blasted Marvin Gaye, 'When I get that feeling, I need sexual healing.' He caressed his breast, and moaned. He torqued and pumped his hips; like a Chippendale dancer. Then he whispered seductively, "Ummm, Boo! Damn, Dimples! Oh, Yomiel! Ooooo, Brighteyes! Do me, baby."

§

Those boys could be heard screaming, coughing and laughing, all the way in the married section.

§

Then Adam dropped it like it was hot and gyrated his butt. He was a natural clown. And he was having a ball!! His cousins were laughing, holding their stomachs. They could envision Brock freaking *out!*

§

Henry leaned over the pool table and wheezed, "STOP!!!" His side was hurting.

§

Adam cut the music and laughed. "I told them I'll be Peeping Tom number one! Every...*damn*...night!"

§

"No you didn't!" Mark laughed. "Boy, you are *sick!*"

"*Da...aaamn!*" Matthew coughed. "That's just wrong, man."

"You are just as nosey as your old man, Dawg," Leroy added.

"Don't think you'll ever spend the night in my house, man," Embry informed him. "Brother-in-law or not. You. Are. Not. Welcome."

Everybody laughed.

Ditto wiped his eyes and looked at Henry. "Have you been schooling him, on how to jack with people's mind?"

"Nah, man." Henry laughed. "Although, I don't doubt he has eavesdropped, from time to time."

Adam stopped laughing. "No I didn't; I'd never do it to you guys."

§

"I wonder what was up with Justin," JR said.

"He did look a little off, didn't he?" Leroy agreed.

"Can you snoop, Adam?" Embry asked.

"I can, but I won't. If he wants us to know, he or his sons will tell us."

"Adam is not going to play the role of spy for us," Henry said. "You wouldn't want him snooping on you, would you?"

"You're right. I shouldn't have asked."

"It's all good." Adam slapped him a high five. "I need to go sit with Mordiree. I'll see you guys in the morning."

§

Brock and Doc were in the conference room watching, and listening to him. They couldn't help but laugh. Adam was going to be handful.

"Man, what am I going to do with your boy?" Doc asked.

"He'll be fine. I laid the real down to him. If he pulls this shit again, I will snatch his powers."

"Good."

"But he's right. We came down too hard."

"You *agree* with him?"

"Yes. He knows he was wrong. He loves Mordiree, as much as you love Kwanita. You worked hard to be able to protect her. He wants to be powerful enough to protect Mordiree, too. He'll follow your directions, for that reason alone. That's his motivation."

"You're right. Being in charge is hard."

"Especially if you have a knucklehead like Adam, on your team." Brock laughed.

They both laughed.

§

Chapter 22

Batman, Jehoel and Araciel landed directly outside of his suite. They hadn't told their wives about their father. They were as nervous as he was. "Stay here for a minute," Batman instructed Araciel.

"Okay."

§

Robyn and Shelonda were watching television. The children were asleep. They looked up when their men walked through the door.

"Hey, Big Daddy." Robyn smiled and stood up.

"Hey, Sweetie. Joy still asleep?"

"Yeah."

Jehoel leaned down and kissed Shelonda. "Hey, Lonnie."

"How was the meeting?" she asked.

"It was better than I thought." He stroked her cheek. "We need to talk."

"What's wrong?"

He didn't respond.

"What's wrong, Batman?"

"Have a seat."

§

"While we were fighting earlier, our father came and helped us."

"Your father?" Robyn asked. "A demon helped you

[212]

guys fight demons?"

"That's what we thought," Jehoel answered.

"What's going on, Joe?" Shelonda asked. "You know I don't like bits and pieces of a story. Just spit it out."

He laughed. His woman did not go for beating around the bush. "Our father put himself in Hell."

Robyn frowned. "What?" She looked at Batman. "What is he talking about?"

"He's not a demon. He was ashamed of his actions. He asked Michael to kill him, but he refused. So he walked *himself*, into Hell."

"You have got to be kidding."

"No, we're not. Kobabiel told us the truth in the meeting."

"He's been in Hell all of this time, Joe?"

Jehoel nodded. "He couldn't face what he did to our mothers. Or that he betrayed the Master."

"Wait a minute. He was a Fallen, right?"

"Yes. But he had a change of heart."

"I didn't know that was possible."

"Neither did we. We thought once a Fallen, always a Fallen."

§

Batman looked over at his brother. *"Here goes nothing."* He looked back at Robyn. "How would you feel if we convinced him to come home?"

Robyn frowned. "Of course you have to convince him to come home. He doesn't belong in Hell, any more so than Akibeel did. Plus, he's your father, Batman. My children's grandfather."

Jehoel stared at Shelonda. She also frowned. "He's been there for so long. You guys think you can do that?"

"We tried," Jehoel responded.

"And?"

"He wouldn't listen to us."

"But, he listened to Akibeel." Batman smiled.

"He did!" Robyn smiled. She felt how much her husband wanted his father. "Where is he?"

"In the hallway."

"What?" She rushed towards the door and yanked it open. "Oh my!" He looked just like Batman. Or Batman looked just like him.

"Welcome home!" She threw her arms around him. "My daughter's grandfather!"

Shelonda stood behind her smiling. She saw his eyes water and that made hers water. "My turn."

Robyn stepped to the side, but held onto him. Shelonda hugged him. "You will be staying with Jehoel and me, right?"

"No!" Robyn objected. "He's home. Right here with me and Batman."

"Y'all got enough family living here. Joe and I don't have anybody. Don't be selfish, Robyn."

"You are tripping, Shelonda. He-"

Shelonda cut her off. "You're the one tripping!"

They started to seriously argue. They were so loud they woke the babies up. But, they didn't hear their children's cries. They were in a physical tug of war; yanking him back and forth.

Batman and Jehoel shook their heads and went to get their daughters.

§

Araciel could not believe his daughters-in-law. He searched their minds. They both genuinely *wanted* him. He put his arms around both of their waists and hugged them. "Please don't fight over me. I'm *not* worthy."

"Yes you are, Father."

Araciel looked up. His sons were standing in front of him with his granddaughters. They were beautiful. Periodically, he'd peek in on them, but he never touched them. He'd always wanted to. He knew Jaz-Mere and Jasmine were Jehoel's; and Joy was Batariel's. He knew their ages and their weights. He knew they all slept on their daddy's chest. He knew they were daddy's girls. He already loved them.

He stretched out his arms. All three of the babies reached for him. His arms were more than big enough. This was heaven enough for him.

Joy and Jaz-Mere started to nibble on his chin. Yeah, this was heaven. How in the world had his sinful acts produced these *beautiful* blessings? He looked at his sons through glazed eyes. "Thank you for this."

"Come on in and have a seat, Father," Batman said and ushered him to the sofa.

Araciel sat down with all three of his grandchildren in his arms. He kept kissing them. "You girls are beautiful," he said in between the hundreds of kisses.

§

Batman wrapped his arms around Robyn. *"Thank you for wanting my father to live here, Sweetie."* He leaned down and kissed her. Then he squeezed her waist and said, *"It had already been decided that Father would stay with Jehoel. He's been in total isolation for thousands of years. He needs to ease into the world. Shelonda is right, we have plenty family; too much for him. He'll be overwhelmed here, Sweetie. Please don't make him feel bad. He is carrying enough guilt."*

Her eyes watered. *"I just want him to know us. I want him to know our children, Batman."*

"Look at Joy; she never goes to anybody. There's no way he's not going to want to be in her life. We will visit them often, okay?"

She wiped her eyes and nodded. *"Okay."*

§

Jehoel had been delivering the same message to Shelonda. *"Please don't gloat, Lonnie."*

"I'd never do that to Robyn, Joe. She saved my

life."

She walked over and hugged Robyn. "We'll share him, okay?"

Robyn smiled. "Okay."

§

Araciel was glad to see them hugging. He didn't want to be the cause of any friction between his daughters-in-law. He smiled.

"How long can you all stay?" Robyn asked.

"It's late and we really should get the children home," Jehoel replied.

"Can we stay a little while longer?" Araciel asked. "I cannot seem to separate myself from any of my granddaughters."

"Of course, Father," Jehoel replied. "We can stay as long as you like."

§

The babies fell asleep in his arms and he still wasn't ready to let them go. "Is there any way possible that you and Robyn can come live with Jehoel?" he asked Batman.

"No sir," Batman replied. "Our home is here. But, we're just a shimmer away. We can be there every day if you like."

"I would like that, very much. I would like to get to know my sons, my beautiful daughters-in-law, and my precious grandchildren."

"You know you have another on the way," Shelonda

told him.

His face lit up. "You are with child?"

"No, Robyn and Batman are expecting a little boy."

"A grandson?"

Robyn sat next to him. "You have to be here when I deliver him, Father."

Araciel's heart damn near jumped out of his chest. She'd called him Father. He leaned over and kissed her cheek. "I will definitely be here to welcome my grandson to the world...*daughter*."

§

As much as he hated to leave, he had to. "I am okay to leave now." He didn't say ready, because he never would be. "Robyn needs to get her rest."

Batman took Joy. She sighed and put her fingers in his mouth. He nibbled them. *"We'll see you tomorrow?"*

"Yes," Araciel replied.

He, Jehoel and Shelonda vanished. Jasmine and Jaz-Mere were still asleep, in his arms.

§

"Are you alright, Sweetie?"

"Yeah. You were right. My family is too big for him to meet right off. I feel sorry for him though."

"I do, too. But, I'm glad my father isn't a Fallen."

"You and Jehoel have the only father that treated you right."

"Well not really?"

"Who else?"

He caught himself. He almost said Azazel loved his wife and son. That would've reintroduced Lilith to the family. Damn! That was close. "Your father treats you right."

"You know what I mean."

"Yeah, I'm just kidding. My father is the only Archangel that has children and grandchildren."

"That is *so* cool!"

"Let's go to bed. We'll tell the family tomorrow."

"So exactly how much power did he give you?"

Batman smiled. "You want to try it out?"

She bit her lower lip. Batman's electricity made their sex life *sizzle.* Now his father had just tripled the charge. Her womb clinched. She breathlessly replied, "Yes."

His canines jumped out and his joystick pulsated. He leaned down and kissed her neck. "Anything for my Mrs."

§

Chapter 23

Adam walked into the ICU. Thank God, Clyde was not in there. When Clyde looked at him, he felt the sting of his burning desire. Desire to kick his ass.

He'd gotten Doc and his father off of his back. That was not going to happen with Clyde. The man had already forewarned him... *'I'll be watching.'*

He looked over his shoulder, to see if Clyde was behind him. The coast was clear. He looked back around. Clyde wasn't in the room, but Rebecca was. No doubt she'd be scrutinizing his every move, too. Damn!

Oh well. He could be as charming as his father. Maybe humble would be better. Yeah, humble. No, contrite was the way to go. That's it, contrite. *'c'mon diaper.'*

§

"Do you mind if I join you?"

"Of course not. I was just checking on her before I reclined for the night."

Recline? That was too formal. She must be really pissed at him. He couldn't *wait* for this day to be over. Everybody, but his boys, had something to say about his behavior. He wondered if Maude was mad at him, too.

Rebecca patted the seat next to her. "C'mon, have a seat."

Here goes nothing. "Yes Ma'am."

[220]

He sat down next to her, and waited. And waited. Man, he hated the quiet treatment more than being reprimanded. At least if someone yelled at you, you knew what they were thinking. If they are quiet, you wonder if they are scheming. You knew when they finally spoke; their thoughts were well organized. Whatever they said, when they finally spoke, they meant every single word.

He held his breath and waited.

§

"You can relax and exhale, Adam. I'm not going to reprimand you."

"You're *not.*"

Rebecca smiled. "Is there anything I can say, that will make you feel worse than you do right now?"

He smiled. "Probably not; but saying nothing is just as bad."

She laughed. "Don't I know it." Then she patted his hand. "Clyde used to glare at our children, with the 'evil-eye'. He'd tell them how disappointed he was in them. How they'd let *him* down. He'd go on and on about how he expected better."

She laughed, again. "I would never say *one* word. It drove my children crazy."

"I know the feeling."

She laughed again. "They'd beg me to tell them how I felt, about what they'd done."

"Would you tell them?"

"No."

"Why?"

"You don't have to tell a person when they are wrong. Everyone has an internal barometer that warns them of their actions, before they act. I never chastised my children, because it wasn't about me. It was about them building character. They needed to find their own way in life."

Adam smiled. He was going to like her. She had wisdom.

Rebecca kept talking. "I've seen parents raise a household full of children. They laid down the same rules and regulations to all of their children. But, when those children grow up; they have different personalities, and values. I don't know a single parent that raised their children to be a thief or murderer. Yet, the prisons are filled with them."

Adam nodded. "That's true."

"Who taught them to go against the grain? Their parents certainly didn't."

"How do you suppose that happens?"

"It happens when you clip your child's wings and force them to *just* follow orders. They can't develop their own personalities, because all they've ever done was follow the rules."

Adam leaned back and crossed his legs. Rebecca had wisdom, he was interested in learning.

[222]

She looked back at her daughter. "Mordiree and Dawn were *wild*. They were a hand full. They did things that they didn't think their father and I knew about. Of course if Clyde had known; he would've had a heart attack. Me on the other hand, I knew every single thing they snuck off and did. Like those foolish body piercings."

Adam's eyes popped. He knew about the one in her tongue; but that was it. "Maude has *body* piercings?"

She rolled her eyes. "In the most *disgusting* places."

"You never said anything?"

"No. If they thought they were doing the right thing, they wouldn't have snuck off and did it." She looked at Adam. "Would they have?"

He smiled. "So you would've let them stick their hands in fire?"

She laughed. "Yes."

"You're *kidding?*"

"I would have. The heat from fire warns you it is hot, long before you touch it. If they were foolish enough to tempt it, so be it."

"So are you upset about Maude and me?"

"Yes and no."

"Meaning?"

"I'm not upset about the two of you as a couple. I'm actually pleased about that." She looked back at her daughter. "But I don't understand why she never told you about the house fire. Why did she feel she couldn't talk to you about that, Adam?"

"I don't know."

"I presume you and she have been talking for months, right?"

"Yes ma'am."

"It feels sneaky to me. That makes me think that maybe my parenting technique was all wrong."

"I don't think so. I think she never thought she'd have to worry about me putting her in danger. She didn't think I'd ever hurt her. But I did."

"On our first date, I told Clyde I was afraid of snakes. I didn't like games. I wouldn't fight over him. If he ever cheated on me there'd be no second chance. He could never hit me. I didn't want more than five children. If, on our one year anniversary, we weren't engaged, it was over. If we were engaged, and not married within the year, it was over. If we were to marry, he could not live off of me. If I rolled out the bed going to work, he had to, too."

Adam laughed. "You laid down the law?"

"Not the law, Adam; an understanding. Clyde also told me what he was looking for. Mordiree should have done the same thing with you. She should have been honest. I don't blame you for what happened. You were basically blind."

"She *did* tell me she was afraid of heights," Adam admitted. "I was just trying to help her get over that."

"No, you were showing off some of the skills you inherited. But, you didn't need me to tell you that."

"No ma'am."

She looked at him. "It has never been my practice to give advice, unless asked for. But, I will make an exception. I recommend you and Mordiree take it slowly. Not for my benefit, or even hers; but for yours.

"Why?"

"You've only been a man for less than a day. You have inherited your father's powers, so of course you can protect her. However, life has to be lived. Certain lessons have to be learned." She looked at him and smiled. "You skipped all of life's lessons, son."

"But I was too powerful to remain a baby, Aunt Rebecca."

She smiled. "Do you imagine Jesus was weaker, as a baby, than you were?"

"No."

"Yet, he followed the laws of nature, didn't he? He went through the physical process of growing up, one day at a time."

"Yes ma'am. But, he had a date with the *cross*. I wouldn't have accelerated *that* destiny, either."

Rebecca laughed. "Point taken."

He looked over at Mordiree. "I couldn't wait, because of her. I didn't want her to see me as an awkward, toothless, pimple faced kid."

"I know that. I know your parents don't get it, but I do. I burned all of my childhood pictures, so my parents wouldn't show them to Clyde." She laughed. "I had knobby knees, buck teeth and coke bottle glasses. There was no way I wanted him to see me like that. I think you did the right thing, Adam. But, those life lessons that you jumped..." She stared at him, "...they've still got to be learned. Your character still has to be built; and not on the back of your father. You've got to make your own mistakes. Find your own way, son. Don't fake it till you make it. Be your own man, not a replica of your father."

She grabbed his hand and squeezed it. "You will learn that we *all* fall down. We all make mistakes. And whether we intend to or not, we hurt the ones we love. So, here's my unsolicited advice: Embrace your mistakes, but don't cling to them. Learn from them, but don't let them define you. If they must define you, let it be for *good* definition."

§

Adam wanted to cry. She just told him not to walk on eggshells. She just told him he was a man, in his own right. He didn't need to be like his father, he needed to be himself. Only time and life would tell who he was.

"You are the only one who gets it. In the meeting, I felt like I would never live it down. Every one of those Watchers made me feel like dirt; and it was their right to walk on my emotions. Even my parents made me feel less than. My cousins laughed with me, and took my side. And I appreciated them for standing with me." He smiled. "But *you!* You've given me permission to be who I am."

"I'm sure no one meant to make you feel bad, Adam."

"Yes they did. They all talked down to me. They used words like: mimic and you are not ready *'boy'.* They accused me of putting their families in danger. Like I wasn't a part of *their* family. And my father *let* them. He treats Akibeel better than he treats me. He doesn't let *anyone* get out of line with his brother. But, he let them rake me over the coals. He let them talk down to me, Auntie. They kicked me out of the meeting, like I wasn't a member of the team. Then to top it off, *Dad* threatened to take my powers, if I don't walk the straight and narrow. That hurt me more than anything. *"*

She felt his pain. "Then you weren't the only one who messed up today; were you?"

She didn't know it, but she just became his sounding board. He leaned over and kissed her cheek. "Thank you for listening to my side. You have eased my spirit."

"Then my job is done." She stood up. "I'll take my leave now. Try and get some sleep, son."

§

Brock and Doc were still watching him. They laughed at his comment about the cross. But nothing else was, in the least bit, funny. They were ashamed of themselves.

Rebecca had just scolded them. He couldn't be who they wanted him to be; and be happy. She was right; he had to find his own way. Hadn't Brock arrogantly told him that he was Seraphiel's son...not Seraphiel? That went both ways.

"She may have eased *his* spirit; but I feel awful," Doc said. "What harm would it have done to let him stay in the meeting?"

"None. It evidently did more damage not to let him stay."

"When I first arrived, I didn't even know how to make a fist. Yet, you let me sit in every single meeting. So I could learn how to be a Watcher."

Brock nodded. "We're going to mess him up if we don't straighten ourselves up. I need to talk with Jodi, too. She and I need to change, not Adam."

"And I don't need to beat him down, just because he reports to me. I need to be there to pick him up, when he does fall," Doc said and looked at Brock. "Just like you have done, for all of us."

"I shouldn't have allowed any of the other team members in the room. It should have been you and him. You should have been the only one to reprimand him. And it should have been words of encouragement, not accusations and ridicule." He rubbed his face. "I have never reprimanded one of my men, with an audience, man.

I can't believe I let that happen. I let Adam down twice today. I should have stood up for my bo...*son*. He's right, I'll never let anyone talk to Akibeel the way you guys did him. I messed up, man. I hurt my son." He frowned, because reality had just slapped him in the face. "He's not a kid, Doc. He's a man. Everyone at the estate has to accept that. Not just in word, but in our interactions with him."

Doc stared into space. Brock wasn't just overly protective of Akibeel. He had admonished Nate, for the way he had spoken to *him* and *Akibeel*. Adam deserved the same consideration, and support. "I'll talk with my team. You talk with yours."

§

Chapter 24

Mordiree woke in Adam's arms. He was holding her protectively. She'd dreamed of mornings like this from the moment he showed her their future.

She hated that she slept through his first day, as a man. He had to face all of *their* anger alone. But, he didn't have to worry, today was a new day. She believed in respecting her elders, but only to a point. If they crossed the line, she had no problem *shoving* them back on their side of it. Her relationship with Adam was just that…hers.

She didn't blame him for what happened. And she wouldn't let anyone else, either; especially Babbo. No doubt he'd given Adam a hard time. His, infamous, evil-eye. No doubt he planned to keep a close eye on him; like he'd done Baraq. It had driven Dawn crazy, but she didn't say anything. At least not to Babbo. She'd complained day and night to her.

She wasn't going to stand for it. She loved Babbo and was grateful that he loved her, too. But, her place was at Adam's side. Just like she was right now.

She rubbed his arm. "How bad was it?"

Adam looked down and smiled. "Bad enough."

"I'm sorry."

"For what?"

"Leaving you to face them all alone."

"I wasn't alone. My cousins had my back."

"Embry and Lamar?"

"Yep! And you know who else?"

"Who?"

"Your mother. She's my NBF."

"What's that?"

"New Best Friend."

"You mean BFF?"

"No. I mean NBF." He laughed. Then he kissed her. "Good morning."

She sighed. "Good morning, Adam."

"Your mother sat with me last night. She made me feel better. But, I'm sorry I did that to you."

"You didn't force me. I agreed to give it a try. I'll try anything once, Adam. Especially, with you."

"I won't do it again."

She stretched. "Once was enough. I'm still afraid of heights."

He rolled over and stared at her. "So I guess you know why the demons were after you."

"Yeah."

"Do you regret us?" He was prepared if she was. *'C'mon diaper.'*

"I regret that I couldn't be there for you. I regret that everyone will be watching us, like hawks. But, as far as you and me…" She smiled. "…I'm *all* in. I can't wait for our first son to be born."

He laughed. "Me either. But, your mother gave me some sound advice."

"What?"

"Take it slow. I need to see what kind of a man I'll become. I was so proud to be Seraphiel's son; I forget to be Adam."

"I can't believe Mamma gave you advice. She never gave me any."

He laughed. "So I heard. Tell me about your body piercings."

"How do you know I have piercings?"

"Your mother told me."

"She *knows?*"

He laughed. "She said they are in disgusting places."

"Oh my God! Does Babbo know?"

"I don't think so. She said he'd die if he knew. So where are they?"

She was about to tell him, but the door opened.

§

Adam frowned. He thought he made himself clear last night. "Man, I know you are not fixin to birddog me, this early in the morning."

Baraq laughed. "Nah man, I came to apologize."

"Say *whaaaat?*"

Dawn walked over and hugged Mordiree. "Mamma

ate Baraq and Babbo up last night. She told Babbo he hadn't seen cantankerous, yet. And if he messed with Adam, she'd take him to the corner of the roof, herself."

"No she didn't?"

"Yes she did. Then she chewed Baraq up…and spit him out." Dawn laughed. "She told him he had a lot of nerve. She said his hands were full enough, dealing with *me*. She told them both to back the hell off!" Dawn laughed. "Then she said, *'I'll be watching!'*"

Adam looked at Mordiree. "I told you she was my new best friend. I love that lady."

"Whatever," Baraq replied. "Anyway, Doc had a talk with the team. We know we were wrong, man. The truth of the matter is; none of it was your fault. They would have eventually come after you guys, anyway. At least last night, all the Ultimate Watchers were here to help."

"But how cool is it that my nephews will be Watchers?" Dawn smiled.

Mordiree smiled too. "I can't wait. I'm already picking out names."

Dawn rubbed her stomach. "I've got Clyde."

"I know. I was thinking Walker Brock, Fred Walker-Brock, and Adam Walker-Brock."

Dawn laughed. "So all of your sons will be named Walker-Brock?"

"Yep!"

"That is so cool!"

"Listen, there's a meeting this morning. You guys coming?" Baraq asked.

"You mean, I'm invited," Adam replied.

"I said we were wrong. You should have been allowed to stay in that meeting last night, man."

Mordiree frowned. "You all had a meeting and wouldn't let him attend?"

Baraq looked down in shame.

"Who's bright idea was that shit?" She was pissed.

§

Yomiel walked in the room. "Mine."

Mordiree jumped up and pointed her finger in his face. "You make that the last time you treat him like that! You will not treat him like a child. And you damn sure ain't gonna yank his chain. Either he's on your team, or he's not. If you can't accept that he's a grown ass man; I will ask Michael to transfer him to another team, my damn self! You understand me?"

Yomiel smiled. She reminded him of Kwanita. Stand by your man, and all. He grabbed her finger. "Yes ma'am."

Adam pulled her back. "He's my boss, Maude."

"I don't give a damn who he is! I won't allow any of them to mistreat you, Adam. We don't need them. I'd rather take my chances with the demons, than to let them treat you like this."

"I'm your uncle first, Adam. I was wrong and I led our team wrong. I'm sorry."

§

The team came through the door: Donnell, Akibeel, Caim and Balam. One by one, they apologized to him.

Then Yomiel said, "We are a team. When one falls, the rest will pick him up. We will stand tall, together. Or we won't stand, at all." He looked at Adam. "You will have to be trained by the Alpha team, but you can use what skills you already have."

Adam's heart leaped. "What are you saying?"

"I'm saying that if there is another battle, you *will* fight, with your team."

Adam stood up. "I won't be confined to the *shelter?*"

Mordiree was getting ready to go off. "Confined to the shelter? What in the hell!"

Adam put his hand over her mouth. She was feisty. And he liked that. "Ssh."

Yomiel shook his head. "You will fight with your team, Adam," he replied.

Then he extended his hand, palm down. One by one they all placed their palms on top of each other's.

Adam wiped his eyes. "What changed your mind?"

Yomiel smiled. "I was snooping last night."

"What?"

"Your father and I heard what you said to Rebecca.

She was right. Whether we mean to or not, we sometimes hurt the ones we love." He frowned. "We had no idea we'd cut you so deeply. We didn't mean to hurt you, Adam."

Then he spoke so only the team could hear, *"We did to you, what the Walker brothers did to Brock and me. We left you hanging out there, alone. As your leader, and especially as your uncle; that will never happen again."*

"And Adam," Akibeel started. "Pops is protective of me, because he knows I'm retarded."

Maria walked through the door. "You are not retarded, Akibeel. Stop *saying* that!"

Akibeel reached for her. "I have a loose lip and I say whatever comes to mind. I offend people more often than not, Maria." He looked back at Adam. "But Pops doesn't love me more than you, man. We all love you. I think of you as my brother. We both have a lot to learn. We'll learn together, brotha. I'm going to train with you."

§

Well hell, Adam had only been a man for a day. He couldn't very well cry, like a baby, this soon. He couldn't speak, or he would. He just nodded.

"And for the record," Donnell added, "Your father has had his share of screw ups, too. We all have." He looked over at Dawn, and then Caim. "Caim reminded us that the garage guards made a mistake that resulted in Dawn being attacked."

"We left her at the park entrance, alone. And demons attacked her. But, we learned a lesson from that mistake. Just like I'm sure you learned a lesson last night," Caim told him.

"Yeah I did. From now on I plan to keep my feet firmly planted on the ground. And if Mordiree and I leave the grounds, I'll take a contingency of guards with us," Adam replied.

"We could double date," Baraq added.

"I don't think so," Adam replied. If he double dated with anybody it would be his boys. "I'd feel like I'm being watched."

"I guess we deserve that," Baraq replied. "But, I wouldn't mind us taking our mates out together. They are sisters, man."

"It'll take a minute for me to embrace that, okay?"

"Fair enough."

§

"By the way, we wanted our team to be the first to know..." Balam smiled. "...Caim and I are mated to Virginia and Grace."

"Say what?" Donnell asked.

The twins laughed. "Yeah man."

"Why the secrecy?" Akibeel asked.

"They weren't ready for anyone to know. They finally agreed, last night, to tell Adabiel and Gabriella."

Doc smiled. Of course he already knew.

"Congrats!"

Chapter 25

Brock wanted to sleep in. As a matter of fact, he wanted to cover his head and not get up for a few days. Yesterday had been a plethora of events. Adam. The party. Adam. Mordiree. Adam. The Fallen. Adam. The Battle. Adam. The children's horror at seeing Seraphiel. Adam. Mordiree's nightmare. Adam. Batman's father. Adam. Justin's revelation. If he wrapped it all up and weighed it in the balance; it was still a good day.

He laughed out loud when he thought about his son blackmailing him and Doc. That boy was going to be more trouble than Elizabeth and Hannah.

Jodi opened one eye. "What are you laughing at, Brock."

"Your son."

"What has he done now?"

He told her and then laughed at the expression on her face. Both of her eyes popped open, along with her mouth. She was horrified. She sat up and brushed her sleep-matted hair out of her face. "He heard us?"

"Yeah," he squealed. "Boo!"

"That boy is nosey, just like his father."

"That's why he'll be sleeping in the single men's area of the estate."

"This is embarrassing, Brock. I don't think I can look in my own son's face."

"Yes you can." He stood up. "C'mon. It's going to be another busy day."

"What now?"

"First, you and I need to discuss our treatment of Adam. Then, there's a meeting with Justin and Batman."

"What's going on with Adam?"

He sat back down and told her about Adam and Rebecca's conversation. "She's right, Jodi."

Jodi was jealous. If she didn't straighten up, she was going to lose her son to her aunt. "I'll work on it."

"We both will."

"What's going on with Justin?"

"It's his story to tell. Let's get showered and dressed." He looked down at her. Matted hair and all; she was *still* the sexiest woman he'd ever seen. "Or we could…"

"No! Don't even *think* about it. Who knows if our son is snooping, this very minute. It's too bad he's too big for me to spank."

He laughed. "He won't be able to hear over the running water," he teased. "C'mon, I'll wash your hair." That always led to other, more exciting, things.

§

Two hours later they walked into the shelter. Everyone was already in there. Jodi saw Adam sitting between Mordiree and Rebecca. Their heads were together, and they were whispering. Then Adam kissed

Rebecca's cheek. He didn't even notice she'd come in the room.

She wanted to cry. She didn't want her baby confiding in a 'play' momma. But, if she didn't get her act together he would. He would turn to his future mother-in-law for advice, instead of her. Her eyes welled.

Brock felt Jodi's heart break. Damn. He didn't like anyone making Dimples cry. But, they'd put Adam in the position to seek solace with a kinder, gentler voice. They needed to make it up to him. And there was no better time than now.

§

"Good morning."

"Hey Brock...Seraphiel...Unc...Pops...Dad," they all replied.

"We have several things to discuss today. Let me start by first apologizing to my son."

§

Everyone looked from him to Adam and back. Adam's head snapped back. He stared at his father, but he didn't say anything. He squeezed Mordiree's hand.

§

"I was *wrong*, son; and I'm sorry. I should not have come down so hard on you. And I shouldn't have threatened to take your powers. I was wrong to allow my team to speak to you like you were a child. You are right, I will never let anyone talk down to Akibeel. I should

[241]

have stood up for you, too. I'm protective of Akibeel and Doc, because I left them alone in the world for so long. Not because I love him more, because that's *not* possible. You are flesh of my flesh. Bone of my bone. But, in here..." He placed his hand over his heart. "...I have three sons. There is nothing I wouldn't do to keep all three of you safe. Because all of you boys own this." He patted his heart. "You *three* boys, *and* your three sisters, control the rhythm, son.

"Up until yesterday, you were my baby boy. My *little* mini clone. Twenty-four hours ago, you went where I carried you. You wore what your mother chose. You ate what she said was good for you. You depended on us for *all* things. You were your mother's and my responsibility. For twelve months we shielded you from the ugliness of this world."

He fanned his hand out towards Adam. "And then this! A grown man. Even though we knew this day was coming..." He tapped his temple. "Up here, it's hard to embrace the drastic change."

§

He walked down the aisle and took Jodi's hand. Then he extended his other hand to Adam. Adam stood up and grabbed it. Brock pulled him into the aisle and then he and Jodi hugged their son.

"Your mother and I are both sorry if we've alienated you. Imagine for a second that the tables were turned.

Imagine if, one day we're your parents, and the next day..."

Brock morphed him and Jodi into eleven month old babies. "...this!"

Adam grabbed them to keep them from falling. "Damn Dad! What are you doing? This ain't right! Turn back!" He was freaked out. So was everyone else.

Brock morphed them back and smiled. "It didn't feel right, did it?"

"Nawl!"

"Unnatural?"

"Yeah."

"You couldn't wrap your mind around it, could you?"

"No!"

"Too much, too soon?"

"Yeah!"

"That's how your mother and I feel. The change is too soon and too drastic."

Adam looked at Jodi and then back at Brock. Then he looked over at Mordiree. He shook his head. "I can't go back, Dad."

"We're not asking you to," Brock replied. "Just be patient with us, son. Allow us the time to wrap our minds around it."

"I don't want to lose you, Adam." Jodi's eyes teared. "I want you to feel comfortable enough to talk to me. Not Rebecca. I'm *your* mother!"

Adam's heart leaped. He'd never do anything to hurt the first woman he'd ever loved. Not his perfect and beautiful mom. He wrapped his arms around her. "I'm sorry, Mom. Nobody will *ever* take your place." He stroked her hair like he always did. "Don't cry. You're still the *best* mother anyone could ask for."

She cried harder.

§

Rebecca wiped her eyes and smiled. She never ingratiated herself in other people's problems. At least not verbally.

When she saw Jodi and Brock walk in the room, she grabbed Adam's hand. Then she deliberately whispered, *'kiss my cheek'*. She knew the minute Jodi saw that, she'd rethink her position. No mother wanted her children going to another for comfort.

She glanced over at Clyde, and winked. She chewed him and Baraq out last night about Adam. But she'd never do that to Jodi and Brock, because he was *their* son. However, she did believe in physiological warfare. Her motto was *'I can show you better than I can tell you'*.

Clyde kissed her ear and whispered, *"Cantankerous woman!"*

She laughed.

§

It took a minute for Jodi to calm down. When she

finally did, Brock perused the room. "Adam is not a baby anymore. He is a thirty year old man. Everyone needs to work on accepting that fact. He is not a *junior* member of Doc's team. He is Grigori...Watcher. Just like his ole man."

Both teams stood up and placed their hands over their hearts. "Semper Fidelis. Always Faithful! Always Loyal!"

Brock nodded. His and Doc's men had all just pledged their loyalty to his son. He smiled. "Indeed."

§

"Next on the agenda," Brock said, and beckoned Aurellia, Akibeel and Yomiel to join him, Jodi and Adam. When they all made it to him, he smiled and said, "Patience has either changed or created your birth certificates. The records now show that Jodi is Aurellia's legal mother."

Aurellia smiled the biggest smile and hugged Jodi. "Thanks, Momma."

"I'm sorry I didn't do it before, Baby Girl. But you know how much I love you, don't you?"

"Yes ma'am."

"The records also reflect that Fred Brock is Yomiel and Akibeel's legal father."

"For real, Pops?" Akibeel smiled and hugged him. Yomiel did too. He was their father. They both wanted that more than anything. They always had.

Adam gave them a fist bump. "Brothers."

Yomiel and Akibeel smiled. "Brothers."

§

Everyone smiled, but H. He was devastated. He should have offered to adopt them a long time ago. He had done it for Nantan, right away. Why hadn't he thought about that sooner?

More than that, he should have stood up for them. He messed up and now it has cost him dearly.

§

Brock felt his angst, but this wasn't about H. It wasn't about what had happened. It was about the meeting they had with Michael. Doc and Akibeel had always felt like *he* was their father; not H. He had always felt like they were *his* sons. They needed this. He needed this.

§

"Speaking of fathers and sons, Batman has some news," he said, and yielded the floor to him.

§

Batman smiled. He reminded everyone about what happened during the battle.

"I was wondering what all that lightning was about," Luther said.

"But why did your father decide to help you and your brother?" Smittie asked.

"I thought all of your fathers were bastards," Elijah added.

"Not mine," Batman replied. "He was good to me and my brother."

"What?" Luther asked.

"He made us promise him that we would accept Michael's offer."

"Why?" Clyde asked.

"He didn't want his sons to burn in Hell."

"What?" Richard asked.

"I thought all the Fallen were evil," JR stated.

"They are."

"I don't understand," Leroy said.

"After five thousand years, I learned last night, that my father is *not* a Fallen."

"He's *not?*" Luther asked.

Batman stared at Luther. Michael had removed the feeling of resentment; but he was still *resentful*. He and the entire team still were. His real father had come up out of Hell to protect him. He'd laid it all on the line and killed his own brothers, for him. That's what real fathers do. He didn't mean to, but he smirked. "He is still in good standing with Heaven. And with *me*. He is *still* an *Archangel*."

"What?" Floyd repeated. This revelation was nothing less than a miracle to the preacha man. He heard his own voice, *'what can separate us from the love of God?'*

Batman told them about their meeting. "Akibeel

was able to convince him to come home." Then he smiled. "Thanks, Kibee. I'll never forget what you did, man."

"No prob. Glad I could help. But, where is he?"

"He is going to stay with Jehoel."

"Why not here?" JR asked.

"It's too many people here. He's lived in isolation for too long. He's not ready for a crowd."

Luther had a twinge of jealousy. Archangel or not; he didn't want to share his son with another man. He was just as greedy as Hezekiah. Hell, H had just lost two of his sons to Brock. Why did he do that? Would he lose Batman to his natural father? His heart clinched, but he said, "I look forward to meeting him; whenever he's ready."

"Batman and I will be visiting him on a daily basis, Father. I'd like for you and Mother to go with us, on some of those visits," Robyn replied.

Oh great. He'd also have to share Robyn and Joy. Batman's father was evidently not going to do like Michael; and stay away. No, he was going to be a part of their lives. Hands on. Besides, he wasn't an adopted or surrogate father. He was the *real*. "I look forward to that, Robyn."

"I do too," Earlie added.

"I'd like to meet the man," Floyd added. "I'd like to talk with him. Seek his counsel, if you will."

Batman nodded. It might not be a bad idea for all of

those Walker brothers to meet his father. He could show them what a real father was. "I can arrange that."

§

Chapter 26

Brock took the floor again. "Next thing on the agenda is Nate's mother-in-law."

Everyone laughed, except Justin, his family and Floyd.

Brock held up his hand. "Justin seems to have insight on her mental state."

"How would he know?" Kwanita asked.

"Have you met her, son?" H asked.

"Ali and Nate took me to her room, last night," Justin replied.

"And?"

"She's *not* crazy."

Layla gasped. "You came to that conclusion after one visit? I lived with her. I've seen her in action. I've felt the pain of her getting worse, year after year. I know she has mental issues, Justin."

He shook his head. "No, she doesn't. Not like you think."

"If she's not crazy, what's *wrong* with her?"

§

He repeated his story to the entire family, up to waking up to his mother hanging from a tree. Everyone looked stunned and grief stricken.

H looked at SnowAnna. "You knew this already, didn't you?"

"Yes."

"What does that have to do with Loretta?" Nate asked.

"My mother told me a story that night. I didn't believe her. I thought she was crazy, too."

"But you don't now?"

"No."

"What did she say?"

He hesitated. "She told me…" He hesitated again. He looked over at Amanda for support. She smiled. He smiled back and said, "She told me that she was in the wrong body."

"What?"

"She told me her host put her in the wrong body."

"Host?"

He nodded his head. "I didn't know what she was talking about. But she kept saying it. She said she was supposed to be put in a *male* body."

"What?" Eugene asked. "Was she transgender?" He knew a few people who had had sex changes. He didn't understand it. He believed gender assignment was a matter of chromosomes. Many people in the gay community disagreed with him. He knew some men that ended up having beautiful and sexy women's bodies. They looked like women, alright. But, he believed it was just *veneer*. If you took a blood sample…*hello* XY.

But, it wasn't his business; just like his sexual

preference was no one's business.

"No."

"Then what are you talking about?"

Justin looked at Ali. "It wasn't until I found out about your alter ego that I understood."

"Oh my God! Host!" Nate shouted. "Who was her host?"

Justin shook his head. "I don't know. I suppose I'll never know."

Layla was holding her chest. "You're saying my mother was a *she-demon?*"

"Yes. Yours and mine."

"What about all the drugs she took?"

"They were to stabilize the raging voices in her head."

"Voices?" Layla replied. "That sounds crazy to me."

"You ever talk to yourself, Layla?"

"Yes."

"I'm not sure, but I believe that's all your mother...and mine...were doing."

"Man, she claimed to be the Virgin Mary," Nate said.

"It was the side-effect of the drugs, Nate. She got confused, just like my mother did. The only difference was my mother was taking prescription drugs."

"Who was the Watcher?" Ali asked.

"She didn't tell me. We won't know until we get her/him out of that body. If we can get him/her out."

Nate was holding his mouth with both of his hands. He felt guilty as hell. "That's why demons are *afraid* of her. Oh my God. I didn't know."

"No demon could hurt her or her daughter. Your children will not be mentally challenged, Nate. They will be like my children."

"How is that?" Nantan asked.

"Demon proof."

§

All of the Watchers remembered how Lilith kept harassing Aden. She threatened him, but she *never* touched him. She couldn't and she *knew* that. The bitch!!

§

"Say what?" H asked. "Did you know that, Snow?"

"No."

"No demon can touch me or *my* children. They can't lay a finger on us."

"Why not?" Henry asked.

"They will die." He looked at Nate. "That's why they ran from your mother-in-law, in Africa."

"How is that possible?" Dan asked.

"I don't know. I was hoping Ali's alter ego could explain it to us."

Ali called out, "Are you here, Leilazeb?"

"Yes I am."

"Have you ever seen this happen before?"

"Yes."

"What happened?"

"I am sorry that your mother could not be helped, Justin."

"Can mine be helped?" Layla asked.

"Yes, but there's a clause I must add."

"What clause?"

"First, let me explain to everyone what happened; and why it happened."

"Okay."

"When a Watcher mates with his 'spirit' mate for the first time, her blood destroys his inner demon. However, there are some of us that are not demons, but an 'alter-ego'."

"What's that?" Dee asked.

"For lack of a better term, we are bodiless Watchers."

"Oh."

"Alter egos are not dispatched to Hell. We have three options. Either we can be reincorporated with our Watcher, or we can remain bodiless spirits. In the latter case, we remain close to our original host; as their protectors. The final option we have is to be placed in a human body."

"Possess them?" Addison asked.

"Yes, but not in the manner you are thinking. We

are placed in newborn babies. Prior to being placed in the babies we advise our host of the gender we'd like to be."

"Get *out?*" Lillian was intrigued. "You get to choose to be male or female?"

"That is correct. It appears that both Justin and Layla's mothers, for lack of a better word, had requested their Watchers place them in male human bodies."

"What?" Nate asked. "Why would a Watcher do otherwise?"

"Their host undoubtedly thought they were putting them in male bodies."

"How would they get that confused?" Eugene asked. "Males have such *wonderful…*" He blushed.

Ali squeaked.

"So y'all just take over some baby's life?" Faith asked. "That doesn't seem right."

"Those who want to be incorporated are put in babies that are dying. At the exact moment the baby dies, the new spirit integrates. That way the parents still have a child, and the spirits have a new home. It's a miracle to the parents, Faith. They have healthy babies. In normal cases the spirit does not remember. But, in a few cases, like now, they are put in hermaphrodites."

Everyone gasped.

"The doctors leave it up to the parents to decide which gender *they* want their child to be," Desiree injected. "I never agreed with it but, that is the normal practice.

There are many cases when the child grows up to be gay."

"What?" Nantan asked.

"Their natural instinct is to be attracted to the same sex. That's because their parents chose the wrong sex for them."

"Why would parents do that?" Robyn asked.

"Those babies have *both* genitals. Their parents don't want their children to go through life ridiculed. Imagine if both parents worked. Their child would be in someone else's custody eight hours a day. Would you risk it?" Desiree asked. "Or what about naming the baby? How would you decide? There are only *so* many unisex names. Even though I don't agree with the gender assignment, at an early age; I understand. I wouldn't risk it, either."

"Are you saying that's the reason for homosexuality?" Henry looked at Sal and laughed. "Is that what happened to the clown?"

Eugene hit him. "Hell nawl, fool!"

Everybody laughed, including Nantan.

Desiree laughed. "Not all, but statistically, some can be linked back. There is even an organization of men and women who were born hermaphrodites. They are trying to get legislation passed that forbids parents from making the decision for them."

"Really?" Eugene asked.

"They say parents should first see which way their

persuasion goes; before opting for surgery. They all believe the embarrassment is the parents burden; not theirs."

§

This revelation had Nate's mind reeling. He was reading between the lines. His mind was screaming *'just before the babies dies. Die! Die! Die!'* He knew what was *not* being said. He rubbed his face again. "Oh. My. God!"

"Indeed. That is why most of us chose to be spirits; instead of being an incorporated corporal."

"Can my mother be helped?" Layla asked again.

"Yes, but at a cost."

"What cost?"

Nate sighed. "If they take Loretta out of that body..." Nate grabbed his wife's hand. "It will die, Laylo."

"That is correct. The vessel will die. And she will become a spirit, like I am. She will be neither she, nor he. We would welcome her into our fold."

§

Justin's heart leaped. "Is *my* mother with you?" he whispered.

"Yes."

"Oh, Sweet Jesus," he whispered. "Can I see her? Talk to her?"

"You have seen her/him. She/he helped protect the

women last night. Every time I've come, she/he has also come."

"Why didn't she say anything?"

"She/he wasn't sure you'd accept the fact that she/he is not female. Or the fact she/he would have preferred to be male."

"I don't care about that."

"Who was Justin's mother's Watcher?" Brock asked.

"She doesn't remember. After a spell, the memory leaves. And since I don't know all of the 'spirit' mates; I can't say."

"Can you examine her memories, Brock?" Justin asked.

"Not a bodiless spirit, I can't. I'm sorry."

"But you know whose Leilazeb was," Amanda reminded him.

"Show yourself, Leilazeb," Brock commanded.

He/she appeared. With everything going on last night, no one paid any attention to his/her appearance. They were all focused on Mordiree and the battle. They all looked from her to Destiny and frowned.

"Understand?" Brock asked.

"My God! She looks just like you," Addison said, looking at Destiny.

Destiny smiled. It was like looking in an enchanted mirror. For the first time she saw how beautiful she was;

through her own eyes. "Yes she/he does."

"So, if we can see my mother, you should be able to tell who her host was," Justin said, hopefully.

Brock shook his head. "Don't get your hopes up, Justin. There are billions of Watchers and 'spirit' mates. It may be someone I have never met."

Justin's continence fell. "I understand."

Nantan had an idea. But, it would only work if... "Can you guys be photographed, Leilazeb?"

"I don't know. Why?"

"If so, Justin can snap a picture of his mother; and Layla's too. I can create a website just for Watchers. It can be used to help identify others that may have the same problem."

"In the end, what does it matter?" Ali asked. "I think it will make the Watcher feel bad."

"It would matter, because my father would know where he came from," Addison replied. "He is related to that Watcher; even if once removed."

"That's a good point," Aden agreed.

"I'd like to try," Justin agreed. "That is, if it is okay with you, Leilazeb."

"Wait a minute."

Everyone turned and looked at Arak.

"Didn't you tell me that you can be in the past, present and future, Leilazeb?"

"That is correct."

"Can't you go back and see who her Watcher was?"

"I could if I had a starting point. But, integrated spirits don't know how long they've been in the bodies."

"How could they not?" Faith asked.

"Somewhere along the line they experience an awakening. Prior to that, they are normal humans."

"I'd like to study that," Desiree replied.

"Very well. But, I'd like to visit with Layla's mother first. Since she is still incorporated, we may be able to determine who her Watcher was. Plus, she's still in turmoil. She can also discuss her options, with her daughter."

Layla looked at Justin. "Please. Can we take care of my mother, first?"

Justin nodded. Loretta's situation was urgent. He wanted to see his mother, but he also wanted to get Loretta out of that mental ward.

§

Chapter 27

Lucifer observed the meeting from his throne room. He was fit to be tied. His second plot had failed. He thought for sure *Rebecca* would be able to create a divide between the boy and his parents. As long as they were at odds, he and Mordiree would take their time.

He used his power of persuasion and whispered in her ear, *'show him kindness.'* Then he whispered, *'tell him to take it slow. Learn life's lesson.'* He went so far as to say, *'tell him his parents made a mistake too.'*

She'd done everything he told her to do. But, dammit! That damn Seraphiel had turned the tables on him. He used his own power of persuasion. His mother's tears had sealed the deal. Now that boy understood his parents' point of view. Dammit!!

He tore his throne room apart. That is all except *his* seat. His biggest secret was that he could release his followers, but not himself. Michael had fixed it so he could not leave unto the final battle.

But, he needed to get out of here. Evidently, his followers were not as strong as he'd hoped. Michael's Grigori were more powerful than any of his soldiers. But, not more powerful than he.

He needed to destroy that boy and his mate. Her name may be Mordiree, but she was the new Eve! He had to kill her.

[261]

If not, the two of them would produce more Grigori than Michael had. After all he was from the seed of that horny dog, Samjaza! And just as fertile!

Not to mention Kobabiel and Satariel's blood ran through that bastard's veins. If they gave him anymore of themselves, he'd be a one man army. Like Michael. Hopefully they wouldn't realize that they could do that.

He thought he had years to kill the boy. Who knew Adam would decide to be a man, on his first birthday? Damn! He should have killed the boy's mother and stopped that birth from even happening. That was a colossal mistake; on his part.

He stopped and looked up. "Daaammmittt!"

§

His imps were scurrying to get out of his way. "What happened, Master?" one asked.

He growled, "That bastard!"

"Who?"

"Araciel!"

"What has he done, now?" another asked.

"He is no longer down here!" Lucifer screamed. How in the hell did he not know his brother wasn't one of his warriors? Hadn't he been here as long as the rest? What was that boy's game?

"Where is he, Master?" one asked.

"On earth!"

"You didn't release him?"

"Shut up!"

"You didn't, did you?" another challenged him.

[262]

"How was he able to get out, without your assistance?"

"He was never one of us!" Lucifer spit out. "He betrayed us!"

They all gasped. "He's still an Archangel?"

Lucifer exposed his jagged teeth. "It would seem so."

"We need *help*. It appears that you can't defeat them alone," his imp boldly replied.

Lucifer hit him with a fireball. All the other imps jumped back and watched him explode into a thousand pieces.

The demon rematerialized and frowned. "That hurt."

"Next time I'll set it at full blast!" Lucifer warned.

But, the bastard was right. They did need help. And at this point he could only think of one person. He vanished.

§

Samjaza had been screaming since the day Seraphiel made him human. You would think one would get used to it, but the pain was unbearable. For some time now he actually felt sorry for women. Childbirth was a bitch! Especially, since he had no womb and no baby. Just the perpetual *pain*. For what amounted to a lifetime, he'd felt like his insides were being ripped apart. If only he could get his spirit back, this pain would go away.

§

But, Seraphiel was as ruthless and as cold as he himself was. Not only had he sentenced him to everlasting torment; he dared anyone to help him. None of his brothers wanted to be in his shoes; so they didn't try. They even put up a binding spell so they didn't have to hear his continued, annoying, screams. Bastards!

§

On top of that, he could look up and see Seraphiel's family. They were growing by leaps and bounds. At least Seraphiel was smarter than he'd been. He didn't give the new Adam all of his powers, right off. Maybe he learned from *his* mistake. Or was he afraid his son would do the same thing he'd done. Turn on his *father!* Wouldn't that be the sweetest revenge?

§

At first he was hopeful; because there was definitely trouble on the horizon. Seraphiel and his team were not happy with that boy. They wanted to yoke his free spirit, but the boy bulked against them. For a minute he forgot all about his pain and anxious waited. But, nothing happened. Damn!

But, it was still early yet. If he could someway influence the kid. Make him believe he was more powerful than his father. Get him to see his father was jealous and fearful of him. Maybe get him to come down and release his grandfather. They could be a team. Together, they could do what he'd set out to do in the beginning.

Create an, all powerful, army.

§

"Well it's about time you stopped all that screaming."

Samjaza had been focused on his new mission and hadn't even realized he wasn't screaming anymore. He looked at the entryway and saw his brother standing in the door.

"Lucifer, you bastard! Why would you show up now? I've been screaming for help for years!"

"I've come to help you now, haven't I?"

"You've come because you need a favor."

Lucifer laughed. "That too. But, we can help each other."

"I doubt it. You want to destroy the boy and his woman."

"Don't you?"

Samjaza smirked. "Hardly. I want him on my side."

"Your side?"

"My side, our side. It's all the same."

"What's your plan?"

Samjaza explained his plan to Lucifer and he smiled. "Good, right?"

"You think it'll work?"

"With your help, yes?"

"What can I do?"

"First see if you can free me."

§

Since key players had been made aware of Lucifer's insidious plan, they kept an eye on him. In doing so, they were one step ahead of his current ploys.

At this moment, Michael, Raphael and Gabriel listened to their conversation, from the balcony of heaven. Araciel listened to their conversation from Jehoel's home, in Kentucky. Seraphiel listened to their conversation, from the meeting.

§

"Alright, let me get you out of that trap," Lucifer

replied.

He swiftly moved across the room with confidence in his abilities. After all, he was 'god', wasn't he? Once Samjaza was freed they could capture the boy, with deceitful kindness. Then the army, he and his wife produced, would be theirs to command.

He got within arm's reach and heard Araciel whisper, *"And his name shall be called..."*

Lucifer pre-maturely trembled. "NOOOOO!"

Seraphiel whispered, *"...Jesus!"*

§

The other onlookers laughed and repeated, *"Jesus! Jesus! Jesus!"*

§

Samjaza could not hear the voices. He frowned. Lucifer was twitching like something had a hold of him. It was almost comical. "What's happening?"

Lucifer was screaming, "No! No!"

A lightning bolt hit him, and he flew backwards, across the room. His hair and clothes were on fire. "Damn!"

He put the fire out and ran out of the tunnel, back to his throne room.

§

"Be careful, Araciel," Michael warned. *"Do not forget, Father does not want Lucifer harmed."*

"Oops."

Seraphiel, Raphael and Gabriel laughed.

§

Chapter 28

Justin, Nate, Layla and Ali arrived back in the ward. Loretta was agitated. Her eyes were just this side of demonic. She was mumbling, cursing and destroying the room. She looked up at Nate and shouted, "YOU!"

He jumped back, and pulled Layla behind him. "*That's* the crazy woman I know."

Then she noticed Justin. She moved away from him. "Don't come near me." Her voice was magnified; with an echo. "Get *out!*"

Justin wondered what had set her off. This was not the woman he'd met last night. She was swinging too violently for him to approach her. "Ease her spirit, Nate."

"I can't. She fights against me."

Layla started to cry. "Somebody stop her!"

Ali tried to calm her down, but could not. "This is her norm?"

"Yes!" Nate replied. "But magnified."

"Can you calm her, Leilazeb?"

Leilazeb appeared in the room. "Not from here. If I touch her, the spirit will follow me out of her body."

"No, don't!" Layla shouted. "I need to speak with her."

§

Raphael appeared in the room. "I believe I can help."

He stilled her storm. Then he walked over to her.
"Hello, Leakah."

Loretta frowned. Then scowled. "Raphael. It's
about damn time you showed up."

He laughed. "Sorry."

"How long have I been stuck in this disgusting
body?"

"I don't know. You hung around with Hakael's
family for about thirty years; so maybe fifty."

"Get...me...out!"

"Not until you speak with your daughter."

Loretta looked over his shoulder. Her face softened.
"Layla."

Layla walked toward her mother. "Momma."

§

"I'm sorry for the embarrassment I have caused you.
I would never deliberately hurt you, my daughter."

"I know, Momma."

Loretta looked beyond her to Nate. "Mister all
powerful voice, should have known what was going on."

"You didn't even know. How in the hell was I
supposed to know?" Nate responded.

"You could've asked somebody, you good for
nothing bastard."

"Who would you have suggested?" Nate replied. "I
got you the best help known to man, didn't I?"

She smiled. "Well that's true." Then she shouted,

"BUT YOU SHOULD HAVE ASKED MICHAEL! YOU...NOT SO FUNNY...IDIOT!"

Ali squeaked. "She's got your number."

"Yeah well if she knows Michael; she knows he *hates* me."

Loretta smirked. "I wonder why?"

Justin laughed and got her attention. She smiled at him. "You're a good boy, Justin." Then she walked over to him. "Here's our secret. Demons can't hurt you, but don't touch one. Or let one touch you."

"Why? Won't I kill them?"

"Yes. But their spirits will *incorporate* with yours."

"What?" everybody asked.

"Demons run from me, because I consume them."

"What?"

"The voices I hear, are the demons fighting to take control."

"I don't understand?" Layla replied.

"Imagine I am a sponge and the demon spirit is liquid. Just as the sponge absorbs liquid; I absorbed them."

"Damn!" Nate replied.

"Shut *up*, you nincompoop!"

"That has never happened to me," Leilazeb said.

"That's because you don't have a corporal body."

"So how many demons you got living in there, 'Linda Blair'?" Nate asked.

"Who's Linda Blair?" Layla asked.

Loretta laughed. Her daughter wasn't even born when the movie "The Exorcist" came out on film. Back then, she was in her right mind. The movie had scared the crap out of her. Who knew she'd eventually experience the twisting head, and green puke, herself. She smirked, and feigned offense. "Enough to take your sorry butt *d.o.w.n.*"

"Really?" Ali asked.

"At last count, it was about a thousand."

"What?" everyone said, even Raphael

"No wonder you're crazy, 'Sybil'." Nate laughed.

"Who?" Layla asked.

"Stop calling me names." Loretta laughed. "And take my daughter to the movies once in a while, you cheapskate."

Everybody laughed.

"I cannot release those demons here," Raphael stated. "I'll have to take this Vessel to the bowels of Hell, and release them there."

"What will happen to my mother?" Layla asked.

Loretta smiled at her daughter. "You know the answer to that, Laylo."

"Hey! I'm the only one who can call her that!" Nate replied.

Everybody said, "Shut up!"

He laughed. Then he walked over to Loretta.

"Before you go, I want to thank you for my 'spirit' mate." He leaned in and kissed her cheek. "Thank you for not giving her your craziness, 'Baby Jane'."

She, affectionately, hugged him. It was too bad she had to leave now. They could have possibly been friends. He had a good sense of humor. In his line of work, it was much needed. "You have been good to my daughter, and I appreciate that. Remember, you can have children."

Then she frowned. "I so wish Michael had given her to somebody else. But, it is what it is." She kissed his cheek.

Everyone laughed at them.

Then she turned to Layla. "I won't have this temple or this face. I will look like Hakael's 'spirit' mate." She pulled Layla's hand to her heart. "But where it counts, I will always be your momma."

Layla was crying. "I love you, Momma."

Loretta wiped her tears, and hugged her. "You are the only good thing that came from my having this body."

Loretta reached for Justin's hand. "You are a good boy. I know your mother is proud of you."

"Do you know her?" Justin asked.

"Not yet. I'm sure I will meet her, in a minute or so."

He smiled. "I'm going to miss you, Loretta."

"I'll be around. I will fight with my kind to protect you and Laylo." She kissed his cheek. "Too bad you couldn't be my son-in-law." Then she raised her eyebrows. "You can't...*can you?* Laylo really is a nice girl."

Nate growled. "Don't start no mess, up in here, Loretta."

Ali squeaked.

Justin laughed. "I think I'll keep my children's mother."

"Too bad. You got a brother or a favorite cousin?"

"Get 'Carrie' out of here, Raphael!" Nate replied.

Justin laughed. Evidently Nate watched as much television as Batman. "No ma'am."

§

"Are you ready, Leakah?" Raphael asked.

Layla jumped. "Wait!"

She hugged her mother one more time. "What will happen to your body? I can't bear for it remaining in Hell."

"We have a memorial tree, at the estate. Brock planted it over one hundred years ago; in memory of his mother. We can lay her to rest there, if you like," Ali offered.

"That is a good idea, Ali," Brock replied. That was the first they realized he was snooping. *"We can even place a headstone, if you like."*

Layla and Loretta both smiled, and said, "Yes."

"Are you ready now?" Raphael asked.

"Yes. Can we stop by Hakael's first, so I can kick his ass?"

Aki squeaked. "You know his granddaughters are married to Kobabiel's grandsons."

Loretta smiled. "Is that right?"

"Yes ma'am."

"Then they are your family too, Laylo. Embrace them."

"I will, Momma."

"I love you, daughter. And you too…you good for nothing, fool."

"Yeah well, now that you are leaving, I love you, too." Nate laughed.

She laughed. "You'd better keep in mind; I won't have a body, in a minute. I'm coming back to kick your ass too, boy."

"Oh damn!" Nate replied. It would be just like her to torment him. And he wouldn't be able to fight back.

§

Raphael and Loretta vanished.

"What now?" Layla asked. Her tears were running full stream. But, at least her mother would finally have some peace.

§

Five minutes later, a she-demon appeared in the room. She/he was a beautiful *brunette,* with short spiked hair. And she looked like a young, *sexy,* Diahann Carroll.

She purposely dressed in a respectable skirt and blouse; because she did not want to offend her child. But she was still unbelievably hot. *Damn!*

§

Layla smiled. "Momma?"

She/he shook her/his head. Then she/he looked at Justin and smiled. "Son."

"Momma?"

She/he smiled. "Yes."

"Oh my God!"

The she demon laughed. "Indeed."

§

Justin was almost speechless. His mother had been a beautiful woman; although no one saw it but him. Marred by the constant inner war, she'd looked wild. Untamed. Mad.

He'd never once seen her with her hair combed, or in decent clothing. It was no secret his father hadn't loved her. He wondered why he married her in the first place.

His mother was listening to his thoughts. "In the beginning we were in love, Justin. And he was good to me."

"Then what happened?"

"The hormonal changes of pregnancy awakened the true nature of my being."

"I did that to you?"

"Of course not. The hormones did."

[274]

"So if you hadn't gotten pregnant, you would've never known?"

"That's right."

"I'm sorry."

"It wasn't your fault, any more than it was mine."

"Did he kill you?"

"No. I killed myself."

"Why?"

"To keep from killing you."

"What?"

"While we were sleeping in the woods, the demons, in me, took over. They were going to kill you and then go back to the house and kill your father. Although, I didn't so much mind them killing him; I couldn't let them kill you. They searched until they found a rope in the woods. They tied a noose and slung it high over a branch. Just when they reached for you, I took control. Thank God. I hung myself. Others of my kind were there to destroy the demons; so they could not get in you, son."

"You died for *me!*"

"I didn't die. No one does. I gave up the body I despised."

"You don't know who your Watcher was?" Ali asked.

"I'm afraid not. But, it doesn't matter. He didn't deliberately put me in the wrong body."

"I think it does matter," Layla replied.

[275]

"Why?"

"So Watchers will know to be more careful. I think it should become a rule that they can't incorporate with a child less than two years of age."

"Why two?"

"Their sex is already determined at that age. Plus, they haven't developed their real personalities yet."

"Hannah has," Ali replied.

"Then what can be done?" Layla asked.

"We'll find a way, Laylo," Nate assured her. Hopefully no others were out there.

§

Justin hugged his mother. "I'd like for you to meet your grandchildren. And your daughter-in-law."

"I'd like that."

"What is your name?"

"I am still momma, to you." She smiled. "And Grandma, to your children. But, to everyone else, I am Nitsuj."

"Nitsuj?" Justin smiled and then smiled bigger. "My name spelled backwards?"

"Yes. Even though I wanted to be male; you were, and remain, my *greatest* love."

"Let's go home," Ali said and reached for Justin.

Nitsuj stopped him. "I will carry my son."

§

Chapter 29

Amanda and her sons were sitting at the dining room table, getting ready to eat dinner. Dee and Celia were doing the cooking.

Aden wasn't sure about Dee cooking. He eased up behind her and whispered, "Are you sure you know how to cook, baby?"

She smirked. "My grandfather never complained."

"Yeah well; he was the donut king, wasn't he?

Addison laughed. "I hope she knows how to cook. I invited Ram and Symphony to join us."

Amanda frowned. "Why?" She thought this was just for her family. "And why isn't Isabella here?"

"She and her parents are coming, too. So, if you don't know how to cook, get *out* the kitchen, Dee!"

Dee laughed. "Listen lil' boy, I…"

§

Adabiel, Gabriel and Isabella teleported in, and cut off her retort.

"Hey," Addison spoke and hugged Isabella. "You smell good."

"It's your favorite."

"I know."

"Hey, Adabiel. Hey, Gabbie." He hugged them.

§

As soon as they finished with all the greetings, Ram

and Symphony walked in the door.

"Hey!" Symphony and Dee said at the same time, and hugged each other.

"What smells so good?" Ram asked.

"Dee is cooking dinner," Adrian said, with a one sided smile.

"Oh." Ram smiled. He knew what they were thinking. She didn't look like the domestic type. She was still as gorgeous and elegant as ever. But, he knew the woman could throw down.

Fried chicken, mashed potatoes, mac and cheese, string beans, fried corn, cornbread muffins, speckle butter beans, scratch pound cake, sweet potato pie…damn! All the things that jacked with a human's cholesterol; she could *cook!* She didn't *eat* it, but she damn sure could cook it.

Of course, he wasn't going to reveal that shit! That would reopen a can of worms.

"Let me help you," Symphony offered. She didn't understand what in the world would make Dee want to embarrass herself. But then again, she didn't know how to cook either. Hopefully, Celia knew what she was doing.

§

The two of them walked in the kitchen talking. Dee laughed. "I really can cook, Symphony."

"Taste this," Celia offered.

Symphony tasted it. "That's good, Celia."

"Dee cooked it. I'm just stirring the pot. She cooked everything."

Symphony raised her eyebrows. "You really do know how to *cook?*"

Dee laughed. "Yeah. It was just me and granddaddy. I did all the cooking."

"Why didn't you tell them?"

"My brothers-in-law are so comical; I wanted to see their faces." She laughed again.

"Does Ram know you can cook?"

Dee frowned. "Do you really want to know?"

"Yes."

"Yes. He probably didn't say anything because he didn't want you to get upset."

"I am so over that, Dee. You need to cook dinner for everyone at the estate; at least once a month."

"I love cooking. You think Chef would let me?"

"I'll handle it."

§

She'd cooked pork chops, smothered in a mushroom, bell pepper, and garlic and onion gravy. Fried cabbage, with stewed tomatoes. Roasted onion and cheese mashed potatoes. Cornbread and yeast rolls. Dessert was lemon pound cake. All from scratch. Her lemon tea would have Chaz and Akibeel doing cartwheels.

§

Everyone was waiting on Aden to take the first bite.

[279]

After all, it was his wife. "Go ahead, Aden." Addison laughed. "You first."

Aden was not about to hurt his wife's feelings. He forked a good measure and stuffed it in his mouth. His eyes bucked and then shut reverently. He chewed for a long time. Not that it was tough; he just didn't want to give it up so soon.

He opened his eyes and licked his lips. "God, baby; who taught you how to cook 'soul' food?"

"My grandfather was from the south. He loved everything I cooked today. Even though he couldn't be here, I wanted to cook all of his favorites."

§

Everybody dug in. And everybody had the same response. Even though there was plenty left on their plates, they licked their forks; after each mouthful.

None of them said a word. They couldn't. Their mouths were always stuffed. Her buttery yeast rolls simply melted in their mouths. The gravy was smooth as butter. The pork chops had just the right amount of tenderness. Her mashed potatoes were seasoned with cheese, onion and bacon bits. They tasted like a baked potato.

"This grub is off the chart, sis," Adrian finally commented and laughed. "You should take lessons from her, Celia."

"It is quite impressive," Amanda added. "I never

would have guessed."

§

After they finished eating, Addison said, "I was hoping Dad would be back by now."

"He'll be back soon, son," Amanda replied. "What's going on?"

Addison smiled and reached for Isabella's hand. "I asked Issie to marry me."

Aden spit out his drink. "What?"

Addison ignored his brother. "She said yes."

"Congratulations," Symphony, Ram, Dee and Celia all said.

Amanda stood up and kissed Isabella. "Welcome to my family. Justin is going to *hate* he missed this announcement."

Adrian and Aden hugged Isabella and smiled. "Welcome."

"When is the big day?" Symphony asked.

"We haven't set the date, but we want you to coordinate the wedding," Addison informed her.

"What?"

"Girl, you know you set it off for Adam's birthday," Isabella added.

Ram smiled. He was so proud of her. Henry had hurt her feelings and pissed him off. But, he hadn't left it there. He helped her find her purpose. "She did, didn't she? Caim and Balam already asked her to coordinate their wedding."

"They did?"

Symphony smiled. "Yeah and Charity and Dawn want me to handle their baby showers. If anything else comes up, I'll need an assistant." She laughed.

"I'll do it," Dee volunteered.

"You will?"

"Yeah, girl. That'll be fun."

"Me too," Celia added. "You can arrange everything. Dee can do the cooking. I can do whatever you guys want me to do."

§

They were in the middle of making plans, when Justin teleported in. They all stared.

§

Justin was smiling from ear to ear. He put his arm around Nitsuj. "This is my mother," he choked. He hadn't thought he'd ever get this chance. Hers wasn't the face he knew, but the touch certainly was. "Momma, this is my family."

He introduced her to Amanda and all of his sons and their wives. Then he introduced her to Ram and Symphony.

"You are beautiful, Amanda. Thank you for loving my son. I've watched you for years. You've always made him happy."

"You were here the other night?" Amanda stated.

"Yes. I helped keep you all safe. Where is Kiah?"

"She's upstairs, in the nursery."

"I'd like to see her before I leave; if it's okay with you," Nitsuj stated.

Then she hugged her three grandsons. "You all are some fine young men. I hope you don't mind me intruding on your lives."

"I'd be upset if you didn't," Adrian replied. "I want you to get to know my family, Grandmother."

"I want that too," Aden added.

"Me too," Addison agreed and hugged her. "You are beautiful, Grandmother."

§

Finally Justin introduced her to Adabiel and Gabriella. Adabiel had a look of concern on his face. He wasn't aware of Justin's story. But he knew this was off.

He looked from Justin to Nitsuj and then at Gabriella. Her expression was just as discontent as his. He looked back at Justin's mother. "Why do you call yourself Nitsuj?"

"I do not know who my Watcher was."

"How did you get out of your human form?"

Justin's head slowly, but purposely cranked. His eyes were piercing. "You know who my mother's Watcher was, don't you?"

Adabiel slowly nodded his head. "How did this happen, Justin?"

Justin told him the entire story of his childhood. He told him Nate's mother-in-law had been trapped, just like his mother had been.

§

Adabiel looked weary, when he sat down. "I am so sorry."

Nitsuj looked at Gabriella. They looked nothing alike. "I couldn't have been yours."

Adabiel shook his head. "No." Then he looked up. "I'll be damned."

"Who was her Watcher?" Aden asked.
"My brother, Sathariel."

"We met his wife. She doesn't look anything like my grandmother," Addison objected.

§

Sathariel and his wife, Angelia, appeared in the room. "What's up, Biel..." Sathariel stopped short. "Oh my *damn!* What are you doing here, Leirahtas? How *are* you here?"

Justin and Nitsuj stared at Angelia. So did everyone in the room. They would have never put it together. Nitsuj was black, Angelia was French. Nitsuj's hair was short and spiked; Angelia's was long and flowing. But their faces... Everyone's mind went to Brock and Doc. Ebony and Ivory.

"How did this happen?" Sathariel asked again.

§

Sathariel was devastated! Remorse was seeping through his pores. "I am so sorry, Lcirahtas. So sorry."

Nitsuj smiled. "It's alright, Sathariel."

"No it's not. Look what happened to you and your son," he growled. "That human bastard abused you both. I would have never let him, and his tramp, mistreat your son. I would have killed him *dead*...if I'd known."

"He did do that. But, you can't change what has happened." Then she smiled. "You can make it up to my son, by making him a part of your family."

"He *is* a part of our family," Angelia replied. "Any son of yours, is a son of ours."

"Your grandchildren are our grandchildren," Sathariel added.

"Hell to the *umpteenth* nawl!!" Addison strongly objected. "Wait one dang-gone minute. That makes Issie and me cousins!"

Ram cracked up. "He has a point."

"It's all symbolic, Addison. There are no blood ties. Justin's blood came from his human mother and father," Adabiel assured him.

"Tell me something, then," Addison huffed. He wasn't into that kissing cousins or incest; but he *loved* Isabella.

"I can't wait to tell Baraq," Ram added. "He'll get a kick out of this."

"Is my boy here?" Sathariel asked.

"Yeah. You want me to call him?"

"Nah. I'll get with him later. Right now I want to spend some time with Justin, and his family. I want you guys to meet your relatives, in Iowa."

Justin was smiling. Sathariel didn't look old enough to be his father and he had no intentions of calling him that. But, he'd like a relationship with him. He hugged Amanda. "It appears my life has come full circle, Mandy."

She sensed the relief he felt. He belonged. She hugged him and kissed his cheek. "Our lives, Justin."

§

Chapter 30

Adam had been training, all morning. He mentally prepared himself for Dan, Chaz and Batman to torture him. He thought for sure they'd beat him to a pulp. But they didn't. At least not like he thought.

For three hours, he and Akibeel had done nothing but run through the preserve, and sub-division. Richard ran with them, because it was his daily routine.

Adam foolishly thought because he morphed himself into a grown man he didn't need to. But, damn, his muscles were hurting. It was hard to tell who was moaning the loudest, him or Akibeel.

"Y'all are some wimps." Richard laughed as he flew past them.

"Kiss my wimp!" Akibeel whispered after him. He was too tired to shout it.

"This is torture!" Adam complained.

"How long do we have to do this, man?" Akibeel asked, feebly.

"Chaz said four or five hours a day."

"That means we have another hour. Hey, let's run to the preserve and hide for a while," Akibeel suggested.

§

They both heard Chaz, Dan and Batman laugh. *"Don't even think about it!"* Chaz said.

"Damn! They watching us, man," Akibeel

[287]

complained.

"Every move you make!" Batman laughed.

"Now speed it up boys!" Dan laughed.

"I can't. My leg is cramping!" Adam complained.

A salt tablet appeared in his hand.

"Squeeze it in your palm and keep running," Chaz instructed. *"Remember this pain now will help you protect Mordiree and Maria later."*

§

That was motivation enough for both of them. Both of them remembered what their women had been put through. They took off in an all-out run. Adam ran the cramp right out of his leg.

§

They ran for four and a half hours. They foolishly thought training was over for the day....

WRONG!

§

They ended up bench pressing, in the training room. Chaz was Adam's spotter, Dan was Akibeel's and Batman was Richard's.

They were both okay with that. Akibeel smiled. "At least we can lie down."

"Uh-huh," Chaz replied, with a smirk.

§

Adam wanted to cry. His arms were trembling and sweat was popping off his face. His shorts looked like he'd taken a dip in the pool. "This is too heavy!"

Chaz laughed. "Just think of the rewards. Next time you won't have to call on your father for help."

Adam grunted, as he struggled to lift the barbells. The salty sweat was running in his eyes and blinding him. "I don't mind asking for my dad's help. I like his help."

Chaz chuckled. Adam was a good sport. Even if he was thirty, he was still a kid, next to him. He reached out and took the weights away from him. "Let's take five."

Adam frowned. "You lifted that with one hand, man!"

"Yep."

"How much can you press?"

Chaz smiled. "One hand or two?"

"Two."

"I can do twenty reps, of a thousand pounds."

"*What?*"

"You heard me."

"Man, how is that even possible?"

"We're not human, Adam."

"I can't do that."

Chaz laughed. "You can't even press three hundred pounds."

"But I'm a Watcher, too."

"True. But you were a baby two days ago, Adam," Batman replied. He bent his elbow and flexed his muscles. "It took years of dedication, and determination, to build these *guns*."

"You're kidding?"

"Did you think we were born with them?" Dan asked.

"Well, *yeah*."

They laughed at him.

"Unlike you, we grew up; one day at a time. Yomiel and I ran and played when we were puny little boys. As we got older, we didn't have the conveniences kids have today. Nobody did. We worked in the fields, with our hands, arms and legs. That started the process of muscle building," Akibeel informed him.

"There were no cars, either. Wherever we went; we had to *foot it*," Dan added. "That strengthened our legs."

"We chopped wood for fire and worked in the fields," Chaz added. "That strengthened our arm muscles."

"But I thought my dad always had his powers."

"Power, yes; but not *might*," Batman replied. "That boy fought his battles with his mind."

"We just found out last year that he even knew how to *fight*," Dan added.

"Really?"

"Yes. But the point is, we've had five thousand years to tune these bodies."

Richard looked at Adam and laughed. "You cheated, Dawg."

"So when I thought I was getting dad's powers; it wasn't physical powers?"

They all shook their heads. "You're gonna have to work at that," Chaz replied.

Adam groaned.

§

Richard sat next to Adam. "Don't sweat it, man. It only took me a year to build mine. You're a Watcher, so it won't take you that long."

"That's provided you have the determination," Dan added.

Adam thought about Mordiree; his future wife. The mother of his seven sons. She deserved better than window dressing. He looked like he-man; but it was just covering. "I'm all in. What's next?"

"Well, alright." Chaz extended his arm for a fist bump.

Adam could not meet his fist with his own. His arms hurt too badly. He wiggled his fingers at him, from their resting position.

They cracked up.

§

He was relieved that the next step was a private soak, in the hot tub. The guys had poured an entire box of Epsom Salt in. They said it was to ease his pain. He hoped so, because even his *tongue* hurt. They turned the jets on high, and man did it feel good.

[291]

§

He'd dozed off when he felt someone slip in the tub with him. It was too painful to open his eyes, but he knew who it was. *"Hey, Shuga."*

Mordiree eased up close to him. *"Was it bad?"*

He gingerly turned his head, and painfully lifted one eyelid. *"Define bad."*

She laughed. *"Poor baby."*

He actually felt worse than he did, when he first got in the tub. *"I can't move."*

"Can you teleport?"

"I hope so. Otherwise I'm sleeping in this tub tonight."

"Teleport us to the room. I will give you a massage."

"Whose?"

"Mine."

That should have motivated him; but pain won out. He still couldn't lift his arms. *"Grab my hand."*

§

Adam had hoped for a softer landing, but he hurt *everywhere*. They landed on the bed with a thud. Before he could apologize, sharp pains accosted his legs, with a demonic vengeance.

The muscles in his thighs and calves seized. His toes turned under and balled. His feet tilted downward. The pain he felt before couldn't touch this!

He screamed, in agony.

§

Mordiree saw the muscles in his thighs ball in a knot. Both of his legs and his feet stiffened. She tried to massage his feet, but it was too painful for him. She panicked, because he was starting to bruise. "What should I do?"

Adam had no clue what was happening to him. He screamed, "DAAAAD!!"

§

Chapter 31

Brock, Ditto and Henry were on their way to the wolf den. He suddenly stopped and frowned. Even though every room was soundproof, he heard Adam's cry. His son was in pain. "ADAM!" He turned and ran back down the hall. Ditto and Henry were right behind him.

§

Before they reached the room, Mordiree ran into the hall. She shouted towards them, "He's having *terrible* muscle spasms, Uncle Brock. His legs are starting to bruise!"

§

Doc was in his room, but heard her shouting in the hallway. He and Kwanita rushed out. "What's happening?"

No one responded, so they followed the crowd.

§

Brock shot straight past Mordiree. When he saw Adam, he came to an abrupt stop. He'd never in his life seen anyone's legs do that! His son's big toes were stiff and standing straight up; while his other toes curled under. The muscles in his thighs looked like they were about to pop. "Son!" he shouted. "What the hell happened?"

"What's happening to him?" Doc asked and moved into the room. "Good Lord!"

He, and Kwanita, rushed to the side of the bed.

[294]

They reached out to touch him, but he screamed. "It hurts, Dad!"

§

Adam was sweating profusely. That was a good thing, because otherwise everyone would know he was crying, too. The pain was unbearable. The legs of his shorts were hard pressed to stay intact. He longed for the comfort of his dad's arms. *'C'mon diaper'* He screamed again, "Help! Me!"

Brock reached out and removed the pain, but the muscles did not relax. And the bruises were almost unbearable to look at.

Ditto and Henry both attempted to massage his feet, but he screamed. The constant pain was gone, but his flesh was tender. "Get Deuce, Uncle Brock!" Henry shouted.

"Deuce, I need you in Mordiree's room! Are you dressed?"

"Yeah, what's up?"

"Adam!"

§

Jodi was in Deuce and Aurellia's room. Aurellia was having a hard time sleeping. She made Jodi promise not to tell Brock what was going on.

"He has enough on his plate with Adam, Momma."

"That may be true, but if you don't tell him...I will."

Deuce quickly stood up and interrupted their discussion. "Brock just called for me."

[295]

"What's wrong?"

"Adam is in Mordiree's room. Something's wrong with him," Deuce replied and opened the door.

Thank God their rooms were only three doors apart. Jodi and Aurellia took off running. "Adam! Adam!"

§

Just as Brock had done, Jodi came to an abrupt stop. His legs were contorting. And by now even his fingers were cramped and stuck in a bent position. "Adam!" she screamed, again.

"Step aside, Jodi," Deuce commanded and pushed her to the side. He looked at Adam and frowned. Not only was his body twisted, his skin was ashy. "He is experiencing muscle fatigue. They worked him too hard today. Plus, he's probably dehydrated. I'll be right back."

Aurellia was trembling. There was always something going on. "Is Adam going to be alright?"

"He'll be okay, Rellia." Deuce hugged his trembling wife. She'd been an emotional mess since the attack. Now this. "Come help me."

"Okay."

§

Dan, Chaz and Batman were on their way to the den, when they saw the crowd. "What's going on?" Batman asked.

Mordiree lit into them. "What the hell did y'all do to him?"

[296]

"What are you talking about?" Chaz asked. When he saw the condition Adam was in he cursed. "Damn!"

"What the hell?" Dan asked.

Pledge be damned, Brock wanted to kill them. "Y'all hurt my *boy*?"

"No, Dad!" Adam replied. "They didn't do anything to me."

Brock growled at Chaz, Dan and Batman. "Where the hell did all those bruises come from?"

"Hell if we know! We would never do anything to hurt Adam. You know that, Brock, man!" Batman responded. "C'mon now; you damn well know that!"

"Then what the hell happened?" Jodi shouted.

"Nothing. After training, we let him soak in the hot tub, to soothe his muscles. That's the last we saw of him," Chaz replied. "We assumed he was hanging out with Mordiree."

"He didn't come to dinner, so I went looking for him. He was in the spa and was still hurting. I had him teleport us here. I wanted to give him a massage," Mordiree informed them. "He was lethargic and couldn't even lift his arms. I didn't know he was in this bad of a shape."

"He was in the spa all that time?" Batman asked. "We helped him in there over three hours ago."

§

Deuce walked back in with an IV pole, in time to

hear Batman's statement. "I know you guys meant well, but that was the wrong thing to do."

"What?" all three said.

"He was probably already dehydrated from the exercising. When you put him in the hot tub, he sweated more. He's lost a lot of his electrolytes."

"What's that?"

"The salt, potassium, magnesium and calcium our bodies need. When it is depleted, our bodies experience severe cramping pains. Plus, like I said; his body fluids, in general, are depleted," Deuce responded. Then he reached for Adam's twisted hand. Adam flinched. He was tender all over. Deuce released it. "I need to give you intravenous fluids, plus a muscle relaxer, okay?"

Aurellia gently grabbed her brother's hand. "It'll make you better, Adam. And probably put you to sleep."

Adam nodded. "Do it. Those big toes are freaking me out!"

§

Everyone stood around the room and watched as Adam's muscles slowly started to relax. But his flesh was still extremely bruised, and tender to the touch.

Mordiree sat at the head of the bed and rubbed his forehead. He was still sweating. "He's still losing fluids, Deuce."

"I know, Cuz," Deuce replied. He took Adam's temperature. "Damn!" It was way too high. Critically high. He turned toward Brock. "Look in my mind and see what I need."

§

Two cases of sports aide appeared at the foot of the bed, along with cooling blankets.

"Help him drink this, Mordiree," Deuce instructed.

§

When Adam finished with the first bottle, Deuce turned to Brock. "Levitate him off the bed so Doc and I can put this blanket under him."

Then he turned to Ditto, Henry, Doc and Kwanita. "Wrap these cooling blankets around each of his legs and feet."

He handed one to Aurellia. "Wrap his wrist, Rellia." He threw one across his chest.

§

"Ahhhhh!" Adam sighed. He could feel his body relaxing. "Those blankets feel damn good."

"Can you bring his body temperature down by five degrees? But at a rate of one degree, every ten minutes, Brock?"

"Yeah." Brock wanted to cry for his child. He reached out and cooled his boy. When he brought it down the last degree, he asked, "How does that feel, son?"

"Like heaven."

"Listen," Deuce said to Chaz, Dan and Batman. "We all know that you didn't *mean* to hurt him. But, you can't work him that *hard*. And you gotta make sure he stays hydrated, during training. How much fluid did he drink today?"

Dan looked down. It never crossed their minds that he wasn't drinking water. "None."

Doc squinted. "NONE?" He wanted to hurt them. How could they not make sure the boy was drinking enough fluids? They heard him growling.

Chaz's eyes were guilt ridden. "We're sorry, Adam. We didn't *know*."

"It's all good, Uncle Chaz." His speech was slurred. That shot was a dose of nirvana. It was doing its job.

Aurellia and Mordiree were rubbing his hands. Their touch felt soooo good. The only thing that was missing... *'C'mon diaper.'*

§

Jodi's heart was heavy. Two days ago he would have drank plenty of water, because she would have made sure he did. Today he was a man and responsible for his own body. She hated this. Nature shouldn't allow you skip the aging process.

She was not going to leave her baby, but she decided to be diplomatic about it. "Do you mind if I stay in here for a while, Mordiree?"

"You and Brock both can," she replied.

"I'm staying for a while, too," Henry informed them. He couldn't believe those guys had been so careless with Adam. They knew he didn't know about the importance of fluid intake. How could they work a man in the sun like that, and not make sure he was properly hydrated. Then again, why hadn't he, warned his Dawg?

"Will you guys move that sofa in here?" Mordiree asked Henry and Ditto.

"Got it," they both replied and walked into the living area of Mordiree's suite.

Brock's mind was on the earlier meeting. He'd told Adam then, that he ate the right amount; because his mother knew what he needed. That included *water*. Then he remembered Rebecca's words *'life's lessons still have to be learned'*. He shook his head. "How are you feeling, son?"

"I'm cold, Dad," Adam whined. He was half asleep.

Deuce took his temperature again. "You can vanquish the cooling blankets now, Brock. And cover him with a sheet."

§

"Oh damn!" Dan cursed.

"What?" Brock asked.

"We need to check on Kibee. He didn't take in any fluids today, either."

§

Brock reached out with his mind. Sure enough Akibeel was moaning and groaning. *"Are you alright, son?"* Brock asked.

"Pop!! My legs are killing me."

"We're on our way, son!" Brock replied. Then he glared at Dan, Chaz and Batman. "I could kick y'alls sorry asses."

"Hey, man. We didn't know," Batman reiterated.

"If I was double jointed I'd kick my own ass, man," Dan added.

"You gotta know we'd never hurt either of them on purpose, Mi Amigo," Chaz said...to Doc.

Doc knew that was the truth, but he was still pissed. Two of his team members were down. His brothers. He didn't like his boys being hurt. He nodded. "Deep down, I know that and so does Pops. But, whether you meant to or not, they are hurt, Chaz."

"I know," Chaz replied remorsefully. He, Dan and Batman were the Ultimate Trainers, but they evidently needed to be trained...on how to train.

§

Brock shook his head. "We'll be right back, Jodi."

She didn't hear him. She was rubbing her baby's forehead. "My poor baby."

Adam was sound asleep.

§

Akibeel wasn't in much better shape. Maria had been massaging his legs all day. As soon as one muscle relaxed, another tensed.

"Let me help you out," Deuce said. "This is a

muscle relaxer."

Akibeel gritted his teeth. "Do it!"

Before he dozed off, Deuce explained the same thing to him that he did to Adam.

Akibeel scowled at his trainers. "How could y'all do that to me and my brother? Y'all know we don't know nothing about nothing. Neither one of us."

No truer statement had ever been made. Adam didn't know, because he was a baby forty-eight hours ago. Akibeel didn't know, because he'd been hiding in a grotto all of his life.

"I'm sorry, man," Chaz replied. "We were not thinking."

"From now on, Deuce will oversee yours and Adam's training routine," Brock told him. "Trust me, son. This will *never* happen again."

"Okay, Pops. Is Adam alright?" His voice was slurred.

"Nah, man. He's in worse shape than you are. They put your brother in a hot tub after he'd already sweated all of the fluids out of his body," Brock replied. He got angry all over again. He could kill Chaz, Dan and Batman.

"Damn!" Akibeel replied and closed his eyes.

"Wait, Kibee." Deuce shook him. "Drink this before you go to sleep." He handed him a sports drink.

§

Brock looked at Deuce; then at his team. "Get with

Deuce and let him see the workout schedule."

"Neither of them will be training tomorrow," Deuce informed them. "Adam's legs are going to be sore for a while. But, I suggest that you utilize my father, not me."

"Why?" Brock asked.

"I'm a *doctor*. I don't know anything about sports training. That's my father's expertise. He trained all the women, and Richard. Not once have any of them come to me with a sports injury."

Brock nodded. James worked the women from sun up to sun down. At the most, they were tired, but *never* hurt. "Get with James. And make sure this shit doesn't happen again."

He walked out the room.

§

Chapter 32

James laughed. As a matter of fact, he fell out. "You idiots!"

"It's not funny, James," Doc said, incensed.

"Damn sure ain't." Brock scowled.

"The hell it's not." James kept laughing. "And by the way, I wasn't referring to Dan, Chaz and Batman."

"Who?" Chaz asked.

"Brock and Doc. Mostly Brock." James looked at Brock and cracked up again.

"Explain."

"Why would you assign your son to fighters, before getting him physically in shape *to* fight?" James asked.

"I..." Brock stopped. James was right. Adam had never used a single muscle in his *manufactured* body.

Even during the battle in the sky he only used his mind to fight. He put up a fire wall around him and Mordiree, to keep the demons away. He'd even thrown fire balls, at the bastards. But the force of those balls came from his mind, not his might.

Adam had screamed when the demon's claws pierced his arm. If his muscles had been as sharply honed, as a Watcher, he never would have felt it. "Damn!"

"Yeah." James laughed again.

"That's what we were trying to do," Batman replied. "That's why we had them run for four and a half hours.

To build their muscles."

"And bench pressing for three hours," Chaz added.

James' chin dropped on his chest. "Seven hours of strenuous exercise; without a break?"

They nodded.

"Without water?"

They nodded.

"No lunch?"

They shook their heads. That even sounded bad to them. It made them feel a hell of a lot worse. Neither of them had slept all night because of the guilt they felt.

Not to mention Brock had accused them of intentionally hurting his son.

"What the hell were you trying to do? Kill him?"

"We work out like that. How were we supposed know it was too much for him?" Batman replied.

§

Brock was snooping. "I'm sorry. I should not have accused you guys. I know this was not on purpose."

Batman smirked. "Please. Let Joy get a scratch and see how I nut up. You did good restraining yourself, man."

"I appreciate you saying that, but I know you guys would never hurt my sons. Not intentionally."

§

"From what I understand, his legs are too damaged to start an exercise regimen, right now," James stated.

"Deuce said he couldn't do it today," Brock replied.

"I'm going to go and visit with him. I want to see for myself. If he was bruising, I'd say he won't be ready for a week. Not physically or mentally."

"Mentally?" Brock asked.

"That level of pain will make him too timid to try again. Plus, spontaneous bruising and dehydrating to the point of needing intravenous fluids..." James looked around the room. "...under normal circumstances he would've been hospitalized."

"Hospitalized?" Dan repeated.

"Severe dehydration can affect your internal organs, man. From kidney failure, to liver damage; and who knows what else. No doubt he had a fever."

"Yeah. Deuce had me cool his body temperature," Brock replied.

"His insides were cooking." James nodded. "I'm surprised Deuce didn't put him in a tub of ice."

"You have *got* to be kidding," Dan replied.

"No, he's not. I didn't even think about that. Thank God Mordiree thought to check on him," Doc responded. "Adam had a *heatstroke. That's* why Deuce used cooling blankets."

"He needed to get Adam's body temperature down *fast*; before it affected his brain," James agreed. "Deuce needs to do a complete work up on him, and Akibeel."

"His brain?" Brock frowned. "We almost killed my

son."

"It's not your fault, Dawg," Dan replied. "We wanted to give Adam his props. But, we didn't take into consideration that his lack of knowledge is akin to Akibeel's."

"Besides, he's Watcher," Chaz reminded them. "He won't die."

"Adam is not as forthcoming as Akibeel. What Akibeel doesn't know, he asks. Adam is afraid of being treated as a *lesser*, so he won't ask," Batman added. "Did you know that he thought we were born with these muscles?"

Brock actually chuckled. "You're kidding?"

"He thought he was inheriting your physical might, man."

Brock shook his head. Doc laughed. "He should have asked me."

They looked at Doc, and all of their minds went to the same place.

When he first arrived he had the same physique he has right now. No doubt his legs were strong from all of the running, but not strong enough. He couldn't even make a fist. His arms had never lifted anything heavier than a petri dish.

"But look at you now, man," James added. "It didn't happen overnight, but it did happen."

"It will happen for Adam also," Brock agreed.

"Have you checked on him yet, this morning?" Dan asked.

"Nah, I wanted to meet with you guys first."

§

Mordiree asked Chef to bring Adam's breakfast to the bedroom. Not only had he not taken in any fluids yesterday; he hadn't eaten anything either. She was angry with him. "You can't do this to yourself, Adam."

"I know. I just wasn't thinking, Maude. I was hyped to start training."

"Yeah well, that's out."

He felt how angry she was at him, and changed the subject. "One good thing came out of it."

"What?"

"My mom was too concerned to notice I was in your room." He smiled.

"She noticed. She even asked if she could stay a while. After everyone left, I told her this was our room, Adam. She's okay with it."

"You did? She is?"

"Yes and Yes."

"You shouldn't have told her that, Maude."

"Why?"

"This is *not* my room. My room is in the single men's section."

"You don't want to stay in here with me?"

"Sure I do, but I won't. I promised my parents I'd

give them time. Plus, I need to work on learning how to be an adult. Yesterday is proof of that. What grown person you know forgets to eat, and drink water?"

She laughed. "None, but…"

"No buts. I know all the basics, but I need to learn how to apply them. I need to get *me* together, before *we* can be together."

She teared up. "Are you breaking up with me, after two days?"

"Nope. Never gonna happen. I love you, Mordiree. I'm just taking *your* mother's advice. When is the last time you've been on a date?"

"The night of Brock's birthday party."

Adam frowned. "What was up with bringing that dude here, anyway? That really pissed me off."

Her eyes almost popped. "You weren't even born, Adam."

"I may have been in my mother's womb, but I was aware. I was trying to get out too, but Michael wouldn't let me. Thank God, because I would've hurt that man."

"Oh my God!"

He laughed. "He'd better hope I never see him again."

"Stop it. He was just a friend of mine."

"Yeah well; you don't need any male friends."

She removed his breakfast tray and sat down on the bed beside him. "So you're going to be possessive?"

"What do you mean, going to be?" He laughed and held her hand to his heart. "I already am."

She didn't mind, because she'd never stand for him having female friends either. She was glad they lived on the outskirts, away from the city girls. Otherwise she'd have to get her 'ghetto' on. "So you're going to date me."

"Yeah. I figure I'll train during the day and we'll date at night."

"I can live with that."

§

Neither of them was aware that Brock and Jodi were at the door. Listening. Jodi squeezed Brock's hand. *"Yea!"*

"You crazy, woman."

"You had twenty-one years to get ready for Aurellia's love life. I had two days with Adam. So crazy or not, I'm the happiest I've been in two days."

"Me too. And just think; he came to that decision on his own."

Adam laughed, *"I...caaannn...heeeaar...you!"*

§

Brock and Jodi jumped. "Damn that nosey boy!"

Jodi laughed. "Good!" She walked in and kissed his cheek. "How is mommy's itty bitty baby?"

"C'mon Mom!"

Brock laughed. "Last night you welcomed us treating you like a baby."

"Yeah well, last night I would have welcomed a diaper, if it would have stopped the pain."

Mordiree laughed. "I would've, too. I hope I never experience that again. I was really scared." Her eyes teared. "It looked so painful."

"All you had to do is see it. Imagine how I felt. It was a good thing I was dehydrated, because no way could I have walked to the bathroom." He laughed.

Jodi touched his leg. Before she could ask how it felt, he flinched.

"Still sore, Mom!"

"Sorry."

Brock reached for his son. "Let me help you to the shower. Otherwise Akibeel will be complaining that you stink."

"How is he?"

Akibeel was standing in the doorway. "I'm better. But Pops is right; I can smell you from here, man." He turned his nose up. "Major rancid!"

Adam laughed. "Shut up, boy!"

Akibeel walked into the room, laughing. "I'll help you, Pops. He smells like a dead polecat."

"Man, I don't smell that bad," Adam objected.

"Yeah, you do. Ask Mordiree." Akibeel laughed.

Adam looked at Mordiree.

She was smiling, and nodding her head.

Adam laughed. "That's cold."

Brock and Jodi laughed. "C'mon, let's get you cleaned up."

"Be gentle," Adam replied. "And please don't make the water *too* hot."

Brock actually felt him tremble. James was right; Adam would be timid, for a minute. "Don't worry, son. Your old man's got cha."

§

While Brock and Akibeel were helping Adam, Jodi and Mordiree changed the bed linen. Jodi embraced Mordiree's hand. "Brock told me if you hadn't gone looking for Adam he'd be in worse shape. Thank you."

"I thought about that. He couldn't even reach for my hand. I had to grab his, Jodi. He would have slept in that hot tub and cooked."

"I know." Jodi hugged her. "I'm glad he has you, Mordiree. I really am."

Mordiree laughed. "Just so long as I don't have sex with him, right?"

"I know that's not fair of me. But, I still need to come to grips with him being a man. Be patient with me."

"No worries. Adam and I have forever, right?"

§

Rebecca and Snow Anna came into the room. "I understand it was a rough night," Rebecca said.

"It was awful," Mordiree replied and hugged her mother.

"It's just a life lesson, baby. There will be many more."

"How is my grandson?" Snow Anna asked.

"Brock and Akibeel are helping him get showered, but he's much better today," Mordiree replied.

"I brought some ointment to rub on his legs and feet. It will heal the bruises."

"Thank you, Aunt Snow."

Jodi laughed. "Don't thank her yet. It stinks like hell."

"But it works," Snow replied.

"Yes, it does," Rebecca agreed.

§

Chapter 33

Brock had mixed emotions. He was torn between two of his children. Both of whom needed him. He promised Aurellia a fish fry at Jodi's house; but he didn't want to leave Adam.

Deuce had given Adam a complete examination. It was determined that he did have a heatstroke. And some internal damage but, nothing that would last; thank God.

Doc came up with the perfect solution. They were in Adam's room now, to get his take on it.

§

"What do you say, Adam?" Doc asked.

Adam turned his nose up. "Get away from me, man! I ain't drinking yours or no damn body else's blood. You can forget that!"

Mordiree was trying to keep from laughing. She thanked God, every day, that Adam didn't have a demon residing in him. She knew she'd never be able to tolerate that shit.

Her sister, and cousins, told her how erotic it was; for their husbands to take their blood. Please! Ain't that much eroticism in the world. How you gon' let somebody puncture your flesh; and then say it don't hurt? She had enough body piercings to know they *all* hurt!

Eventually she and Adam would get around to making love. She wished he would try to bite her; she'd kick his ass! She wasn't about to play that shit!

§

Nosey Brock heard her thoughts and squealed. "That's just wrong!"

They all thought he was laughing at Adam.

§

"Laugh all you want but, I ain't doing it, and that's that. I ain't ever going to be that thirsty, okay?"

Doc looked at Brock. "I tried, Pops."

"If you don't, it'll take a minute before you can start training again, son."

"Oh well," Adam replied. "I got a minute."

Brock and Doc laughed. "Alright, son. Listen, I'm going to be out for a few hours. If you need me call, okay?"

"I'm good, Dad."

§

When they left the room, Mordiree looked at Adam and cracked up. "I guess you told them, huh?"

"They meant well. But listen, I heard your thoughts. You don't have that to worry about. I wasn't born with a demon; so I won't need to take your blood."

"Yeah well, Maria told me that Akibeel didn't *need* to take hers, but he *did*. And still does."

"What? Why?"

"She said, he said, it was as natural for him, as breathing."

[316]

"I don't get it."

"I don't either. But, I'm telling you now; you'd better put your fangs up!"

They both laughed, but Adam was concerned. He needed to talk with his brother.

§

Henry, Sam and Matthew knocked on the door. "Can we come in?" Henry asked.

"Yeah, man. C'mon in," Adam replied.

It was good to see his boys. Henry had stayed most of the night, but he slept through the visit. "What's up, Dawg!"

"You look better," Henry said and extended his fist.

Adam extended his, but when Henry saw how bruised his hand was, he jerked his back. "Man, your hand looks awful."

"I know. They say it came from the intense, and prolonged, cramping."

"Damn," Sam replied. "They look like you hit a brick wall or some shit."

"Do they hurt?" Matthew asked.

"My dad took the pain. But they are still sore, to the touch."

"That's messed up," Matthew stated. "Sorry I wasn't there for you."

"No prob." He was good with Mordiree and Henry being there for him. Mordiree hadn't left his side once.

[317]

"So how long are you going to be down?" Matthew asked.

"Deuce said I had some damage to my kidneys; so it'll be a minute."

Mordiree laughed. "Tell them about Doc's offer."

§

Adam told them, and they all laughed. They thought the blood thing was freakish too, but Adam was a Watcher. That made it all the more funny.

"Man, you've got to be the only squeamish Watcher, in the world," Henry told him.

"Whatever. Say what you want, but I was not about to be sucking on Doc's wrist. Or no other part of his body, for that matter."

His boys squeezed their eyes shut, and screamed. Adam was a laugh a minute. Even in pain, he could still make them laugh.

"You better be glad he didn't try it last night, while you were in pain," Matthew teased him.

"I still would have rejected it. I'm telling you, there ain't enough pain in the world for me to do that shit."

§

Mordiree stood up and kissed his cheek. "I'm going to see if Chef will fix us something to eat. I'll be back in a few."

"See if he'll fix enough for us too," Sam asked.

"Okay," she replied, and left the room.

§

Once she was gone, Matthew asked, "Okay, how bad was it, man?"

Adam got real. "I wanted to die. Look at my hands and legs. I look like I was in a fight…and lost. Truthfully, I was in a fight. My muscles were pissed and kicked my ass. I said I hadn't drank anything, or eaten, in twenty four hours. But that wasn't the truth, man."

Henry scowled. "It wasn't?"

"It was longer than that. I hadn't had anything from the time I morphed into this body," he confessed.

"You didn't eat, or drink, anything at your party?"

Adam shook his head. "I didn't think about it. Mom and Dad went off, remember? Then there was the battle, with the demons. Then I had to deal with Baraq birddogging me. Then I was worried about Mordiree. I had too much on my plate." He frowned. "How does a grown man forget that he needs sustenance?"

"Seems like your stomach would have growled," Matthew stated.

"It probably did. But, since I'd never been hungry I didn't know what it was. Mom fed me at the same time every day. Dad was right; I didn't have to worry about anything, because they took care of me."

He actually looked sad. "Do you guys think I made a mistake?"

"Hell Nah," Henry replied. "Listen, we got your

back, from now on. I know you won't feel comfortable asking the team anything…"

"Damn straight," Adam replied. "They'll start treating me like a kid again."

"But we won't," Sam stated.

"Open a link between the four of us, Adam," Matthew requested. "That way we can talk in private without those other birds knowing."

"Okay."

"And we've already told James that when he starts your training; the three of us will train with you."

"The four of us."

They looked up and saw Akibeel standing at the door. "Am I intruding?"

"C'mon on in. I need to talk with you anyway," Adam replied.

§

Akibeel sat in the chair next to the bed. "What's up?"

"Where did Dad go?"

"He and his team are spending the evening with Aurellia. They are having a fish fry at Jodi's house."

"That's good. She needs that. But listen, what's up with you taking Maria's blood."

"It is erotic as all get out, man." Akibeel smiled. "I spent my entire life thinking I was doomed to Necrophilia. I couldn't make a booty call, *unless* it was with a cold dead nasty body. Then I couldn't make a booty call, *because* it was cold and dead. That really sucked! But, Maria is nice, warm, soft and sweet tasting. I can't get enough of it, man."

Adam shook his head. When he got through clowning Akibeel; his posse was on the floor. Adam was funny as hell. Tonight, they were the ones experiencing cramps. Their stomach muscles were balled in knots. They were so loud; Adam reached out and closed the door.

§

Adam was like, "How ya'll gon' get offended by somebody calling y'all Dracula; when you act like his ass?"

Henry's crystal blue eyes were swimming. He'd never seen or heard anybody as quick witted as Adam. He groaned, because his stomach muscles were really paining him. "Oh God, please stop!"

Akibeel laughed. "Just wait, lil' brother, you'll see."

"Maybe you needed it because you had a demon. I *never* had one. Therefore, there is no reason on earth for me to be sucking on my woman's bloody neck."

God he hoped that was the truth. If it wasn't, he and Mordiree were in trouble. Not only did he not want to do it. She wasn't about to *let* him do it. They'd be the only celibate couple at the estate. But then again, holding hands was nice.

Akibeel cracked up. "We'll see. Besides, it ain't her neck you'll be sucking."

§

Chapter 34

Chef had fixed dinner early, at the estate, so that he could be at Jodi's house, for the fish fry. He'd been looking forward to this, as much as the team had.

He was surprised that all of their 'spirit' mates understood. Maybe they needed a break, too.

He knew for a fact Lorraine did. They spent every waking hour together. She'd been timid when they first met. She had since come out of her shell. Her confidence was through the chart.

When he told her what they were going to do, she said take the entire day. Evidently, all of the other 'spirit' mates had had the same sentiment.

Or maybe they finally saw the same, overwhelmed, look in Aurellia's eyes that the Watchers saw.

§

Aurellia was in seventh heaven. For a little while, at least, she'd have her daddy to herself.

Ram had the pleasure of teleporting her to Jodi's house. She almost didn't want to let go. It had been four years since he'd done that. She laughed. "Do it again, Ram."

"Do what?"

"Teleport me back to the estate, and then back here."

He did, because it made her happy. "You are still a *trip*, Baby Girl."

She kissed his cheek. "Thank you, Ram."

§

Arak, Chaz, Ali and Dan were downstairs, playing bid whist. Batman and Ram were watching a movie on the tube.

They hadn't realized how much they'd also missed their small circle. This serene and familiar quiet was a welcomed old friend.

Prior to Anakim's attack, they'd *all* been bored. They'd gone *decades* without flexing their muscles. They'd spent night after night in an eventless park. No action, no 'spirit' mate; just them and Baby Girl.

Then Brock found Jodi; and the unending battles started. With each new discovery of another 'spirit' mate, a new battle line was drawn. They'd had to fight demon and human, alike. Since then, it was a weekly, and in some cases, a daily occurrence. They could honestly say they *missed* the quiet.

They loved their 'spirit' mates and children. But, this gathering was as therapeutic for them, as it was for Aurellia. For a brief moment in time, it got their minds off the endless battles.

§

Brock and Aurellia were upstairs, lying across the bed, talking. They hadn't had a father and daughter moment since the day he split himself. That was four years ago. He missed it as much as she did.

[324]

§

After her birth parents died, she became his shadow. She was afraid he'd die and leave her, too. He had to come off the battlefield and work on her emotional state of being. Back then she'd climb in his bed, just to talk. They had no secrets. She'd ask him personal things that she'd never asked in front of the team.

'Who will take care of me if you die?'

'I can't die, Baby Girl.'

'When you find your 'spirit' mate, will I still be your baby girl?'

'No matter what; you are stuck with me, Aurellia.'

'When you have your own children, will you still love me, Uncle Brock?'

'You are my own child. And they will be your sisters and brothers. And I will always love you.'

'What if your 'spirit' mate doesn't like me?'

'If she's my 'spirit' mate, she'll love you.'

'What if your kids don't like me?'

'You mean your sisters and brothers? Of course they will like you.'

'When you have your own children, will I still be your daughter?'

"Smh! You will always be my daughter, Aurellia. Why are you worried about that?'

'I'm afraid of being orphaned, again. Where would I go? Who will take care of me?'

'You're being silly. I could never love anyone more than I love you.'

'But what if they are mean to me?'

'I would never let anyone mistreat you. Don't you know that?'

'Promise?'

'I promise.'

'But, what if they are mean when you are not around?'

'I'll always be around, Aurellia.'

§

She'd been so insecure about the future. Her future. Their future. Didn't she *know*…?

§

Brock looked at her, and smiled. "I heard your thoughts, at the party, Baby Girl."

"I'm sorry, Daddy."

"For what?"

"I know that you spent your life looking for momma; and I'm glad she's in our lives. I love my sisters and brothers, too. I just get overwhelmed sometimes. You never have time for me, anymore."

Brock sat up, and squealed. "Oh *please!* You decided you were *grown*, remember?"

"I am grown. But, being grown doesn't mean I was ready to give this up." She fanned her hand across the bed. She was lying on her stomach, propped up on her elbows;

with her legs hanging over the edge.

"Why didn't you say anything?"

"Everyone seems to require all of your time. I didn't want to be in the way."

He frowned. She'd gone from being an only child to having five siblings in four years. Not to mention all of the extended family. No wonder she was overwhelmed.

She kept talking. "Even though they've moved into their own homes; they still hang around."

"But…"

"Not to mention all the fighting, Daddy. It was never like that before."

Good; she was talking. That always helped. He leaned back against the headboard and folded his arms across his chest. And listened.

"I love James. I love our entire family, but…" She paused and looked at him. "It was easier back then. I didn't have to worry about anything. But now, sometimes I'm so fearful, I can't sleep at night. And when I do, it's riddled with nightmares. James has to wake me up, some nights, because I'm screaming in my sleep." She took a deep breath, and her eyes watered. "He said I have a bleeding ulcer."

"What?"

"I'm afraid *all* the time, Daddy."

Brock frowned. How could that be? How could he not know that? He hadn't snooped on her since she'd gotten married. He hadn't wanted to accidently get a visual of her and Deuce's intimacy. God he'd die if he ever saw that shit! He'd straight up kill his own damn self! Right after he killed Deuce.

But all of this time, his daughter had been emotionally, and physically, suffering. It was no wonder she had a breakdown.

§

He opened his arms, and she crawled up in his lap. He wrapped his arms around her, and kissed the top of her head. "You know that I will *never* let anything happen to you, don't you?"

"I *used to* know that. But your attention is divided these days. You have small children that need you. I am a grown woman, with a husband."

"You are *still* my daughter. You are my first and last thought every day, Aurellia. No matter how big our family gets, you're my number one concern. Didn't I put Addison in check for making you feel uncomfortable?"

She laughed. "Yes."

"I wanted Akibeel to live with us. But I asked you how you felt about that, remember?"

"Yes."

"If you had said no; he would not be here today, baby. I'll never put *your* security and peace of mind at risk. You should have told me you were struggling."

"Do you ever *regret* keeping me?"

"Why would you *think* that? Don't you know how much I love you?"

"Face it. I'm your only human child. I'm a burden more than anything else."

"You think you're a burden?"

"Sometimes."

"Your mother told you about the argument she and I had, right?"

"Yeah."

"What all did she tell you?"

"That you accused her of not really being my mother." She looked up at him. "That was wrong of you."

"Yeah, yeah." He smiled. "Is that all she told you?"

"Yes."

Brock opened up his mind and let her hear some of the argument. *'Baby Girl was and always will be my number one concern. I wasn't about to subject her to a bunch of strangers; without checking them out, first. When it comes to my oldest daughter, that's how I roll. Get mad all you want; I am six degrees separated from giving a good damn!'*

He kissed the top of her head and hugged her tighter. "Like I said; you're my first and last thought. Everything I do...I do for *you*. You have *never* been a burden to me. It has been my *pleasure* to be your father."

He kissed the top of her head, again. Only this time he let his lips linger there. *"I don't make a move without considering your best interest. Other than my mother, and my sister, you were the first person who ever loved me."*

Aurellia laid her head on his chest, and wrapped her arm around his waist. *"I still love you, Daddy."*

He felt it when her spirit eased; and her body relaxed. *"Back at cha, Baby Girl."*

§

They'd fallen asleep by the Chef came to let them know dinner was ready. It was a beautiful sight. He decided not to interrupt them.

Aurellia needed this, more than she needed food. They'd all been remiss in seeing after their girl. He made a mental note to store this information; so he'd never do it to his own two daughters.

He threw a blanket across them; and eased the door closed. Dinner could wait.

§

"Are they coming down, or what?" Chaz asked.

Chef put his finger up to his lips and gave them all a visual. *"Keep your voice down."*

"WOW!" Ali whispered. They looked like the old days. Peaceful.

Ram smiled. This really was like the old days. He and his team busy on one end of the estate; Brock and Baby Girl, on another. But, they always came together to eat breakfast, lunch and dinner.

He laughed out loud. "Ya'll remember the first time

Brock washed and tried to comb her hair?"

Ali squeaked. "He had that poor little girl looking like a plucked chicken."

"She was screaming and running, *'you hurtin' me! I want my mommy!'* It was sad," Batman replied.

"He kept trying though, didn't he?" Chaz laughed.

"He still couldn't get it *right,*" Ram reminded them. "And he kept hurting her."

"Then he sent for Donnell." Arak smiled.

"Who would've guessed that boy was braiding his own hair."

"Brock didn't guess; he snooped," Ram replied. "Donnell was still leery of Brock, at the time. He thought he was being setup."

"You would've thought that, too. None of the field guards had ever been invited to the estate. They didn't know about the Brocks. They certainly didn't know about Baby Girl," Dan reminded them.

"Plus, Brock was bald, so whose hair was he going to comb?" Ali asked.

"When Donnell saw Baby Girl, he was like, *'Oh my goodness. What happened to her?'* Then he sat down and combed her hair. She didn't cry one time," Arak said.

"I can still hear her, *'thank you for not hurting me, and making me look pretty',*" Ram reminded them. "Then she hugged and kissed his cheek."

"He fell in love with her that day. And she with

him," Arak added.

Ram looked toward the stairs and smiled. "It was so easy to love that child. She was spoiled and a brat; but she was our spoiled brat."

"She still is," Chef added.

They all smiled.

§

"Anywho, I'm hungry," Chaz said and walked into the kitchen.

"You'll have to wait. This dinner is for Baby Girl, Dawg," Arak replied.

"Besides, you aren't starving. You're just greedy." Dan laughed.

"I haven't eaten all day, waiting on this fish fry. I'm hungry," Chaz replied.

"Sit cha butt down, and deal the cards," Ali ordered.

§

Aurellia woke up and stretched. She hadn't felt this relaxed in a long time. The comfort of her father's arms was just what she needed. She looked up and smiled. "Hi, Daddy."

§

Brock smiled. He'd been awake for a while, but hadn't moved an inch. He just sat there with his baby girl in his lap, and watched her sleep. He'd eased into her dream to be sure it wasn't nightmarish. It wasn't.

She'd gone from being an only child to having two

sisters and three brothers. All of them more powerful than she would ever be. He understood why she might feel like she was a burden. But, please…

He hadn't just spouted words. She had always been *his* Baby Girl. He'd held her ten minutes after she was born. When he'd looked in her face, she gazed back at him; and smiled. At *that* moment, she imprisoned his heart.

Prior to her birth, many Brock babies had been born, lived and died. But, none had captured his heart like Aurellia had.

Back in the day he'd acted just like Batman did with Joy. If you saw him, you saw her in his arms.

Her natural father was a good man, but not hands on. As much as the man loved his family; he loved the bottle more. When he wasn't asleep, he was drinking. He drowned himself in his self-inflected sorrow.

He was the last of the Brock line and didn't have a son to keep the line going. He always said, *'I'm the last train to pull out of the station! No more Brocks!!'* The fact that he wore the Brock 'name' was not legitimate enough for her father. It had to be true blood to count.

The man really believed teleportation was the cause of his failure to reproduce. But Brock knew better. It was the *alcohol* that had affected his fertility. It was impotence *not* infertility.

He was grateful Aurellia was conceived before her

father started his downward spiral. He was even more grateful she hadn't been on that airplane. That would have destroyed him, for sure. He couldn't imagine his life without her. Sure he had Elizabeth, Hannah, Adam, Yomiel and Akibeel; but one child couldn't replace another.

He loved all of his children, but Baby Girl *needed* him more.

§

He laid there and listened to his team reminisce about Donnell combing her hair. It was true he didn't have a clue about a little girl's hair. But, he learned. She was *his* daughter and his responsibility. It took him about a month to get the hang of it. Before it was all over, he was better at it than Donnell.

§

He ruffled her hair. "Hey, Baby. You feel better?"

"Yeah, but I'm hungry now."

"That's good, because the guys are starving, waiting on you." He laughed. "Chaz is pouting."

§

The minute they made it downstairs, the team jumped up, and moved towards the kitchen.

"It's about time," Chaz complained.

Brock smoothly pushed them back to their seats. "No one gets their plate before Aurellia."

"I was going to fix her plate, for her," Ram lied.

[334]

"I was going to get her tea. Don't you want some tea, brat?" Chaz sheepishly smiled.

Aurellia laughed, and sat at the table. This was the best day she'd had in a long time. "Okay, you guys can wait on me, and Daddy."

They did just that. Her wish was their command. And it felt *right*. Her smile was no longer forced. Her shoulders no longer tense. She was relaxed and at ease.

She and Ram made plans for their next get together. It would be just the two of them. Chef said he wanted a night at the show with her.

Brock promised his room door was always open. "You should have known that."

"She knows now," Chaz responded.

§

They all prayed for a break in the attacks; for Aurellia's peace of mind.

§

Chapter 35

The minute they returned to the estate, Brock went to check on Adam. This was what parenting was about; the welfare of his children.

After he checked on Adam, he needed to check on the twins. He hadn't had any time for them, lately. Aurellia was right, it was always something. He was thankful that Jodi didn't want any more children, after this one she was carrying. He didn't think he could stretch himself any wider.

While at Jodi's house, he'd come to a decision. He was going to have Ditto and his boys turn one of the cabins into another 'wolf-den'; and the other into a theatre. He was going to have them build a school for the children. The spa would remain where it was, because it was for the 'spirit' mates.

There was going to be no more open door policy, inside the estate. The Walkers and their children had moved into their own homes, on the property.

He had provided all the security and safety they needed; and would continue to do so. But, the *estate* was his, his team, and their families', home. He couldn't continue to allow all of the foot traffic. He couldn't continue to be distracted from the needs of his wife and children. They were his first and primary concern.

§

When he reached Adam's room, Jodi, along with all of his sons and daughters, were in there. Justina was in there, too. Evidently they'd kept him company, while he and Aurellia were away.

§

Adam was in the bed because his energy was still zapped. Hans, Lizzie and Justina were in the bed with him. They were talking up a storm.

§

"I'm your nurse and you have to do what I say," Justina demanded. She was going to be as bossy as all the other women at the estate.

Adam laughed. "Yes ma'am."

"He not gon' do what you say!" Lizzie objected. "I can make him better."

"No you can't," Justina replied. "I'm his nurse."

"Yes I can. Watch this," Lizzie said and poked his hand.

"I can do that, too," Hans declared and poked his thigh. "See?"

§

One by one the adults in the room surrounded the bed. They watched as Lizzie and Hans continued to touch one place after another on Adam's bruised body. Every place they touched instantly *healed*. When they finished, Lizzie smiled. "I told cha!"

Hans giggled. "Told cha."

"Oh my goodness," Brock whispered. His daughters were even more powerful than he imagined. "How do you feel, Adam?"

Adam rubbed his once bruised hands. "They aren't tender anymore." He was just as freaked out as everyone else in the room. He rubbed his thighs. "It doesn't hurt to touch them."

Jodi looked at her daughters. "This is amazing. How long have you been able to do this, Lizzie?"

"I don't know. I just wanted Adam to feel better."

Adam sighed. "I do feel better, Squirt. But, I'm still a little tired."

"Oh, I forgot," Lizzie replied, and placed her hand on his stomach. "Hans, put your hand next to mine."

Hans did and everyone witnessed an energy source leave their bodies, and enter Adam's.

Doc pointed. "Look at *that!*"

Adam's stomach bunched. He started squirming and laughing. "It's feels like they are tinkling me! Stop!"

His laughter was contagious. He made everyone else laugh.

§

Brock picked his twin daughters up and kissed their cheeks. "You girls did real good. Aurellia's tummy hurts, too. You think you can help her?"

Both girls nodded.

He put them down. "She's in her room. Go help

your sister."

"Okay, Daddy," both girls replied and ran to find her.

"Hey, wait for me," Justina yelled behind them.

§

"What's wrong with Aurellia's stomach?" Doc asked.

"She has a bleeding ulcer, man," Brock replied.

"An ulcer?"

Brock nodded. "She's scared to death over all of these attacks."

Jodi sighed. "I'm glad she told you."

Brock frowned. "You *knew*, Jodi."

"I found out last night; just minutes before you called out for Deuce. He made her tell me because she wasn't getting any better. He was concerned about her."

"Why didn't you tell me?"

"Adam was hurt, Brock. So was Akibeel. They required immediate attention," she replied defensively. Brock had already accused her of not being Aurellia's mother. She didn't want him to think that Aurellia wasn't as important to her as Adam. "I made Aurellia promise me that she'd tell you today. Or I would."

Doc didn't want them to get into another argument, especially with both of their oldest children needing unity. "I could offer Aurellia some of my blood."

"Man, ain't noooo…*body* trying to drink your damn

blood, up in *here!* What the hell's wrong with you? You act like you're offering a cup of coffee or a soda!" Adam responded. "What's up with that?"

Mordiree was cracking up. "You tell 'em, baby."

"Please don't get him started." Akibeel laughed. "Otherwise, he'll never *shut* up."

Brock's lips were twitching. He hadn't told Jodi about Adam and Mordiree's aversion to blood foreplay. If they thought his taking Jodi's blood was bad; what would they think about her taking his?

He laughed out loud. "Let's see if Hans and Lizzie are able to help her first."

"Alright," Doc replied. He looked at Adam and laughed. "You are a new breed of Watcher; that's for damn sure."

"That's right, Dracula!" Adam replied.

"Hey boy!" Brock frowned. "That's derogatory and offensive."

"Why? Y'all do drink blood, like Dracula."

"First of all, there is no such person as Dracula, Adam!"

"Then why is it offensive?"

"It's right up there with racial slurs. We didn't choose to be born cursed. We didn't choose to have a demon in us. We *needed* our 'spirit' mate's blood to redeem us, son. It's only because of your mother's generosity to me, that you could be born, in the first place.

[340]

And not just born, but born *without* the curse. You can walk in sunlight, because I took your mother's blood. Don't you understand that, son?"

Adam realized he'd just hurt his father's feelings. He'd never do that intentionally. Before he could apologize Brock started scolding him, again.

"Let that be the last time that offensive word crosses your lips; you understand me?"

"I'm sorry, Dad. I *am* grateful for you and Mom. But, I'm *really* grateful I don't have to drink blood. If I did, I'd puke."

Doc laughed. "Don't knock it until you try it."

"Then I'll never knock it again. Because I damn sure ain't gon' try it."

Akibeel squeaked. "That boy is as retarded as I am."

"Not quite." Adam laughed.

Brock couldn't help but laugh at his son. He looked at Jodi and showed his pearly whites. "He's *your* son, Dimples."

Jodi cracked up. Adam was a handful. But when Brock first told her about the blood exchange, she'd had a similar reaction. "Remember what I wanted you to do, when you first told me?"

"What?" Doc asked.

Brock laughed. "My woman was like *'can't you just go to the blood bank'*.

Doc squealed. "No she didn't!"

"Yes she did, man."

"I was serious. I'd only *seen* Brock at night. So, when he told me about the blood, visions of 'Bela Lugosi' swarmed in my head. I freaked out."

Everybody laughed.

"At that point, Brock hadn't told me that he could read my mind. He knew what I was thinking and deliberately drank his coffee; so I could see he wasn't the *undead*."

Doc squealed. "The undead!"

"Man, my woman was tripping. That is after she got past lusting after my body."

Jodi hit him. "BROCK!"

"Am I lying?"

"Shut up!"

"Nestlé's makes the…"

She put her hand over his mouth.

§

Mordiree and Adam were intrigued. Neither of them knew Jodi had had reservations about it. What had Brock done, or *said*, to convince her? Certainly he hadn't forced the issue, had he? Was the desire, or need, overpowering and he couldn't stop himself? Had it been a sort of a *rape* of her blood?

"How did he get you to accept it, Jodi?" Mordiree asked.

"No one had ever loved me more, Mordiree." She looked at Brock and smiled. "He gave me back my self-confidence. He made me feel like I deserved to be loved. I would've done *anything* for him. Still will."

It was like Jodi could read Mordiree's mind. She kept talking. "He didn't force me. I offered. In the beginning it wasn't about sexual pleasure; at least not for me. It was about being all Brock needed me to be. I would have sacrificed anything to ease his pain; because I loved him. Four years later, I have no regrets. I love him more today, than I did back then. I'd do it all over again."

Brock smiled and kissed her cheek. "I love you too, Dimples. I always have."

"Aw, how sweet," Akibeel voiced. "My Santa Maria loves me too."

"I sure do, baby," Maria said, as she walked into the room with Kwanita. "I missed you, too."

Doc pulled Kwanita into his embrace. "Hey, Brighteyes."

"What's this, a family meeting?"

Brock looked around the room and smiled. "Yeah."

§

He told them about his plans for the wolf-den. They all, adamantly, objected.

"We like the den right where it is."

"Listen. We've gotta stop allowing this house to be a revolving door. Aurellia needs stability and so do the twins. People running in and out, makes this place seem like a hotel."

"Brock is right," Jodi agreed. "It's time for everyone to *live* in their own homes. They can visit, but we've got stop letting this be Grand Central Station."

"But what about the ICU," Kwanita asked. "We still have Dawn and Charity expecting their babies; real soon, I might add. They need to be close to Deuce."

"Charity doesn't live in this house now, Kwanita. What would be the difference?" Maria asked.

"That's true."

"I don't want to be the one to make the final decision. I'll put it out there and let everyone voice their opinions," Brock decided. "In addition, we've got to come up with a plan to keep the demons out of the preserve. I'm worried about Aurellia. She doesn't feel safe anymore."

"She's been struggling for months, Pops," Maria volunteered.

They all looked at her. "Months?" Jodi asked.

"Really, ever since Akibeel and his brothers broke in," Maria replied.

"Thanks for bringing that up, Maria." Akibeel looked guilty.

"No, baby. She knows it wasn't your fault. I'm just saying that's how long she's been struggling."

"She's afraid that the demons will eventually get her little sisters, too," Mordiree added.

Jodi was concerned. "What can we do to help her, Brock?"

"The first thing is make this house a home; and not a hotel. Secondly, we gotta work on the preserve."

"Aurellia needs normality," Adam told them. "Dad is right. She needs to feel like this place is her home, again."

"Let's discuss it in the morning," Brock suggested. "I need to check on her and the girls."

The truth was; he knew his boys wanted him *out* of the room. He knew why, too. And he wanted out! He never felt comfortable discussing that crap.

He and Jodi left, holding hands.

§

Doc, Kwanita, Akibeel and Maria stayed. They wanted to spend some time with Adam and Mordiree. All three of them liked that they were *legally* brothers now.

Plus, with Brock and Jodi gone, they were going to school this boy on the art of making love. And the sexual pleasures of the blood exchange.

§

"Okay now that the prude is gone, let's talk," Doc said.

Akibeel laughed. "Pops was most definitely uncomfortable."

They all laughed.

§

[345]

Deuce and Aurellia walked in the room. "What's so funny?" Deuce asked.

"Dad." Adam laughed.

§

Brock and Jodi were in their room with the twins and Justina. But he was snooping. He looked at Jodi and laughed. "Our children are getting ready to have a…" He spelled it out because of the twins and Justina. "…s.e.x. education class."

"That's why you sent Aurellia in there?"

"Yeah. Hopefully her presence will force Doc to be less graphic. That boy has a colorful mouth when it comes to s.e.x. Plus, those boys are her siblings. She needs to get as comfortable with them, as she is with my team. They can do for her, what I can't."

"What's that?"

"Make her *feel* like she's a part of this ever growing family."

"She doesn't feel like that now?"

"She thinks she's a burden, because she's human."

"A *burden?*"

"She asked me if I had any regrets about keeping her, after her birth parents died."

"Is she serious? Doesn't she know we couldn't imagine life without her?"

"Her brothers will help her to see that," he replied. "Parenting is hard, isn't it?"

"Momma used to say, when they're small they lay on your lap. When they're grown, they lay on your heart."

"Ain't that the truth? Except that, *we* have two grown and two small children. Plus, *I* have Doc and Akibeel. Our laps *and* hearts are both full," he replied, just as Hans, Lizzie and Justina crawled up in his lap.

"But, I'd have it no other way," Jodi replied.

"You're finally accepting Adam as a man?"

"I was afraid he wouldn't need me anymore. But, Aurellia still needs us, doesn't she?"

"No matter how old they are, they'll always need us, Jodi. We will always be their solid ground."

She displayed her dimples. "I'm good with that."

§

Chapter 36

Brock and the men were having a breakfast meeting in the conference room. Even Chef was included in this meeting. After all, this was his home, too.

§

As usual, the Watchers, and Walkers, were sitting at the table. The nephews were sitting on the barstools around the walls.

§

They didn't need the air conditioner this morning. Thanks to his and Doc's teams, the atmosphere was quite chilly. You'd have to be self-absorbed to not realize something was off.

Brock smiled. "I wanted to have this meeting to toss something out at you guys."

No one asked what or said anything.

He looked around the table. "The entire family is here. There are no more 'spirit' mates, to be found. There are no more family members that need to be brought home."

Everyone nodded.

"It's time for things to level out."

"How?" Elijah asked.

"My children, especially Aurellia, need stability. The estate is no longer going to be a revolving door. It's our home."

James looked at Deuce. "What's going on with Aurellia?"

Deuce told them how stressed she'd been. He also told them about her bleeding ulcer. "Brock is right. My wife needs to feel like she's at home, and not at a hotel."

"Why didn't you say anything?" Elijah asked.

"It wasn't your business," Deuce replied. "Even if she is my wife, and your niece; I'm still bound by patient confidentiality."

Elijah frowned. All he heard was *'it wasn't your business'*.

"I made *her* tell her parents, because I was worried about her," Deuce continued.

"Does that mean I can't live here?" Addison asked. He actually looked sad.

Brock shook his head. "This is your home, too, son. Tim and Paul are also welcome to continue to stay; that is until they get married."

Tim and Paul smiled.

"I'm getting married," Addison replied.

"And you and Isabella will still live inside the estate," Brock reiterated.

"Cool." Addison smiled.

Justin smiled, too. He wasn't jealous of his son's affection for Brock. He was grateful, because his son had grown up under Brock's tutelage. He knew he'd never let him be a man.

§

"So are you saying we can't utilize the wolf-den anymore?" Eugene asked.

"No," Brock replied. He saw the look of despair on all of their faces. "However, I'd like for you guys to turn one of the cottages into a second den. That one will be a community den."

Their eyes lit up. "That's a great idea," H voiced. "That way we don't have to worry about having to leave, until we're ready."

"And..." Ditto added, "...it'll be larger. We can add more pool tables."

Adam offered his fist. "For sure." He liked the game as much as Ram.

"And since it will be a community den, our wives will be welcome," Aden added.

Everyone nodded.

"We can do that today," Sam agreed.

§

Brock couldn't believe they all understood where he was coming from. They seemed to be more excited about it, than he was. "This was easier than I thought."

"Man, we understand," Floyd replied. "This is *your* home. We have intruded long enough."

"You're not an intrusion, Floyd," Brock responded. "But, I have to think about my children's wellbeing. I'd also like to commission Ditto, and his boys, to build a school, an office building and a church."

"We should have them build a clinic, too," Smittie suggested.

"And a library," James added.

"A day care, too," Adrian input.

"What about a spa?" Addison asked.

"Nope," Brock replied. "We'll keep the spa where it is. That'll be our room to get together as a family; for things like baby showers and birthday parties."

"Instead of using one of the cottages; why don't we use the basements to *our* houses? They are all communal anyway," Nantan suggested.

"That's true. It's a mini city down there. We already go from house to house through our basements," Clyde agreed.

"We can put the school, the clinic and library down there," Howard suggested.

Henry smiled. "We can have an indoor basketball court."

Matthew offered his fist. "With bleachers, too."

§

Brock sat back and listened to them make plans about *their* sub-division. "I'm good with anything. That is provided it doesn't spill over into the tunnels that lead to the estate's basement. That passageway has to remain open, and unobscured."

"Don't worry, Unc. We won't block our escape

route," Henry assured him.

§

"Okay, now that that's settled. My brothers and I would like to speak with Brock," H informed his nephews and grandsons.

Brock squinted. He started to read H's mind, but decided against it. He hadn't read the man's mind since that life altering day.

§

When all the nephews left, H looked at Brock. "Would you put the cone of silence up, please?"

"What's going on?" Brock asked.

"Please."

Brock honored his request. Then he asked, "What's going on?"

"My brothers and I wanted to apologize to our sons."

Brock frowned. He knew damn well H hadn't told his brothers what happened. He looked under eyed at H. "For *what?*"

Hezekiah held his ground. "Listen. Everyone knows something's up. Everyone feels the strain. And, by the way my brothers' sons-in-laws are treating them, it's obvious that you've *told* them. It's only fair that my brothers know why their sons are giving them the cold shoulder."

"What is he talking about?" James asked Ali.

Ali shook his head. He was going to take his lead from Brock. But, he thought all along that they should know. Both teams thought they should.

Sal looked at Baraq. "What's going on, Pup?"

Baraq didn't answer, either. He just looked at Brock.

§

Brock wanted to kill Hezekiah. They were having a staring contest. Neither said a word and neither looked away. The room went '*eerily*' quiet.

Brock never diverted his gaze. *"Shut down your links,"* he commanded all of the Watchers. Then he closed off the links between the Walkers and their wives.

§

"Alright, if you insist; have it your way. I hope you explained the consequences if their wives, and children find out."

"They know how Snow is treating me. I told them their wives all felt the same way."

"And their sons and daughters?"

"They know how bad it was. They know what the loss will be, if they ever say anything."

"Very well. Let's have an open discussion." He looked at his men. "A respectful discussion."

§

Akibeel was the first to speak. "I'm glad you know. Now I can tell you how I *really* feel!"

Brock growled, "Respectful, Akibeel."

Akibeel ignored him. His already dead eyes turned dark with resentment. "You ungrateful bastards! You stood there, and let Lightwings attack my brother and my Pops?"

"What?" Justin asked. "Lightwings did *what?*"

Sal's *jaws* jumped. He looked at Floyd. "When in the hell was this?"

Akibeel answered. "After our fight in the preserve. He knew my Pops didn't have his powers. And he viciously attacked him!" Akibeel replied. "And y'all *encouraged* him!"

"I would *never,* stand by and, let that happen," James responded. "No way in hell, I would have encouraged that, either."

"You didn't. You, Justin and Sal tried to help him. Even the nephews tried to help. They stopped him. But, these Walker bastards just stood there," Ali replied.

§

That's all it took and, one by one, all of the Watchers went off. They lit into the Walkers like nobody's business.

"Baby Girl had a nervous breakdown," Ram said angrily, and hit the table.

"Aurellia?" James questioned. "My daughter-in-law?" He looked heartbroken.

"She lost her mind! You understand!" Ram hit the

table again and again. "She! Lost! Her! Mind!"

"Snow Anna had to jump time to save our girl," Chaz informed them.

"I can forgive anything but that," Batman added.

"Michael tried to justify your behavior, but I ain't buying it," Baraq informed them.

Ali frowned. "I've tried to come up with a plausible explanation…"

Arak glared at Smittie. "There *ain't* one!"

§

The Walkers did not try to defend themselves. They just let everyone have their say. But, they were heartbroken and disappointed in themselves.

§

When H first told them, they refused to believe it. It was hard to believe Lightwings would do such a thing. It was even harder to believe they'd encouraged him.

There was no way they wanted their sons and daughters to remember that event. If they ever remembered, they'd all lose their children's respect.

They were grateful that even though the Watchers were mad at them; they were *still* protecting them. That made them feel even worse.

§

When the Watchers ran out of rant, Elijah said, "I am the most ungrateful. I'm sorry for my lack of action, Brock. I can't imagine why I would've done that. You've never owed any of us anything. Not the security you provide, and certainly not the friendship you've offered."

§

Smittie looked from one son-in-law to the next. Arak, Sal and Akibeel angrily stared back at him. "I can't handle losing any of you boys' respect. What can I do?"

Neither responded.

§

Each one of the Walkers offered their remorseful apologies. They all fell on deaf ears. H nodded. "It's apparent it will take some time. I'm okay with that, because at the end of the day you boys know we love you. We made a mistake."

He stood up to leave. Brock stood and extended his hand. "We'll talk later, H."

H shook his hand, nodded and walked out. His shoulders were stooped and his steps weighted down. Just like they'd been when they all first met him. His brothers stood up and silently followed him. Brock's heart went out to them; because he loved those men.

§

When Floyd reached the door, he turned back around. With sorrow in his eyes, he said, "Then Peter asked; how many times must I *forgive* my brother, who has *sinned* against me." He turned and walked out the door.

§

Brock responded to the closed door, "Seventy times

seven."

§

Chapter 37

Brock stayed in the conference room. He had one more meeting scheduled. This one was with the Ultimate Watchers.

Floyd's words, although softly spoken, had teeth. They weren't self-serving; but were spoken with heart and conviction. They were not only mindful; but a *reminder*.

Hadn't he challenged Symphony regarding her forgiving spirit? He'd been right to challenge her; but what about him? Wasn't he charged to live by the same 'fruit of the spirit'? In particular...longsuffering?

Floyd and Howard had almost come to blows, over Howard's attempted attack on Mark. They'd said some terrible words to each other. Lucinda had said despicable words to Candice; hadn't she? Yet, none of them had let the sun go down on their wrath. They hadn't even let an hour go by without reconciliation.

Henry had spewed awful condemnations at Symphony. It had been too much for even him to hear. Yet, in less than an hour they were hugging each other.

He needed to examine his *own* self. His *own* heart. Could he afford to let the spirit of *hurt* reside within him? Spirits fester and grow, when you don't deal with them.

It was time to put an end to this nonsense. He needed to lead, by example.

He quietly sent a shout out to Symphony.

[358]

§

Lucifer sat on his throne and growled. He needed them to stay at each other's throats. If Seraphiel forgave the Walkers too soon, it would ruin his plan. "I thought you had this under control, Division!"

"I thought so too, my lord."

§

Brock stood and smiled, as the Ultimate Watchers started to teleport in. "Hey guys."

They all embraced his forearm. "Good to see you, Seraphiel."

Lightwings was apprehensive about extending his; and for good reason. Brock extended his own arm; as an olive branch. Lightwings gratefully accepted.

Brock spoke to his mind. *"We'll talk later."*

Lightwings nodded.

§

Brock introduced Doc and Lightwings to the Ultimates who hadn't yet met them. "This is my son, Yomiel. He is my co-Ultimate Watcher. And this is Spirit Warrior. He is co-Ultimate Watcher with his father, Kobabiel, in Ohio."

"I remember the day you were born, Hania," one of the Watchers said. "I told your father, back then, that you were *destined* for greatness."

Lightwings smiled. "I don't know about greatness."

§

When they finished with the meet and greet, Brock got down to business. "I called you guys here, because we need to discuss several things."

He glanced around the room. He thought about it long and hard. He knew what his commission was and he accepted it. But, after Aurellia and Adam's health scares, he put things in perspective. No *one* man could do it all. And he wasn't arrogant enough to try.

"As your leader, I will endeavor to always be patient. I will listen to all of your recommendations. We will work, together, as a team. And I pledge my commitment and allegiance to every one of you. I will never do any of you emotional or physical harm."

They frowned at him. "We already *know* that, Seraphiel," Satariel replied.

Brock nodded, but kept talking. "We have enemies out there that have ramped up their attacks. We are brothers, with a commission to keep God's *'so loved'* safe. We can't do that with *division* amongst us."

"What division?" another asked.

Lightwings stood up, and put his hand over his heart. "I pledge my allegiance to you, Wolf."

One by one all the Ultimates followed his lead, and reaffirmed their allegiance.

That is, everyone *except* Kobabiel.

§

Like Seraphiel, Kobabiel could read everybody's thoughts, including Seraphiel's. He was curious why Spirit Warrior felt the need to pledge an allegiance that had been unspoken for centuries. Every Watcher in this room was devoted to the man.

Back in the day, he had been brutal. He was a bully and no one liked, or respected, him. But life and times bring about a change.

He examined himself, and experienced an enlightening; an awakening, of sort. He found out that *fear* was not *respect*. He embraced the cliché *'no man is an island'*; and capitalized on it.

From then on, he changed. Instead of spouting demands, he solicited other's advice, and opinions. And more often than not, he acted on their advice. That act had engendered loyalty from all who knew him. Those who didn't know him personally sought him out. Instead of being ignored; he became the 'go to' man.

Word soon spread that his alley, and garage, teams were the happiest teams across the country. They all boasted about his fair treatment of them. Average Watchers, all over the world, wanted to be on *his* team.

Every Watcher standing at this table, wanted to be a part of his inner circle of *close* friends. So what was this pledge all about? He eased into Seraphiel's mind.

§

Kobabiel frowned, and then his eyes gradually bucked. He looked shocked, offended and royally upset. And he was. He snapped his head around, and stared, at his only son. *"WHAT HAVE YOU DONE, SPIRIT WARRIOR!!"*

Lightwings did not respond to, or look at, his father. In all of his life, his father had *never* raised his voice. For the first time in his life, he felt his father's rage *and* anger. He looked down at the floor.

§

When Kobabiel spoke again, it was with closed eyes and acute sorrow. *"I am sorry for what my son has done, Seraphiel. I am ashamed."*

Brock smiled. He knew Kobabiel was reading his, and Lightwings', memories. He welcomed it. *"Be easy, Kobabiel. All is well."*

"How can it 'ever' be?"

"You, my friend, taught me how to let bygones, be bygones. You taught me to embrace every situation, as a learning experience."

"But this?"

"Including this."

"I noticed arrogance in your son; but did not see it in my own."

"Do not judge him harshly, Kobabiel. We all make mistakes."

"I have never laid a hand on my son; but right now, I want to beat...his...ass!"

Kobabiel never *ever* used foul language. Brock inwardly laughed. *"Our children can work our nerves, can't they? I wanted to do the same thing to Adam."*

"We will discuss this later, Seraphiel."

"Indeed."

§

"Kobabiel, Adabiel, Satariel, Nate, Hasdiel, Ezeqeel and Jehoel will be my inner circle of Ultimate Watchers," Brock informed everyone. "They will be my moral compass and advisers. And in the event we have to take down a Watcher; they will fight at my side."

Nate smiled. "When did you decide *this?*"

"My oldest daughter reminded me that I can't be all things, to all people." He told them of both Aurellia and Adam's health scares. "My children need their father's presence. I am not a deity. I can't do this job alone. I'm asking you guys to partner with me, because I *need* your help. Are you willing?"

They were all gleeful, but they tried to hide it. They wanted to be his inner circle. They were all more than willing to add their input. They wanted to add value and purpose to the cause. Not to mention, they felt the humility in his voice. The Great Seraphiel was asking for *their* help.

"I'm all over it, Dawg," Nate replied.

"For sure," Satariel replied.

"You know how bored I've been. Nothing will make me happier, my friend," Hasdiel replied.

"You know I'm in," Adabiel added.

"Same here," Ezeqeel agreed.

"Count me in," Jehoel added.

"It will be an honor," Kobabiel replied. "But why us?"

"Besides the fact that you guys are the oldest; you all are the obvious choice, Kobabiel." He gazed around the table. "Wisdom, voice command, lightning, emotions…" He didn't need to go any further.

It wasn't a slight on Lightwings or Yomiel; and neither took it as such. Everyone knew what everyone else's gifts were; and he was right. They were the eight oldest. Their combined gifts were *formidable*.

§

"Michael doesn't like me. What will he think of your decision?" Nate asked.

Brock, and every one at the table, laughed. But, it was time to put an end to Nate's myth, too. "Man, why do you think Michael doesn't like you?"

"I *know* he doesn't," Nate replied. "He thinks I don't take my responsibilities seriously."

Brock smirked. "Please, stop jacking with my boy and end this, Michael."

They all heard Michael laugh. Most of them had *never* heard that sound before. *"That was true at one point, Nate. But, I was wrong. I admire the way you embrace your responsibilities. Seraphiel has chosen his inner circle wisely. In coming days you will all need to embrace Nate's sense of humor."* Then he laughed and said, *"Sayō-nara..."* good-bye.

§

Nate couldn't believe Michael had admitted he was wrong. He even laughed and acted like he had jokes. He looked at Brock, and smiled. "He was still cryptic, though. What's going on?"

Brock told them about Lucifer's plan to take Mordiree. "He even tried to release Samjaza from his chains."

"What?"

"He's upped his game." Brock went further to tell them about his future grandsons. "Lucifer will be pulling out all the stops from here on out. He wants to build a new army, with the seed of Seraphiel. *My children.*"

"Damn! That's why you need to stay close to home?" Nate stated.

"Yeah."

"We've got your back, my friend," Hasdiel told him. "I enjoyed the battle the other night."

"I did, too." Nate smiled.

"Besides, your future grandchildren are *my* future grandchildren," Satariel reminded him.

"And *mine*," Kobabiel added.

"Mine, as well," Lightwings echoed.

"Not to mention, all of my children are now living at your estate," Adabiel reminded them. "If they come for Mordiree, they won't stop with just her."

"And my brother and his wife," Zeek added.

"My baby brother, and his family, as well," Jehoel added.

Nate stopped smiling. "Don't think for a minute I hadn't considered my nephew, his wife and little Alyni. I'd kill Lucifer himself, for those three."

Everyone realized that it made perfect sense for Seraphiel to choose those birds as his inner circle. However, they assured him that they were available, at a moment's notice.

"Plus, don't forget my father is on board," Jehoel reminded Brock.

"Your father?" one of the Watchers asked.

Jehoel smiled so wide, his jaw cracked. "May I?" he asked Brock.

Brock nodded.

Jehoel told his father's story, with pride. "He helped us the night of the battle. Before he left, he gave Batariel and me a mega dose of his powers." Then he sounded like a child. "My daddy *loves* me and my brother. He always has. He'll never let any harm come to his grandchildren."

§

Chapter 38

After everyone got over the shock of Jehoel's revelation, Brock said, "Next on the agenda is rogue Watchers."

"I've got a few in my territory," Hakael informed him.

"We all do," another added.

§

The door opened. Brock and Yomiel's teams entered the conference room. He introduced everyone. "These are my other two sons, Adam and Akibeel. Both of them are on Yomiel's team."

They all stood and greeted the new comers.

§

"Dang. Samjaza had some strong genes, Seraphiel. Both of your boys look just like you," one of the watchers said.

"I look like him, too," Doc insisted. "I'm the white sheep of the family."

Everybody laughed.

"Indeed. But you are family, nonetheless, Yomiel," Adabiel replied.

§

"Ram and Akibeel are our '*Diplomatic Persuaders*'." He explained what they'd done for

Lightwings' new inner circle. "Their experience will be our first attempt at rehabilitating the rogues."

"They must be really powerful if they were able to turn those birds around," another one replied.

"You mean if they could undo the damage I did," Brock corrected him.

Everyone nodded. They all knew those boys' behavior was a direct result of his iron fist. They'd healed physically, but emotional scars are lasting. Over three thousand years later and they all still looked nineteen or twenty. They were stagnant and hadn't thought to age. Not physically and not emotionally. Lightwings had his hands full, for sure.

§

Next Brock went on to explain what his team's new responsibilities were.

Finally, he said, "If there are any in your areas that Ali and Arak think are ready; we will move them to either inner circle or Ultimate Watcher status. Based on their recommendation."

"Say what?"

"Twenty-one Ultimate Watchers are not enough. Since Lucifer has upped his game; it is only prudent that we do likewise. My plan is to have two Ultimates in every region. Plus, reduce the size of some areas; and increase the size of others. I will maintain the United States. All other countries will be broken down into *seven* zones. My

[369]

inner circle of Ultimate Watchers will each be over one of seven. They will be your first line of defense. I will get with them later on how to break the zones down."

§

The door opened again. "These are my nephews, Nantan and Henry."

Everybody spoke.

"They are in the process of setting up a website for Watchers. We will be able to trace our children for generations to come. There will be no more lost children."

"I hear ya," Adabiel said. "That is a *great* idea."

"I came to that decision with your situation in mind, Biel."

"As well as Hakael's," Nantan added.

"What situation do I have?" Hakael asked.

"You put your alter-ego in the wrong body, you jackass!" Nate replied.

"I did *what?*"

"I was going to talk with you about it later, in private, Hakael." Brock smirked at Nate. "Shut up, before I sic Michael on your ass."

Everybody, including Nate, laughed.

Brock went on to tell Hakael about Nate's mother-in-law. "You have a responsibility to Nate's wife, Layla."

"And I will honor that responsibility," Hakael replied. Then he looked at Nate. "I look forward to meeting her."

§

Adabiel informed them that the same had happened to Justin's mother. "She was my brother's. He was devastated, and has embraced Justin and his entire family."

"So you see why it's important," Nantan asked. "We'll be able to keep a record of any baby a Watcher puts his she-he demon in. If it appears that they've made the wrong choice, we'll be able to correct it while they are still very young."

"How?" Kobabiel asked.

"By swapping one she-demon with another that has been misplaced," Henry responded.

"So you'd have to be aware every time a Watcher meets his mate?" Hasdiel asked.

"Hence the website," Nantan replied. "It will be a secured database. We'll be able to gain access to the babies' medical records."

"Man, that's a good idea," Satariel replied. "Plus, we'll be able to keep track of our issues." He told them how he'd just found Mysia and Nikki. "Nikki was dying. Thanks to Batman, and his 'spirit' mate, I got to her just in time."

"If there is anyone in your family that is computer literate; Nantan and I will train them on our program," Henry informed them. "We are setting up a training facility to train a group of the women that live here. We can work out a schedule that includes anyone you want us to train."

"I'd like Isi and Una to train," Lightwings offered.

"My granddaughters?" Hakael asked.

"Yes. They are staying with me and my father."

"I wasn't aware of that."

"Oops," Brock replied.

"Oops what?"

"I thought they informed you that they'd been kidnapped," Brock responded.

"Say what!"

Dan spoke up. "My demon brothers kidnapped them and their children. We got them back."

Hakael looked like he wanted to kill Dan. "Those son of a bastards better be dead, Denel!"

"Yomiel, Lightwings and I handled them."

"You still should have told me." Then he glared at Lightwings. "Don't ever keep anything from me that concerns my grandchildren. You understand?"

"I assure you, it will never happen again," Lightwings replied.

"Seraphiel, are my grandchildren still in danger?"

"All of our children are in danger, man. You know that. And for the record, it is not Lightwings' fault that you were not in the loop. Michael blocked your granddaughters from reaching out to you. So, back up off of him, man. If you have a gripe, take it up with Michael."

"Why would Michael want me out of the loop?"

§

As angry as Yomiel was at Lightwings, he didn't want Hakael attacking him. That was a strange feeling to him. "They were after *my* wife," he informed Hakael. "Her brothers and their families were bargaining chips. The retribution was Lightwings', Denel's and mine."

§

Dan felt the same way. Which pissed him off. He wanted to stay mad at that old Indian. But he didn't like someone not related giving the man a hard time, either. "But, like Brock said, if you got a problem with it, don't blame Lightwings. You take it to Michael!"

§

Both Brock and Yomiel's team was glaring at Hakael. You could feel the anger radiating off of them. Hakael threw his arms up. "Whatever."

Lightwings' heart broke. He knew they all knew what he'd done; yet they were standing by him. That made him feel, all the more, guilty.

Brock smiled, but he needed to get one more point across. "Back down, everybody. As your leader, I won't tolerate infighting. Not physically and not verbally. That will only make it easier for Lucifer to infiltrate our ranks. Understand?"

§

Lucifer growled, "That bastard!" Now he needed to

change his plans.

§

Chapter 39

Jodi was meeting with the wives of the Ultimate Watchers. She was aware of Brock's plans and wanted to get to know the other wives.

Her grandmother, Kiche, introduced her and Kwanita to all of the women. "These are my granddaughters. Jodi is Seraphiel's wife; and Kwanita is Yomiel's wife."

"Jodi is also *my* granddaughter; on her father and mother's sides. And Kwanita is *my* granddaughter, on her mother's side," Sarah informed the women.

Like Kiche, she'd known these women for years. It was beneficial to have other women to talk with. Especially when you take in consideration the nature of their existence.

§

Jodi smiled. "It's good to meet all of you."

"So tell us, what is it like living in the same house with a slew of "spirit" mates?" Hasdiel's 'spirit' mate, Sonji, asked.

"We get along really well," Jodi replied. "It doesn't hurt that we are all related. We also babysit each other's children."

"Plus, we support each other when the men are in a battle," Kwanita added.

"I imagine it's helpful to have others who know

[375]

what you are going through," Layla stated. "In Africa, it was sometimes unbearable. I had no confidant."

"Same here," Sonji agreed. "Hasdiel's inner circle didn't live in India. Once my children grew up, I was alone."

"Same for Jehoel and me," Shelonda added. "His team was just starting to find their 'spirit' mates."

"I knew all of Satariel's team's wives; but we didn't live in the same house. Sometimes the battles were frightful. I'm grateful to have Gabbie; and her sisters-in-laws living with us."

"Fortunately for me, I had all of my family in Iowa. Adabiel's brothers are his inner circle, so I had my sisters-in-laws close. Not to mention the thousands of their children, who chose to stay with us," Gabbie added. "My house in Iowa was always filled with our grandchildren. I miss them dearly. But, I am glad to have Sarah and her girls."

"Kobabiel and I had our grandsons and their wives, but I missed my son. He never let us establish a relationship with his children or grandchildren."

"I never understood that," Jodi replied.

"He and Kobabiel both knew that you all were 'spirit' mates. He didn't want to tip his hand."

"Oh."

§

"Do any of you have a problem with the way they

snoop?" Shelonda asked. "Jehoel drives me crazy sometimes."

Jodi looked at Kwanita and laughed.

Kwanita smirked. "Brock is the worst."

"Leave that young man alone," Sharon said. "He was good to me, before he even knew me."

"He was?" Sarah asked.

Sharon told them about her children. "They abandoned me, after their father died." It was obvious she was still hurt. "My oldest was fourteen, and the youngest was seven when their birth mother died. I raised them, as my own. Then when they realized their inheritance wouldn't be in one lump sum, they turned on me. They had me tied up in court for three years. Then out of nowhere, Brock comes along and settles all of my problems. He bought my children out and paid me more than my husband's buildings were worth."

"He did?" Jodi asked. She had never heard that.

"Yes ma'am, he did. Not to mention, he was going to offer me refuge at this estate."

"He was?" Sarah asked.

Sharon nodded her head and laughed. "That was until he snooped on me; and got more than an eye full."

"Oh my God. You *know* about that?" Kwanita asked.

"Of course I do. They can tell when someone is snooping on them. Hania was fit to be tied. He was ready to beat the crap out of Brock, and Yomiel. But, Snow Anna told him he had better not *touch* her sons."

"What did he see?" Shelonda asked.

All of the other 'spirit' mates laughed. Sharon looked at her under eyed. "Use your imagination, child."

Shelonda frowned. Then the lights came on. "Oh no they didn't!" She slapped her hands over her eyes. "I'd just *die!*"

"It was quite embarrassing." Sharon laughed.

"That may have been uncomfortable, but I'll take snooping, any day, over not," Gabriella said.

"You *would?*" Shelonda asked.

"Two of my daughters ran away in the middle of the night. I lost them for over fifty years, because I wouldn't allow Biel to snoop." Her eyes watered. "I never knew my two granddaughters, because I insisted our family would be better off without it. My brothers-in-law's grandchildren are little tramps, because they didn't keep a watchful eye on those hussies. My sister-in-law's brother stalked my youngest daughter; and we had no idea. Seraphiel's nephew found our daughters, living right here in Indiana."

"Really?" Sonji asked.

"That same nephew found my three great-granddaughters. They'd been working for Seraphiel all along. Their mothers worked for him too, but both of them had died. Biel would have been able to save them, if he'd snooped."

She looked over at Jodi and Kwanita. She knew how they felt. "I know you all don't like all the snooping, but imagine not knowing where your children were. Imagine years upon years worrying about them every single day."

§

Kwanita thought about Abe. Would she be able to survive one day, let alone fifty years? She shook her head. She wouldn't and she'd blame Yomiel and Brock, for the loss.

§

Jodi's mind was in the same place. Just because her children were Nephilim and Watcher, didn't mean they wouldn't walk away. She'd almost pushed Adam out the door. She'd lose her mind if she didn't know where her children were.

She needed to rethink her position on Brock snooping. "You know Brock and I just found out a day or so ago that our oldest daughter has a bleeding ulcer."

"He didn't know?" Kiche asked. "I thought you said he snoops *too* much?"

"Evidently he doesn't snoop enough," Sarah added. "How bad is it?"

Jodi laughed. "He's afraid he might see our daughter doing what Sharon and E-du-di were doing."

Everybody laughed.

"Anyway, Aurellia has been struggling for months, and Brock didn't have a clue. Her husband finally confided in me, and I made her tell her father."

"How is she now?"

"She's better. But my point is; I may be wrong and unfair."

"I know you are," Sarah replied. "You didn't marry a human, Jodi. You didn't even marry an average Watcher."

"Or Ultimate Watcher," Kiche added. "You married *Seraphiel*, granddaughter."

"I know."

"As 'spirit' mates we give up the right to total privacy," Sarah added. "Besides, is there anything you don't want him to know?"

"Not really," Jodi answered.

"What about you, Shelonda?" Kiche asked.

"Yes, there is."

"May I ask what?"

"I don't want Jehoel to know how much he has blown my mind," she replied.

"Why wouldn't you want him to know that?"

"Men take advantage when they know how much you care," Shelonda replied. Then she told them about her first husband. "I gave my heart to him, and he used it against me. I hold back sometime, with Joe, because I don't want to be hurt again."

"I was the same way at first," Jodi told her. "My first husband was awful to me. He always had a woman on the side. He treated me like I didn't have feelings. I was afraid to trust or love again."

"But you know Jehoel already knows how much you love him, Shelonda. He feels what you feel," Kwanita reminded her.

"Unfortunately he does, and it scares me sometimes. My first husband sold me a bill of goods; then he cheated on me, with my best friend. Then he tried to kill me, because I left him. If Jehoel ever cheated, he wouldn't have to kill me; because I'd die."

"That's never going to happen," Kiche assured her. "Not even time will make him love you less; or risk losing you."

"You've only been a 'spirit' mate for four years. I have been with Satariel for almost two hundred. It just gets better with time," Sarah assured her.

§

Chapter 40

Everybody at the estate was busy. The Watchers were all in a meeting. The nephews were arranging the tables in the basement, beneath their homes. The nieces were cooking at Henry and Pia's house; because it was closest. The Walkers were setting up a dance floor, a few feet away from the tables. Their wives were making flower arrangements, to sit on the tables.

§

Michael, Gabriel and Raphael were taking care of all the children. That was a treat for Gabriel and Raphael. Both of them envied Araciel and Michael, their grandchildren. They'd never thought to develop that type of relationship with their warriors: The Nazarites and She-demons.

They could not believe how relaxed Michael was. All the children were jumping on him, like he was a bean bag.

§

Brock left the menu up to Symphony. She utilized Aurellia because of her history with the team. Aurellia rattled off a lot of different things. It appeared that they all had different favorite dishes. Each of their 'spirit' mates co-signed what Aurellia said.

Then she had to make sure Dee could fix everything. Dee was tickled pink. She replied, "If it's eatable, I can cook it. But, with this big of a crowd, I need more help, than just Celia."

All of the 'spirit' mates jumped in to help. They were all surprised that their mothers hadn't taken over; especially Snow Anna. Of course, they didn't know she was pissed at H. She hadn't cooked a morsel for him in a week.

Symphony, Aurellia, Celina and Celia were the only ones who did not know how to cook. "What happened to us?" Symphony asked them.

Aurellia laughed. "I had Chef. I don't know what y'alls excuse was."

Celia laughed. "Celina and I ate frozen dinners every day."

"I ate can soup and sandwiches," Symphony admitted.

"That's a shame." Robyn laughed. "What's even more shameful is..." She looked at Dee and laughed, "...This girl cooks better than *all* of us!"

Hope's mouth was full; but she nodded and said, "Uh-huh!" Then she demonstratively gave Dee a thumbs up.

Faith smiled. "Momma taught Maria and Charity how to cook."

"Yeah, and we had to cook for the zombie," Maria replied.

Charity hit her. "That's not nice, Hermana

Pequeña." *Little sister.*

"Don't pay her any attention, Charity. You know *she's* the one with the screw loose." Faith laughed. "This dinner was a really good idea."

"Especially since Adam's birthday party was ruined," Lillian agreed. She, Dawn and Patrice were lighting the candles for the tables.

"I know, right," Naomi agreed. "A sit down dinner, with the entire family, is a nice change."

This family loved to gather together.

§

Lucifer was sitting in his throne room, smiling. What humans called busy, he called something else. Even Araciel was busy with his three granddaughters. His sons had left him alone with their three daughters and his mind was solely on them. The old fool was acting like they were precious metals, or something. The more they talked, the more he enjoyed it. Although most of what they said was not coherent.

He gave one of his most faithful vassal's an order. "You know what to do, Distraction."

"Yes, my Liege"

"You help him, Gluttony."

"As you wish, my Liege. However, may I make an observation?"

"What?"

"Seraphiel has more brothers than those in the ice

block, sir."

Lucifer frowned. He'd forgotten all about *that*. "Bring them to me! Now!!"

§

"Is anybody stacking the CD player?" Symphony yelled out.

"Geno is handling it," Ditto responded.

"Oh hell nawl!" Mark objected. "That clown is gon put some shit like 'YMCA' on!"

"I was thinking more like 'I will survive'," Eugene replied.

"Move away from the stereo, Eugene!" The Walker brothers shouted.

Everybody laughed, including Eugene.

"Let me handle it, son," Sal said and pushed him aside.

When he saw the songs Eugene had selected, he smirked. "How in the hell does Nantan put up with you?"

"What did he have, Sal?" Sam asked.

Sal started calling off the titles. "Rubber band man. I'll take your man…"

"Enough said," Leroy stopped him.

"Oh wait," Sal said and looked up. "YMCA."

Everyone laughed again. Eugene was cracking up. "I was just playing. I wasn't really going to put those songs on the track."

Ditto smirked. "Yeah right."

§

"Let's start setting the table. They should be down here in a little while," Symphony instructed everyone.

They'd brought the good China and crystal from inside the estate. Since it was a sit down dinner, each table would have enough food already available. Chef and Lorraine were not expected to serve, because this was a family gathering.

They had one table reserved for the children, Michael, Raphael and Gabriel. Those Archangels insisted on sitting with the children. They would not indulge in the meal, but had requested a full pot of coffee, just for them. Raphael and Gabriel insisted on it. They were caffeine junkies.

Batman's father had declined the invitation, because it was too many people. However, all of the Ultimate Watchers in the meeting with Brock would be joining them.

Everyone was distracted, because they wanted this dinner to be perfect. The Walker brothers felt like they owed it to their sons. They'd even offered to work as the waiters, but Symphony said no. Brock wanted everyone seated.

He'd given her specific seating arrangements. Patience and Mordiree had placed the laminated name plates in front of all the seats.

§

Lucifer watched his brothers gulp that coffee down like they were humans. "Good. They are all distracted."

He tried to solicit the help of Seraphiel's brothers, but they flat out refused.

"Once was enough, Uncle Lucifer," Arba said. "Besides, Batariel's father has given him even more of his powers."

"That's right," Gibborim agreed. "Not to mention that little bastard Akibeel is now on their side. He always could make us fight each other."

"And he'd come away without a scratch!" Ertael added. "I ain't doing it."

"Besides, have you seen what Seraphiel did to Amazarak?" Arba asked Lucifer. "I ain't doing it either."

"Don't forget that punk ass Yomiel," Awwim added. "How did he get so powerful anyway?"

"It doesn't matter how. He is and I'm not for going up against him again."

Lucifer growled, "You deny my demand."

"Yep!" Ahiman replied.

Lucifer formed a fire ball in his hand. "Are you sure?"

"Either your fireball, or Seraphiel's wrath. Right now I'm more afraid of him, than you, Unc," Talmai responded.

"Look at what he did to Turiel and his group! The way I figure; ice and fire *both* burn. Either way we are screwed," Arba added.

"And we still can't figure out what he did to Amazarak. He's been running around with all those worms on him, since the battle."

"So do to us what you will," Gibborim added. "I'll take my chances with you."

Lucifer's eyes turned red. "Get out of my throne room, before I set you all on fire!"

They all slightly bowed. "As you wish," Arba said and walked out the door.

§

Lucifer was outraged. He was about to tear his room up again.

"I'll help you," a voice said from the door.

He looked up and smiled. "You will?"

"Yes. I have a bone or two to pick, Bruh."

"Sit down with me, and let's prepare." Lucifer smiled again. This was even better.

§

Chapter 41

The tables were set and everything was ready to go. Symphony sent a shout out to Brock. *"Dinner is served."*

"We are on our way," Brock responded. Then he sent a shout out to Jodi. *"Meet us in the basement of the sub-division."*

Jodi replied, *"We're on our way."* She knew about the dinner, but the other wives did not. She thought this was a good idea. She knew Symphony was in charge, but hoped she hadn't done the cooking. That girl could not cook.

§

Everyone was seated in their designated seats. Per Brock's instructions, every Watcher was sitting at the table with his father-in-law. Those boys were *not* happy.

They were all talking at the same time, in his head.

§

"Whose bright idea was this?" Ram asked.

"Mine," Brock responded.

"What the hell is wrong with you?" Ali asked. Brock had sat him with H and Lightwings.

Brock laughed. *"That was a mistake, Ali. I meant for you to just be with H. Doc was supposed to be with Lightwings."*

Yomiel laughed. *"I dodged that bullet, didn't I?"*

"I've lost my damn appetite!" Ali said and then

[389]

frowned. *"You bastard! You changed these seating arrangements, didn't you?"*

Yomiel laughed, again. *"Yep!"*

Brock cracked up. *"Doc!"*

"This changes nothing," Dan added.

"Yeah it does. Try and get along," Brock replied.

"I have nothing to say to Elijah."

"Try, for Lilia's sake. She feels your emotions right now. All of your mates feel your discontent."

"It's mighty strange you aren't sitting with them," Arak said.

"Ain't that the truth?" Chaz replied.

"What were you thinking, Pops?" Akibeel asked. *"Do you want me to hit Smittie?"*

"You'd better not."

"I'm glad I don't have one." Donnell laughed. He was sitting with his brother and sister-in-law.

"We like ours," Caim said.

"We sure do," Balam added and laughed. They were both sitting with Adabiel and Gabbie.

"That's because Biel is a good guy. He'd never do what Lightwings and those Walkers did," Baraq replied. *"I should be sitting with him; instead of being stuck with Clyde."*

"Ya'll shut up and eat your food before it gets cold," Brock demanded. *"Symphony went through a lot of trouble to make everything perfect. I cannot believe that

skinny little stick, Dee, can cook like this."

They all laughed.

"She can throw down," Akibeel said with a mouthful. *"I've never tasted most of these dishes."*

"That's because you only like steak, boy," Doc replied. *"But no joke, that woman put her foot in this food."*

"Did y'all taste the tea?" Chaz asked.

They all nodded.

§

Dee had fixed country fried chicken, meatloaf, ham, turkey and cornbread dressing. Four cheese macaroni, broccoli and rice casserole, candied sweet potatoes, potato-salad, mashed potatoes and smothered potatoes and onions. Fresh mustard, turnip *and* collard greens. String beans with Rotel tomatoes. Buttermilk cornbread, hot water cornbread and yeast rolls. Fried apples and peach pies.

§

"It's a good thing she doesn't live in the estate," Chef replied. *"Otherwise, my job would be in jeopardy."* He never cooked like this because first of all it was too heavy. Secondly, his men had always liked quick meals; or bar-be-que. This was definitely a treat.

§

Lucifer was smiling. "Good job, Gluttony, Distraction and Discontent. They are all distracted and stuffing their pie holes. Even Michael, Gabriel and

[391]

Raphael are busy drinking that coffee. None of them are aware of what's happening around them. Not to mention the Watchers are all discontent with their seating arrangements."

§

Brock stuffed his face until he couldn't anymore. He could hardly move. But, he stood up and walked to the middle of the dance floor.

"May I have everyone's attention?"

Everyone looked up, with their eyes; while they continued eating. He laughed. "That dinner was outstanding Dee. Symphony, you did a wonderful job pulling this together. I had no idea it would be this much food." He rubbed his stomach. "I'm stuffed, but want to keep eating."

Everybody laughed.

"I want you all to look around you."

They all did.

"Everyone has found their 'spirit' mate or soul mate. My old friend Solomon said, "When a man finds a wife, he's found a *good* thing." He looked at Jodi and smiled. "That *is* the truth. However, my friend failed to warn us about what else happens, when we find her."

He gazed around the room and smiled. "Throughout history, man has acted a plumb fool for the woman he loves.

"We can't tolerate her being hurt or disrespected.

Can we?"

All of the men looked at their wives and smiled. "No," they said in unison.

"We are willing to go up against our worst enemy..." He paused and looked at Ram. "...Or our closest friend."

Ram smiled and nodded.

"We'll put their fathers and brothers in check..." He paused and looked at Chaz, H and Henry. "...if they step out of line."

"We give up growing up one day at a time..." He looked at Adam. "...because we can't wait to *be* with her."

Adam kissed Mordiree's hand, and smiled.

"More often than not, we will stand by and let our friends fight for their woman's honor..." He looked at all of the Walkers. "...because we know we'd do the same, if it had been ours."

"We call our behavior..." He looked at the Watchers. "...*'righteous retribution'*."

Chaz remembered how upset he'd been while they were on vacation. He'd wanted to hurt Hope's cousins for seeing her partially naked. Her body was his to see, and no-one else's.

Ram remembered how he'd disrobed Symphony in front of the entire team. He'd freaked out because her scars were vanishing right before his eyes. He'd forgotten they were not in the room alone. But, the team had respected him, and her, and turned their backs.

The Watchers and Walkers looked at each other for the first time, in a day or so. And smiled.

§

Michael nodded. He'd gotten it all wrong. They hadn't stood idle, because Lightwings was their father. They'd stood by, because they would have been just as outraged, if it had been their wives that had been spied on. This was humanity. Thank God he didn't possess those emotions.

§

Brock kept talking. "When we *really* love our women..." His gaze fell on Lightwings. "...we will fight a battle we *know* we cannot win."

Lightwings closed his eyes and nodded.

§

Kobabiel was astonished at Seraphiel's analysis. After all, *he* was superior intellectually than Seraphiel; but he hadn't put that together.

§

"We are willing to walk away from our brothers..." He looked at Dan and Ali. "...if we imagine even the slightest perception of disrespect."

§

Dan and Ali both nodded. Dan thought Brock didn't like Lillian. He was willing to walk away without looking back. Ali was going to fight Brock first, and then walk away.

§

"No one can truly explain why we act like we do…" He looked at Ram, Batman, Ali, Chaz and Akibeel. "But, we lose our minds, *don't we?*"

§

All of the men reached for their wife's hand. Even Snow Anna smiled at H. Never once had he let anyone get out of line with her. Not in fifty years. She remembered the time he beat a man up, just because he was cursing in front of her. He said the man had disrespected his wife.

§

Brock smiled. "They are bossy…"

"And cantankerous!" Clyde shouted out.

Rebecca hit him.

Everybody laughed.

"But we are theirs to boss."

All the men squeezed their women's hands and said, "Yep."

§

He looked over at Jodi. "They lock us out of our rooms…" He looked at H and then Elijah. "…and kick us out of our own beds."

"They kick us out of our own homes." He looked at Howard and laughed. "But we'll sleep in the car… just to be close to her."

Howard kissed Lucinda's hand.

§

He looked at Baraq and cracked up. "They entice us to pierce our bodies…"

Dawn smiled.

He looked at Batman. "…And foolishly carry them piggyback."

Batman and Robyn smiled.

He looked at Arak. "They bring out the best in us."

Arak kissed Faith's hand.

He looked at Akibeel and Maria. "They help us overcome our past transgressions."

Akibeel's eyes watered. He kissed Maria's cheek. "My Santa Maria."

He looked at Doc and Kwanita. "They help us to become all that we were destined to be."

Doc kissed Kwanita's hand.

§

"They labor to bring our children into the world…" He looked across the room at Sal. "…So that our footprint isn't washed away by the sands of time."

Geno smiled.

§

"They bring out the gentleman…" He looked at Jodi. "…And the beast, in us…"

"…And we *crave* their love..." He reached for Jodi's hand. "…like a *junkie*."

§

Lucifer jumped up. "Hurry up, get going! We're going to miss our chance!"

"I'm going," his demon replied.

§

Chapter 42

When Jodi stood up, he wrapped his arm around her. Then he caressed her 'adorable' dimple and whispered, "Percy Sledge understood what you women do to us."

§

The stereo cranked and Percy crooned: *'When a man loves a woman, can't keep his mind on nothing else. He'll trade the world for the good thing he's found'.*

He leaned in and kissed her. Then they started to slow dance.

§

One by one the couples made their way to the dance floor. This was it. This was why they acted the way they acted. No man worth his woman's love would act any other way. It was their *caveman* nature.

It had been ingrained in them since the beginning of time. No matter how *liberated* a woman wanted to be; to her man, she was a damsel.

That's why there were no female Watchers, and there never would be. Women were created to be loved, protected and cherished.

That was the reason Naomi and Ditto didn't tamper with gender roles. They understood each had their own responsibilities in the relationship. And even though Henry had disapproved; once he found Pia, his opinion had quietly changed.

[398]

That was the reason Brock so graciously pulled the women's chairs out so they could be seated.

That was the reason H and his brothers always carried the heavy loads for their wives. And why they walked on the street side, when out in public.

§

In the end, even Lillian realized that chivalry was *not* dead. Discretion was *still* the better part of valor. And gallantry was still the *sexiest* side of a man.

§

When Percy crooned, *'He'll give up all his comfort, and sleep out in the rain'*, Howard whispered, "I'll give up everything for you, Cindy." Then he kissed her cheek.

§

Percy soulfully crooned: *'He can do her no wrong'*. Jehoel lifted Shelonda's chin. "Stop trying to hold back on me. On us. Don't you know I don't need to look to another?" He leaned down and kissed her. "I need *you*. You are all I will ever need, Lonnie. You're my whole world."

§

Percy crooned: *'When a man loves a woman, down deep in his soul; she can bring him such misery'*. Hezekiah hugged Snow Anna tighter. "I'm miserable, Wife."

Percy crooned: *"Trying to hold on to his high class love."* H whispered and crooned, in Snow Anna's ear,

"Baby, please don't treat me bad."

Snow Anna's eyes watered. She'd been giving him fits since he let her father beat her sons. "I'm sorry, Hezekiah."

Hezekiah kissed the top of her head. "I'm sorry, too. I should have done something to help our sons."

§

Adam and Mordiree were dancing on the edge of the platform. She looked up and smiled. "No regrets?"

Adam kissed the tip of her nose. "No regrets-"

§

Everybody was preoccupied....
Everybody's guard was down...
No one was prepared...

§

The dance floor rumbled and fell apart. Everyone thought it collapsed because there had been too much weight on the stage.

They women screamed, as they lost their footing. All of the men reached for their 'spirit' mates and wives, and tried to keep them from falling through the openings.

Brock was concerned about his pregnant 'spirit' mate and daughter. He was paying no attention to what was really happening.

Batman, Sal and Baraq had the same thought. They were holding their pregnant wives up in the air.

§

Michael, Raphael and Gabriel were trying to quiet the screaming children.

§

None of them felt the true danger that had just infiltrated the basement.

§

While Mayhem kept everyone busy, Barren eased through the break in the concrete floor. None of them were paying him any attention. He didn't even have to touch the Vessel. All he had to do was touch her clothing; and she'd *never* be able to bring forth the new breed of Watcher.

All he had to do was press his way through the crowd. And he was *almost* there! He had to be careful though. If he were caught, it was his ass. Unlike other demons, he only got one shot. If he failed, he would be dispatched to nothingness.

He reached for Mordiree...

§

Brock teleported Jodi, Aurellia and Deuce to the table. Then he reached out and lifted everyone else off the stage.

§

"Damn!" Barren whispered. He almost had her. They were still distracted, and didn't see him. When Seraphiel lifted everyone off the stage, he lifted him, too. However, he was further away from the Vessel than before. And much too far away from his escape route. "Damn!"

Well, he had to finish what he started. He was just about close enough to touch her, with the tip of his finger. If he could just touch the hem of her garment. *"Al...most there..."*

§

Lightning crackled, like it had the night of Adam's party. That was the first clue that something sinister was going on. Everyone jumped, and looked around.

Michael, Raphael and Gabriel jumped to their feet. They recognized where the intensity came from. Michael threw up a shield around the children.

§

Standing in the door was Araciel, holding his three granddaughters. "If you all will pardon me..." he said, and shot a lightning bolt into the crowd. It slithered through the crowd, not hurting anyone he didn't *want* it to hurt.

§

Lucifer shouted, "RUN!"

§

Barren tried to duck out of its path, but to no avail. Lightning lassoed his hands and feet. That bastard wrapped himself around and around his fingers. He couldn't reach out and touch himself; let alone the Vessel.

Then lightning lifted him up and suspended him in the air. The women screamed and the men gathered in front of them.

§

Brock had never seen Barren. He was as handsome as any other demon; a little short though. He wasn't five feet tall. "How in the hell did he get in the crowd?" He certainly hadn't felt him enter the premises. And who the hell was he?

Michael blasted the dance floor into nothing. They all saw the gaping hole. "It was not the weight. That bastard came up from the underworld," Michael informed them. "He doesn't have the ability to teleport."

"He doesn't?" Brock asked.

"No!"

"Who *is* he?" Brock asked, again.

"Barren!" Araciel growled. "If he were allowed to teleport he'd bring humanity to a screeching halt."

"Barren?" Brock asked. Then it clicked. Infertility. "Oh my God! *Barren!*"

"He is the only other Fallen, besides Lucifer, who didn't father a Nephilim. If he were to touch a woman, she instantly becomes infertile. Lucifer commissioned him."

"For what?" Kobabiel asked.

"His job is to destroy the Vessel's *womb*. Make sure she never conceives," Araciel replied.

§

Everyone looked at Mordiree. She was trembling. Adam put his arm around her, just as her legs gave out.

[403]

Adam lifted her and sat her in a chair.

Clyde knelt down beside her. "Will it never stop? WILL THEY FOREVER BE AFTER MY *CHILD*?" he shouted.

"They will never stop. And they will never win," Araciel replied. Then he looked at his sons. "Take my granddaughters, please."

Batman and Jehoel both took their daughters, and handed them to their mothers. Then they stood on each side of their father.

§

Lightning reeled Barren back to stand in front of him. "Was it worth it?"

"Why do you care? I cannot hurt your sons, Araciel!" Barren asked.

"You were too close to my daughters-in-law. If you accidently touched any of these women, you would doom them to *childlessness*. And you know that. I warned Lucifer, did he not tell you?"

"No."

"Too bad." Araciel magnified his lightning and burned Barren to a crisp. Then he looked at Adam. "He will not bother you anymore."

"Are there others like him?" Adam asked.

"Yes," Araciel replied. "That Fallen split himself into millions of Barrens." Then he stretched his hand forward and closed the hole in the floor.

He looked at Seraphiel. "If you will allow me, I can secure this entire basement floor."

"Please."

"I'll need everyone to move to the tunnels, except my sons." He smiled at Jehoel and Batman. "You both have the power put up a shield."

"How?" Jehoel asked.

"Follow my lead."

§

Once all the humans were in the tunnels, the Watchers stood in the doorway. They watched as the three men stretched their hands out.

Lightning danced, like a snake, back and forth, up and down the basement. It hit every basement of every house.

They covered the floors, and the walls. They covered the stairs that led to each house. They were proficient, and left no spot untouched.

§

Once they finished, Araciel turned toward Adam. "I cannot stop them from coming for your 'spirit' mate."

"I know."

"However, I can *anoint* her so that no other *Barren* will be able to touch her."

"You *can?*" Brock asked.

Araciel nodded once. "That is if Adam permits me."

"Let me get her," Adam replied.

[405]

§

Mordiree was nervous. But, she wanted her future children. Adam's sons and daughter. "Okay."

§

Clyde and Rebecca walked back into the basement with them. They were going to witness what this Archangel did to their daughter.

Embry, Lamar and Dawn all came along. Everyone else was watching from the tunnel.

§

Just like he'd done to Jehoel and Batman; Araciel lit Mordiree up. She was glowing, as bright as the sun.

Everyone squinted. The Watchers closed their eyes and watched through their 'spirit' mate's eyes. It looked like it was hurting her, but she didn't even flinch.

"Does that hurt, Maude?" Adam asked.

"No." Mordiree smiled. "It's warm and soothing. It feels like a warm liquid is flowing through my womb."

§

When Araciel finished, he toned down his lightning's glow. He bowed his head slightly toward Adam. "If any other Barren attempts to touch your 'spirit' mate, they will burn to a crisp."

Everyone breathed a sigh of relief. Adam embraced his forearm. "Thank you."

§

Araciel reached for Mordiree's hand. He held it in

both of his, and smiled. "Thank you for this first step towards *my* redemption."

Mordiree's eyes glazed. She squeezed his hand. "Thank you for my future sons and daughter."

He reached for Adam's hand, and joined it with Mordiree's. "Many are called, but *few* are chosen."

Then he looked around the crowded room and pledged an oath. "Be at ease. My brothers and I will keep a watchful eye over these *chosen* Vessels."

Michael, Raphael and Gabriel nodded.

He leaned down and kissed Adam and Mordiree's hands. "Be fruitful, multiply and replenish the earth."

§

Then he smiled at his sons. "You both have that gift."

They knew he meant the gift to destroy a Barren. "We *do?*" Batman asked.

"You do. And you will need it," he replied and vanished…with his three granddaughters.

§

"HOT DAMN! HEEEE'S *BACK!!*" Raphael shouted.

§

Lucifer roared so loud, they heard him in the basement.

"BASTARD!!!"

§

NOTE FROM THE AUTHOR

Adam's story could not be told in one book. Stay tuned for the second part of his story.

COMING SOON

DESIREE'S SWEET BABY

DONNELL

MORDIREE'S HEART

ADAM

Made in the USA
Columbia, SC
04 July 2022

62782978R00228